MW00681963

A
STANDARD
Arises
BOOK 1
THE AMATTA VALLEY CHRONICLES

S.C. DUCOMMUN

A STANDARD ARISES

This is a work of fiction. Names, characters, places and incidents either are the product of the author's imagination or are used fictitiously, and any resemblance to actual persons, living or dead, businesses, companies, events, or locales is entirely coincidental.

Printed in Canada

ISBN: 978-1-4866-2343-3
eBook ISBN: 978-1-4866-2344-0

Word Alive Press
119 De Baets Street Winnipeg, MB R2J 3R9
www.wordalivepress.ca

Cataloguing in Publication information can be obtained from Library and Archives Canada.

For Pastor Alex

— 1 —

A Camp Like Any Other Camp

Ra'ah stirred the pot of simmering broth absently as he stared into the deeper shadows of the late afternoon forest. Of all the campsites that they frequented on their routes between the villages of the Amatta, this was one of his favourites. The earthy smell of evergreen forest was heavy in the air. The breeze blew cool off the higher slopes and chased away the muggy summer heat that hung heavily over the great valley floor. He could hear the deeper purr of the creek as it cascaded over falls some way up the slope, and then danced down in laughter as it sought to join with others in community, forming the great valley river many miles away.

The word "community" made him grimace, leaving a sour taste in his thoughts. It seemed like an eternity ago since he'd left his village and the community that he had grown up in. An eternity since his dissatisfaction with the life plan that had been laid on him. He knew he had disappointed many when he left. Few understood the restlessness in his spirit; fewer still understood his need to pursue that restlessness. His parents had, thankfully—although they were reluctant to let him go.

Quiet laughter brought him out of his brooding. Daskow and Angelis were laying on top of their bedrolls a little way off. Daskow was explaining clouds to the petite bard, his brows furrowed with all of the seriousness he could muster as a tutor. Angelis, however, was demanding he explain how each cloud could look like a rabbit or a deer, her good-natured giggles mixing with his soft baritone and carrying across the clearing to blend with the creek and the breeze in a quartet that brought Ra'ah a deep sense of peace.

He hadn't remained alone long after leaving his village. In fact, he hadn't even made it to the next village before stumbling upon four friends camped together. It had been Ange who had immediately insisted he stay with them when he apologized for intruding. She was the most gregarious of them. Skilled in music and dance, she made her way by entertaining in marketplaces. Frequently they all had her to thank for a roof over their heads and food in their stomachs when they visited a settlement. Angelis seemed to possess endless energy for people.

Daskow was her opposite in many ways. Quiet and often withdrawn, Daskow was easily the smartest among them. Ange had once said he had left a very promising career as a tutor in the city of Kathik. Apparently he had simply heard the Call one day, packed his few belongings, and left the city. He tutored whenever he could, but never seemed to consider any offers for more permanent employment. He was always ready when the group decided to move on.

Movement through the trees brought his attention around in time to see Nebaya step into the clearing. She carried her bow and quiver loosely in her hand, a small deer draped over her shoulders. He always marvelled at the graceful strength of the group's main hunter. Nebaya had been the most distrustful of him that first night—she also served as the group's self-appointed protector. But once she had made up her mind about him, she fiercely adopted him as one of their own.

"Time to do your work, little slacker," Nebaya teased as she set the dressed deer beside him. He regarded the meat thoughtfully, already working out how to divide it and which parts he would roast and which would go into the stew. "I shot you a smaller one than last time so I wouldn't have to hear you complain," she called out as she made her way across the clearing toward the creek.

"That last one was an elk, Neeba," Ra'ah protested. "How was I supposed to properly prepare an entire elk in one night?"

"That elk fed us the entire week and we still had meat to sell in Cardaya!" she called from the forest. "So quit your complainin'."

"My pack still smells of week-old meat!" Angelis chimed in from across the camp. She suddenly elbowed Daskow and pointed upward, "Oh, look, that one looks like an elk!".

The deer was already cut up and Ra'ah was slowly turning a beautiful roast over the fire when Anatellia returned to the camp. She just suddenly appeared in the clearing from the forest, ducking under a low tree branch like the wind itself, and made a beeline to the fire like her nose was leading her. She crouched and picked up the spoon he used to stir the stew and drew off some of the simmering broth.

"Your cooking could lead a blind woman home." She gave him a wink and a grin as she wafted the broth under her nose. "How long till we eat?"

"Soon," Ra'ah said firmly, taking the spoon from her and stirring the pot to reveal the small chunks of deer he'd added earlier.

Anatellia looked around the camp, silently taking stock of her troop. The fifth member of the group, she was also the most enigmatic. A gifted leader and negotiator, she had given up a very promising future with her family's silk trade to wander the length and breadth of the valley as a travelling merchant. When asked why she had given up wealth and luxury for such a simple life, she would just shrug and blame it on the Call. She was the official leader of the Five, which had become their new name when Ra'ah had joined them. As such, she was fiercely protective of them, calling them her family.

"What's the plan?" Nebaya called from the creek side of the camp, where she was busy repairing several arrows from her quiver.

"There is something stirring in the forest." Anatellia's face clouded as she sat with Ra'ah beside the fire. "I thought this morning that we would make our way to Pethe, but the Call is disturbed in a way I have not felt before."

"What do you mean?" Ra'ah felt butterflies in his stomach every time that the subject came up. He didn't fully understand the Call himself. Where he only felt it as a kind of pull, the others seemed to regard it like a conscious force that guided them.

"There is almost a warning voice in the Call today." Anatellia's gaze was locked on the flames. "I've never felt anything like it—it's unprecedented."

Ra'ah stared into the fire. Tentatively he reached out with his awareness, trying to feel what the merchant sensed. The breeze picked up, stirring the flames that drew him into their dance. He was so engrossed in his meditation that he jumped when Nebaya spoke from right beside him.

"What do you sense, little cook?" she asked as she sat down.

"Nothing," he admitted—and then realized that wasn't entirely true. He did feel something. A nagging pressure, like an unused nerve that had suddenly been pricked. "Nothing I can understand, anyway."

"You can hear the Wind of the Living God better than you realize," the huntress assured him. "You just have to learn to trust. Have faith."

"All my life I was taught that the Living God doesn't speak that way," Ra'ah admitted, looking sidelong at Anatellia. "That the Call was emotional immaturity."

"And yet here you are, out with us, following the Call," Nebaya teased gently.

The fire popped loudly, throwing embers out of the stone ring Ra'ah had carefully laid. Anatellia used her boot to snuff them out before they had a chance to cause mischief. Even as she did so, the breeze died away. The clearing settled into a deep silence, with only the crackle of the fire and the distant creek as background.

"Anatellia..." Daskow's voice was low and strained, carrying across the camp from where he sat reading. His head was cocked to the side as if listening.

"I hear it," Anatellia whispered, her hand dropping to where her knife lay in a sheath at her side.

"What?" Ra'ah looked at her in alarm, straining in the sudden silence to hear what had alarmed them.

Nebaya touched his arm and put her fingers to her lips. She had the look of a feral animal as she regarded the darkness of the forest around them. He was about to ask again when he realized that the forest was silent. Completely silent. It was like the forest and all of the life in it had suddenly stood still, holding their collective breath. Nebaya slowly stood up, her eyes on her bow halfway across the clearing from them.

Ra'ah was about to speak again when darkness exploded into the clearing.

2

Uninvited Guests

The creature broke into the clearing with a snarling howl. It was covered in densely matted black fur, and the light of the campfire refused to reflect off of it. Red eyes took in the entire clearing before they fixed squarely on him as he sat dumbstruck across the fire, and in that instant he recognized something that froze his heart: intelligence. Pure malevolent intelligence.

The instant was broken by a scream—one so full of the fear he felt that for the briefest moment he thought it was his own voice. But as the blackened beast turned to regard Angelis—the source of the sound—the fear suddenly burned out of him. Something new took its place; an awareness that felt distinct from his own took hold and shook him. Anger like a suddenly kindled fire rose in him, fuelled by the thought that this creature meant to harm his friends. This creature meant to destroy his *family*. Without realizing what he was doing, his hand grabbed the end of a burning brand from the fire, and in one fluid underhand motion sent it spinning across the clearing and into the side of the monster's head.

The flaming branch struck the beast squarely over its eye with a sickening thud and the hiss of burning flesh. The animal let out a snarl and shook its great mangy head, sending embers flying. A madness then seemed to overtake it, and it turned back toward Ra'ah with murderous intent in its eyes. It coiled its body, which looked to be nothing but solid muscle, and leapt the width of the clearing between them.

Time slowed and the beast seemed to hang impossibly in the air. Even as a part of himself screamed frantically into his head, telling him to move, a feeling of intense peace came over him. He suddenly had no fear of this creature. It achieved the top of an arc that would surely end with its impossibly long teeth and claws rending him apart. He saw his four friends, moving impossibly slowly at the edges of his vision, warning him to move even as they manoeuvered to defend him. He almost fancied he heard another voice say "Wait."

A bolt of white suddenly shot past Ra'ah's head, so close that he felt the wind of its passing in his hair. With a heavy thud it embedded itself in the form of a great white arrow deep in the monster's throat. With almost careless ease, he stepped aside as the suddenly lifeless body sailed over the campfire and past him to tumble in a heap at the clearing's edge.

Everyone stared in shocked silence at the now dead creature and then turned to look as a tall figure, clothed in bright armour and with a great bow in hand, strode out of the forest and coolly regarded the carcass for a long moment before turning her gaze on them.

Ra'ah's mind raced as he beheld the warrior before them. Not only was she adorned in bright armour, but everything about her was radiant. Light fell from her as if she herself glowed. Realization blossomed in him: their deliverer was no simple soldier, but a Maylak of the Living God.

The Maylak's gaze caught his own and locked, making him suddenly feel known and laid bare. The feeling lasted only an instant and then her gaze moved on to the others until they finally rested on Anatellia.

"I have been sent with a message from the Living God." The voice that came out of the warrior was shockingly deep and full, penetrating to the core.

Anatellia stood before the softly glowing warrior, a look of wonder on her face as Nebaya, Daskow, Angelis, and Ra'ah came to stand with her. The Maylak simply stood beside the beast that she had so effortlessly killed, waiting for a response.

Finally, the tall leader cleared her throat. "Who are we, that the Living God would send us a Messenger?" she spoke softly.

"Greatly favoured of the Living God"—the declaration cut through them all—"It is not for me to answer such questions. But know that I have been sent to you in this hour with both a warning and a charge. It will be up to you to heed the warning and accept the charge."

The four friends looked at each other in confusion behind Anatellia's back, but the tall woman kept her gaze locked on the Maylak, lost in thought for long seconds before she spoke.

"Though I would find it difficult to deny both my eyes and my very heart, I would be remiss if I did not ask you for some token of whom you serve." The others looked at her in shock, and Nebaya started to speak but was silenced by the lifting of a hand. "What I mean is, it is said that often those of ill intent clothe themselves in well-meaning righteousness. And your arrival right when that… thing… attacked us was either divine providence or careful deceit."

"I am a servant of the Living God," The warrior stood tall and grew suddenly brighter, so that they could not look directly at her. "Let those who know the Living God hear His message and judge accordingly.

"A shadow has fallen over Amatta," the Maylak continued uninterrupted. "The enemy of the Living God has set a great army against the valley and all who dwell there. Its intent is to raze the valley to its foundation stones and leave nothing living. This will happen before the next new moon."

Shock flooded through them all. Ange collapsed in a heap on the ground, tears welling up in her eyes. Ra'ah's mind rolled from shock to denial to a desperate wellspring of urgency and need. Even as the others went through similar silent thought processes, words blurted from his mouth.

"They have to be warned! The villages and the cities have to be warned!" Hot tears poured down his cheeks. "We have to save them. As many as will listen! We have to find a place to hide, to make a stand!"

"Indeed." The bright warrior regarded him; her eyes seemed to bore into his soul. "And so with the warning comes the charge. You five have been chosen. Go to the villages of the valley. Go to the city. Give them this warning. Tell them to leave behind all that hinders and anything that weighs them down. Tell them to come to the Mountain of the Living God in all haste."

"How?" Ra'ah blurted out again, frustration riding the turmoil of emotions as he considered the monumental task they were being given. "No one knows the way. No one has seen the Mountain in a dozen generations!"

"I have." Anatellia's voice cut quietly through his objection, silencing any further outburst.

"Indeed," the warrior nodded, her head turning to regard her again. "The way is cleared when the One who made it clears it. And none can block it again."

"Two fortnights to warn the entire valley and get to the Mountain," Anatellia mused, making calculations in her head. "Wouldn't it be better to raise an army to stand against this enemy instead of just fleeing up the valley?"

"Daughter of the Living God"—the warrior's tone carried an edge—"what you say may be true. But know this, even if the people of the valley could be united, they would need a greater strength than they currently possess. All paths now lead to the Mountain of the Living God. The charge is given. It is yours to accept."

"What of that thing?" Daskow nodded to the dead beast. "That has something to do with all of this, surely. It is neither bear nor wolf. It has the feel of something unnatural."

"The beast served the enemy." The Maylak stooped with a hand over the fell beast and spoke a word of command. Instantly the carcass ignited into blinding flame and was consumed. "It was sent to find you all and destroy you. The enemy knew you would be no match for it. The Living God would not let you face anything you were not strong enough to face, however."

Once their eyes readjusted to the night, they discovered they were alone. The Maylak was gone.

3

Plans in the Night

They banked the fire against the darkness, which suddenly seemed more sinister. The new moon gave no light to their thoughts, but instead reminded them of the limited time they had for the task that had been thrust upon them. The messenger's final words did not fully prevent the fear of the darkness that hung over the clearing. They talked over, at length, what had just happened and the Maylak's charge.

"We can't reach everyone," Angelis lamented quietly during a lull. "Surely He knows that?"

"We have to try," Ra'ah insisted, even as he realized that she was probably right. The valley was easily crossed in a day at its widest point, and in three days down its length. But there were many, many people spread out in hamlets and settlements around the four villages, and of course there were many more in Kathik, the City of the Holy.

"We don't have to reach everybody," Daskow corrected softly. "We've been charged with going to the villages and the city, that is all."

"But what about everyone else?" Ra'ah turned to him in protest. "We can't ignore half the valley."

"We must do what we've been asked to do, Ra'ah," the usually quiet man insisted. "Ange is right that we can't reach everyone in only one month. There are simply too many places to visit. So we must follow the instructions we've been given."

"Daskow is correct," Anatellia cut off Ra'ah as he opened his mouth to continue his protest. "We've been told to go to the villages and the city. To the villages and the city we will go." She raised her hand to further forestall the young cook's objections. "We will tell those who listen to tell whomever they meet along the way to go to the Mountain. That way each village can warn the surrounding settlements and homesteads."

Mollified, Ra'ah nodded. The wisdom of the plan seemed suddenly so plain he felt foolish he hadn't seen it himself. But the task ahead was still daunting. He knew that the villages would not easily receive them, a group of wanderers. With a sudden sinking feeling, his thoughts went back to his own village of Bato. A new thought then rose to the surface.

"Anatellia, you've been to the Mountain of the Living God?"

Everyone turned their questioning gazes on their leader.

"Yes," she admitted. "A very long time ago." Silence followed until she realized they wouldn't accept so short an explanation.

"I went hunting with my brothers when I was ten. They were much older and I was the irritating little sister. They did not want me tagging along, but I made such a fuss that our mother insisted they take me." She seemed lost in the memory that she was invoking and was silent for a moment. "They were very angry, but no one argued with our mother.

"We were two days up the Valley River, climbing into the Shaar Pass, when the weather turned bad. I remember sitting in my saddle, soaked through to the core, feeling quite sorry for myself. I wasn't paying attention to my brothers and they weren't paying attention to me. And then suddenly I was alone." Raising her hands in helpless surrender, lost in the memory, she paused only briefly before she continued.

"At some point in the rain and mist, my horse had taken a different path than the others. It always was a bit scatterbrained. But there I was on a steep path, mountain on my left and fog-draped forest dropping away to my right, and not a brother in sight. When I realized I was alone I panicked a little, screaming my brother's names until my horse started to dance nervously. A quick survey told me I couldn't simply turn back. The path was too narrow and the drop on my right too great. I realized that I would have to keep going forward until I found wider ground."

The fire popped, causing everyone to start. Looking into the sparks that rose from their fire, she sighed deeply.

"If I had known where the path was leading me, I probably would have attempted to turn around despite the obvious danger. The trail rose up the mountain, hugging it closely, and the rain and fog closed in around me. I couldn't see more than ten feet in front of that stupid horse, and the trees on my right disappeared into shadowed gloom. I could tell we were climbing but I had not realized how high we were getting until the rain started turning to snow." She shivered involuntarily. "I was already soaked, as I said, and now the temperature was dropping. I was shivering and scared. In my own miserable self-absorbed state, I hadn't noticed the path had steepened considerably. It wasn't until the horse slipped on a loose stone and I bumped my head on its neck that I realized how drastically we were actually climbing."

She paused her story long enough to add more fuel to the fire. They all waited impatiently for her to continue—everyone except Daskow, who seemed to be distracted by the fire and his own thoughts. But that was typical for him. Ange and Nebaya sipped quietly on cups of stew. Ra'ah tried to imagine riding any kind of animal on a mountain path. He was not a fan of travelling on a mount.

"We climbed for what seemed like an eternity," she finally continued. "I wasn't nearly as scared as I would have been if the snow and fog hadn't blocked my view. But even as we ascended, I noticed the snow was lessening, and it suddenly stopped all together. The path became level and I saw the dark shadow of stone rise up on my right hand from an abyss of white fog. In that instant, I realized that what I thought was a slope down into the valley was actually a sheer drop. Even as I looked back and down into the white abyss, the light suddenly grew and the sun broke through over the peak to my right. The fog just melted, like snow in Ra'ah's cooking pot, and the most terrifying view was laid out before my eyes."

Anatellia paused to ladle some of the stew into her cup. Everyone stared. Even Daskow was now watching her, waiting for her to continue. When she did, they could hear the strain of her voice, like she was back on that mountain top.

"That stupid horse had brought me right up the side of a mountain on a path no wider than its fat butt." She shook her head in wonder. "I looked back down the trail we had just come up, and I honestly couldn't even recognize it as a trail. It was more like a crease or a goat trail, spiralling dizzily down and around a corner hundreds of feet below where we currently stood. The cliff on my left dropped a thousand feet into a stone valley that also fell steeply down and away. We were at the summit of a high pass between two peaks, the path leading into a narrow cleft between them. As I looked down from that mountain pass, I realized I would never be able to go back the way I came. I didn't know how we'd even made it up. I had no choice but to go forward.

"My horse seemed eager to get away from the dizzying drop behind us, and walked with more confidence than I felt into the tight defile. The path very soon started to angle and descend. I struggled to stay in the saddle at many points as the trail twisted and turned. A great tiredness was on me, which I only later realized was the beginning of a fever that I had caught from being so wet and chilled. That last thing I remember clearly about that trail was coming out of the gap between the peaks and seeing a great valley below me—and at the end of the valley was a mountain greater than any I had ever seen."

"The Mountain of the Living God?" Ra'ah ask, his voice betraying a slight incredulity.

"Even if you had only seen that mountain," she continued with a nod, "you would know. But wrapped across its lower spurs was a city of great size, with shining walls of white marble. And a road paved in similar stone wound from great gates in the walls and along the valley floor. It passed below me and into another pass rising up at the opposite end of the valley. The path I was on wound down a steep slope in switchbacks to disappear into the tree line, where it obviously met up with the road below."

"What do you mean that it was the last thing you remember clearly?" Daskow interjected as she paused. He seemed to be troubled by something in her story, and his brows were furrowed in thought.

"Well..."—she seemed reluctant at first to answer—"apparently at some point down the slope my horse slipped and I hit my head." She raised her hand and waved off Daskow's next question. "The memories that follow that image of the valley and the mountain are disjointed and hard to explain. I remember waking up next to a fire beside quickly moving water. A damp cloth was over my eyes and I heard beautiful voices around me talking softly, but when I tried to move the cloth, a hand took mine and told me to leave it and go back to sleep, which I did. Another memory is of a voice telling me that I was very blessed to have survived what I did, and that the Living God had placed a great calling on my life. There are others, but they are too muddled even to this day to remember.

"The final memory I have is of being carried down an uneven trail into a deep canyon with water on one side and an echoing roar all around me, but I couldn't move and the cloth was still bound over my eyes." She shrugged in apology. "The next thing I remember is being woken up by my older brother, with my other brothers standing around me looking both relieved and angry. Apparently they had been looking for me for the better part of two days after they discovered we had become separated. They were on their way back to get help when they came across smoke from a campfire at the base of Gellah Falls, a full day's ride from where we had gotten separated. And that is where they found both me and my horse, banged up but bandaged, sleeping on a bed of fern boughs beside a well-banked fire. I tried to explain what had happened, but they didn't believe me. They outright called me a liar at first, but simply settled on the idea that I had fallen off my horse somewhere up the Shaar Pass and had wandered back down in my delirium until I had been found by another group of hunters.

"Their story had more holes in its logic than mine, but it still made more sense to them. To this day I wonder if they even believe that God is living and active…" She trailed off as they all stared into the fire.

"Could you find that trail up into the high pass again?" Daskow asked pointedly. "Because I've never heard of any road, path, or deer trail other than the main one up and out of the Shaar. The cliffs are sheer and unscalable."

"I don't know, Daskow." Anatellia shook her head in frustration. "My brothers said the same thing when they called me a liar. I don't know where the trailhead started. I don't know what path it took up the mountain. I don't even know what direction I actually went once I was separated from them. I've told you everything I remember."

"Even if we could find the trail that no one else has ever seen," Daskow outlined his thoughts out loud, "how would we direct people up such a trail? From what you are describing there is no way that the elderly and children could make a climb like that."

"I don't know," she admitted again. "I honestly don't think I could do that climb again, knowing what I know now. But you heard the Maylak's words."

"The way is cleared when the One who made it clears it," Ra'ah repeated softly, almost to himself.

"What?" Anatellia's head spun toward him. "What did you say?"

"It's what the Maylak said. Right after you admitted you'd been to the Mountain." Ra'ah watched confusion dance across her face. "You said 'I have' and she said 'The way is cleared when the One who made it clears it. And none can block it again.' Don't you remember?"

"Remember…" She looked down, realization dawning on her face. "Yes, I do remember those words, but not from the Maylak."

"What do you mean?" Daskow asked for all of them.

"I've heard those words before, on the trail when I was being carried along the water, right before the roaring grew too loud to hear. Except the words were 'The way *will* be cleared' and 'None *will* block it again.'" She looked at them in confusion. "What could that mean?"

"Well, don't you see?" Daskow nodded to himself as if everyone suddenly understood. "It's all right there in your story." Anatellia returned a blank stare. The others just waited for him to continue. He gave a small exasperated sigh.

"Listen," he switched to his tutor voice, making sure they were all paying attention. With a barely perceptible nod, he continued, "It's all there in Anatellia's story. She saw a road. A road that went past the pass she had just come out of. That road obviously comes out onto the Valley River somewhere between the head of the Valley and the Shaar Pass."

"But there is no such road," Anatellia insisted, shaking her head emphatically. "The peaks on either side of the Valley River don't have a pass through them until Shaar. And there are certainly no roads that branch off the main one, especially none like the one that I remember in that valley."

"That's because the entrance to that road is hidden," Daskow declared triumphantly. "But the clues are all there, and I'm sure the entrance is there, as well."

Blank stares were the only responses he got. He sighed again. Searching the ground, he picked up a small stick and proceeded to draw what quickly became a passable map of the upper valley to the Shaar Pass, complete with labels written in his flowing script.

"Nice," Angelis complimented him.

"It's not to scale, but it'll do," he said absently, and then dropped back into his tutor voice. "The road goes straight up the valley till it reaches this point"—his stick jabbed at the dirt map for emphasis—"where it crosses the Valley River and continues on up into the Shaar Pass. It's at this point, based on Anna's story, that I believe the secret road to the Mountain starts."

"But there is no place for a road there," Anatellia countered. "There is nothing but a wall of impassable mountains and Gellah Falls. Sure, there are a lot of deer trails to be followed, but there is nothing but cliff after cliff rising above the treeline. My brothers once climbed above the falls to find the source of Gellah Creek. There's nothing but a deep lake in a great bowl of mountain peaks. There is no pass over the mountains beyond that point."

"Not over, no," the young tutor admitted.

"I don't understand." She shook her head in confusion.

"Oh, I see!" Angelis clapped excitedly. "It's all so plain!"

"It is?" Anatellia continued to shake her head, looking back and forth between the two.

"A tunnel?" Ra'ah guessed. He'd only been to Gellah Falls once, when he was very young. It flowed from the high cliffs in a series of seven drops, finally falling with a constant thunder of water into the bottom basin below. The memory still filled him with awe.

"Exactly!" Daskow pointed toward him, but kept his eyes on their tall leader. "You remember being carried down an uneven trail into a deep canyon. What made you think it was a canyon?"

"I don't know—it just sounded like a canyon," she admitted in frustration, trying to remember details of an event two decades old.

"The roaring echoed back off stone walls, but it was muffled. I heard water running beside me. And it was very humid. There was a cold breeze that blew constantly. That's all I remember. Except that right at the end, when I heard those words, the roaring increased in volume and wasn't muffled. Like we turned a corner and the source of it was suddenly right there."

"Or like a door was opened, letting the sound in," Daskow countered. "I believe the entrance to the Mountain road is behind the third fall."

"I know there is a cave behind the third fall, Daskow," Anatellia scoffed. "Everyone who visits Gellah goes behind the falls to explore that cave. But everyone who has explored it also knows it's no more than ten feet deep at its deepest."

"Yes," Daskow nodded, "it's about ten feet deep and ends in a tumbled pile of stone. But that's why I know it's there. Think about it, put it all together. Whoever found you and tended your wounds brought you also to the base of Gellah. They brought you through, by your own accounts, a deep canyon. But you couldn't have told the difference between a cave and a deep canyon, blindfolded as you were. I'm telling you, there is some kind of doorway in that cave. A doorway they took you through to get you back to the valley, where they made sure your brothers found you. A doorway that the Maylak has all but said is now open."

"It's a lot to gamble on," Nebaya said, breaking her long silence.

"Do we follow the Call?" Daskow asked them all in exasperation. "Is this not the very thing we've longed for since answering that Call? To be used by the Living God?"

"Peace, Daskow," Nebaya raised her hands in mock surrender. "Do not hear what I have not said. What you have said rings true to me. I believe you are correct about this door or passage or whatever it is. But our belief in it is only the beginning. We have to convince everyone in the valley to believe as we do."

"Let faith arise," Anatellia breathed a prayer as the realization of what they had been charged with sank in.

"Let faith arise," they all agreed together.

The fire, the wind through the trees and the distant creek were the only sound for some time. Finally, as if they had all received a silent, agreed-upon cue, they made their way to bedrolls, and each fell into restful sleep.

The Maylak regarded the five slumbering forms around the fire with unreadable eyes from her vantage point in the forest. Then she signalled the others who accompanied her, and they all spread out around the clearing to keep watch during the night.

—— 4 ——

A Plan Is Made

The sun rose in a firestorm of reds that morning. After a short breakfast and a quick discussion, they all agreed that the first village they would visit would be Cardaya. Although it lay a day back, it also lay on the side of the valley they were currently on.

Daskow laid out a detailed map and drew what he considered to be the most efficient route with his finger. "Cardaya and Pethe on this side of the river," he outlined, highlighting with finger jabs to the parchment map. "Cross the river at Kathik, which will also be our greatest delay or I'm a donkey. Then Meletsa, and finally Bato."

Ra'ah did the math in his head. One day back to Cardaya and then three days down to Pethe—that was assuming they made perfect time. One day from there back to Kathik, another day to Meletsa, and then three days up to Bato. Eight days of perfect travelling to cover the five main settlements of the valley. Two days per village to meet with and convince the elders of the importance of their message. Probably twice that to get the message out in Kathik. Eighteen days; it would take eighteen perfect days to accomplish their charge. And he knew that it wasn't going to go perfectly. A sense of urgency hung over his heart.

"The way I figure," he spoke his concern out loud, "we've only got a ten day buffer for things to go wrong. Any more than that and whatever army is coming will be at our heels."

"Don't look for trouble, little brother," Nebaya chided. "There's plenty of trouble natural to life without looking for it in advance."

"Nebaya is right," Anatellia agreed as she considered the map. "Although you speak my fears out loud, Ra'ah. We must move forward as if the Living God goes before us. We must move forward knowing that this task is ours to complete, and we will complete it. But we must be prepared for opposition and setbacks. We will keep our faith in the One who sends us. I know in my heart we will be sorely tested in the next weeks. It will be for each of us to decide how much is too much to give, but as for me, I will give everything to this. It is the least I can give. It is all I can give."

They all looked at her in sober silence until Nebaya extended her arm to the tall merchant, who grasped it tightly. The other three joined them, locking arms so that the five of them stood in the silence, clasped tightly together. In that moment Ra'ah felt a connection with these four friends in a way that he had never felt before. His heart stirred and suddenly he felt it, more powerful and obvious than ever before. The Call reached up from the depths of him, grabbing threads of understanding and bringing them together in an awareness that suddenly made everything so clear, so obvious. In that moment, he knew his place. He finally understood his role in this group. No matter what, he'd care for these four friends with everything he had within himself. His smile beamed around the circle.

"What's gotten into you now, little brother?" Nebaya teased.

"You should have shot us another elk," he teased back.

"You're impossible to please!" Her laugh was loud and heartfelt.

They all laughed then, arms gripped tight, unwilling to let go too soon. The spirit of the Living God bound them together in purpose, in family. Finally they released each other, moving to pack the camp and get moving. But even as she walked away, Angelis patted Ra'ah on his arm and whispered to him.

"I'm never putting meat into my pack again."

The day remained clear and warm and they made good time through the alpine forest that lined the valley sides. They often travelled between the villages this way, as most of them appreciated the solitude and relatively untouched beauty of the higher slopes. As they descended toward the village of Cardaya they first came across scattered hunting lodges and woodsmen's cabins, then farms cut out of the forest. The deer trails of the high country gave way to broad trails cleared of obstacles and great wood beams laid across creeks and gullies. Finally the trail became a road, carefully banked and reinforced against erosion, with evidence of cart use abundant on its scarred surface.

The entire time the paths, trails, and road remained surprisingly free of traffic. It was not uncommon to meet a woodsman and his wife, or a group of older children about on errands, but today they met none of these as they descended toward the village. Every so often they would see a farmer working in his yard or a haggard wife standing in a distant doorway, but their eyes would just follow the five as they passed with wary glances and a perfunctory return wave. As they started to get to more populated areas, they were surprised to find some farmyards watched over by young men with bows, looks of nervous vigilance on their faces.

"Something has got people on edge," Nebaya noted as they passed the fifth such yard in a row. "They're watching for something other than people, though."

"What makes you say that?" Daskow asked quietly.

"Because even though people are obviously on edge, we haven't received a single challenge," she pointed out matter-of-factly. "If they were looking for someone, they'd be asking us our business at every settlement we passed."

"Do you suppose there are more of those creatures about?" Angelis asked nervously. "I mean, what are the chances there was just one?"

Nebaya nodded. By the look on everyone's faces, Ange had spoken what they were all thinking.

They came to look down slope towards a treeline that marked the main road between Cardaya and the rest of the valley. Although partially obscured by the trees, they could tell there was very little movement on it for the time of day. Usually the road would be packed with people from the surrounding area heading to and from the village.

"There is the main road," Anatellia pointed out. "We'll know soon enough what is up."

She was right, of course. No sooner had they reached the road and turned toward Cardaya than a group of mounted men hailed them from a pond at the side of the highway. They had the same watchfulness as the young men of the farms and were taking turns watering their horses and keeping an eye on the fields on either side of the road. The leader of the group called again and motioned them over. As they approached he sized them up and shook his head in disapproval.

"You pick a bad time to come to Cardaya, my friends," he spoke as they got close.

"Why? What has happened in the three days since we left, Deacon?" Angelis immediately recognized the weathered sheriff.

"Wolf attack, Miss Ange." The sheriff brightened a bit in recognition as he turned his attention to her. "The night before last. A terrible incident with a young shepherd and his flock down by the river." He shook his head in sadness. "People have been shut up in their homes in fear since yesterday, while those of us who can handle a bow have been hunting the creature, but it's a wily and wholly evil thing, and has eluded us."

"Evil, you say?" Nebaya eyed the surrounding fields. "More evil than a normal marauding wolf?"

"No, miss..." The sheriff faltered momentarily before continuing. "Not to put fear in you all, but it's not at all a normal wolf. I myself caught sight of it last night at dusk. Scared me to my core, it did. Bigger than any wolf I've seen, and blacker than the Pit."

"Stands about here?" Ra'ah cut in, holding his hand at chest level. "Black matted fur that seems to suck all light into it? Eyes that tear into your soul with hatred?"

"Aye," Deacon nodded blankly, staring at each of them with new appreciation. "You've seen it, then?"

"We've seen a creature much like it, at the very least," Anatellia confirmed. "It's partly because of it that we've come back."

"So you didn't kill it?" the sheriff asked hopefully.

"We didn't—the Maylak did," Ange blurted before Anatellia could give her the "keep silent" look.

Silence fell around them. The sheriff's eyes moved back and forth between the two women.

"What Ange said is true," Anatellia confirmed quietly, "although the beast that died in our camp last night is not the beast you are currently hunting. We've been given a dire warning and have made incredibly good time returning here with it."

"A message from a Maylak?" The sheriff shook his head in wonder. "What on earth is the message?"

"The message"—she glared sharply at Ange, who looked ready to tell the whole story right there—"is one that would be best shared with the village elders as soon as possible."

"Very well." The sheriff nodded over to the other sentinels, who led their horses over and took up positions around the five. "We were on our way back to the village ourselves. Let us escort you, and you can tell us this astonishing tale as we walk. We'll be back to the village before the new moon sets."

"That would be welcome." Anatellia nodded in thanks. "I admit the thought of camping, even on the highway, lost its appeal after your news."

They set a brisk pace, flanked by the sheriffs with their bows. The oppressive feeling seemed to hang over them all as they walked, everyone's attention split between watching the fields and hedgerows along the road and Angelis's expert retelling of their encounter the night before. Ra'ah walked at the back with one of the sheriffs, his imagination playing havoc with the soft sounds of the country around him. As he looked back up the hill from where they had come, he thought for the briefest moment he caught a flash of white at its summit. He mused at the thought of the Maylak continuing to watch over them, and with a sudden renewed peace he returned his attention to Ange's story.

5

Cardaya

True to his word, Deacon got them to Cardaya as the sliver of a moon followed the setting sun over the western peaks. The few people out and about watched them as they passed, a mixture of wariness and curiosity in their expressions. The sheriffs with them dispersed once they reached the village, but Deacon insisted they meet the elders before settling in for the night. Anatellia's open relief at his insistence was shared with the group. The realization that there was more than one creature in the valley laid seeds of urgency in their hearts.

Cardaya's village square was usually bustling, even into the evening, but it was muted and sombre as they entered it. Knots of people went hurriedly about their business and a hush was over the entire place. A group of sheriffs stood in a cluster at the base of the broad stair that led into the banquet hall, their leader talking to two elderly men standing above them on the broad landing that stretched the length of the hall. One of the men on the dais looked up as they approached and raised his hand to the sheriff.

"Deacon," his voice carried across the square, "what news do you bring?"

"We saw no sign of it, Elder Breck," their guide admitted as they drew closer, adjusting his volume as they approached the group of men. "But these hawkers have news that I deem to be of greater importance."

"Is that so?" Elder Breck's eyebrows raised in surprise. "Something of greater importance than a rabid wolf running loose, killing and destroying unchallenged?" His penetrating stare fell on Anatellia, waiting.

"Elder Breck." She lowered her head respectfully.

"Miss Anatellia," Elder Breck nodded. "What brings you back to us so quickly?"

"We had an encounter last night while we camped in the high country," she started to explain.

"They were attacked by one of those creatures and were rescued by a Maylak of the Living God," Deacon cut her off. "And the Maylak gave them a message for the villages. I'm sorry to be rude, Miss Anatellia, but I thought I'd save you the trouble of having to tell your story to each village elder one at a time."

"A Maylak of the Living God? That is quite a claim!" The man beside Breck stepped forward into the conversation. He was older than Breck, with a deep and intelligent gaze that pinned first Deacon and then Anatellia down before he turned his attention to Nebaya. "What do you have to say about this, Nebaya?"

"It is the truth, Uncle." Nebaya met the older man's stare with one of her own.

"Breck"—he put his hand on his colleague's shoulder—"let us send for the rest. Deacon, send sheriffs to collect the other elders. And have someone arrange some food in the hall."

"Yes, Elder Shamar." Deacon nodded and starting dispersing men.

"As for you five," Elder Shamar smiled at them, "come into the hall and you can give Elder Breck and I the highlights before the others join us.

The meeting hall of the elders was a comfortable room with a great table lined with high-backed chairs and woven tapestries that helped retain and reflect the heat from the great fireplace at one end. Ra'ah studied the worn needlework that had once been bright but now showed the wear of many years. Ange was retelling the tale of the previous evening for the third and hopefully final time, now that all of the elders and the various village leaders were all present. The room that was meant to accommodate thirty had twice that in attendance, and he had long before given up a chair to find himself seated on a bench against the wall. Everyone in attendance stared fixedly at the young woman as she told of their harrowing encounter with the dark beast and the sudden appearance of the Maylak. He marvelled at how she seemed to stretch an event that in truth had taken only minutes into a fifteen-minute battle with death and revelation.

The promise of food had died a quick death at the very first moment of her retelling, and Ra'ah was wondering, not for the first time, if they'd be eating at all this night. He smiled ruefully as she finished up her tale with the dramatic incineration of the beast and the disappearance of the Maylak in a flash of light. He shifted uncomfortably on the bench and waited for whatever reaction would be forthcoming from the crowd, but for many long seconds there was just silence and then dozens of people started speaking out loud. Elder Breck stood with hands raised, and as quickly as the noise broke out it was silenced. He shifted uncomfortably as Breck's eyes fell on him and each of the other four in turn.

"The first thing that must be decided," he declared solemnly, "is whether the witnesses before us are trustworthy. Who will vouch for these five vagrants?"

Ra'ah felt offence rise inside himself at being called a vagrant. A murmur passed through the room but he couldn't tell if it was for or against them before it was quickly silenced as Elder Shamar stood. He looked at each of them, as Breck had done, and then his eyes rested on Nebaya. She returned his stare in silence, her head high and confident. Somehow satisfied with what he saw, he turned a withering gaze to Breck.

"Elder Breck, your words are, as ever, a reflection of your experience as one of us." He nodded at his peer, who flushed perceptibly but sat down immediately. "I will vouch for Nebaya, who is kin to me, being the daughter of my deceased sister. Normally that alone would be enough, but each and every member of this peculiar nomadic troop is known to us. We have trusted each one of them at one time or another. They have never been given to gossip or wild exaggeration. They have not cheated or stolen from any of you. They have proven themselves on every visit. Where is the wisdom in distrusting them now?"

"But what they are proposing is insane!" one elder, a woman named Deatre, protested from her seat by the fire. "They may speak truth as they understand it, but they themselves could be deceived. They could be duped by an elaborate hoax, designed to fool us all."

"We are not deceived, for our part," Nebaya spoke up. "What we saw last night was not a hoax. I know of no way to create the illusion of what we all saw. And apart from that, our hearts were not deceived." She looked at each of her friends as they nodded in agreement. "The Calling within each of us confirmed what we saw with natural eyes and heard with natural ears. For our part, we have shared true what we have been charged with."

"So what then?" Deatre persisted. "There are probably two dozen swords left in the whole valley. We have no army—no weapons except bows. Do we just pack ourselves up and flee into the high country looking for a path to a mountain that is straight out of legend?"

"I have seen the Mountain," Anatellia insisted.

"And we believe we know where the beginning of that path is," Daskow added from where he stood across the room from Ra'ah.

"Apparently the tale is not finished." Elder Shamar looked at them with renewed curiosity. "And since we cannot make any kind of judgment on what to do about this warning without the knowledge you say you have, I suggest you finish your tale."

He sat down with a motion for Anatellia to stand before the table. Everyone's eyes were on her as she collected her thoughts. She may be their leader, Ra'ah realized, but she didn't enjoy being put in front of these people. That was Angelis's strength.

He smiled at her as she looked around the room. He put all the encouragement he could into his expression. She smiled back at him and then looked squarely at Elder Shamar and spoke directly to him.

"I was ten years old when I went hunting with my brothers," Anatellia began her story.

It was late when the council finally adjourned for the night. Anatellia's account of her journey to the Mountain of the Living God and their theory of where the trailhead lay sparked a heated debate among the elders and other village leaders. Many argued that there was not enough evidence to warrant the risk they were being asked to take. It took Elder Shamar standing in the midst of them all and pointing out that the choice was actually a simple one. If they chose to believe the warning sent through the Maylak messenger, then they would have to move in faith that they would also in some way find the Mountain. The entire decision hinged on choosing to heed the warning or not. In the end the elders held it to a vote, five voting for accepting the warning and two elders abstaining, submitting instead to the will of the majority. Ra'ah found it telling that Breck and Deatre were the abstainers.

The breeze through the village refreshed and roused him from the heaviness that had fallen on him in the council hall, and he stood for a long time staring up at the stars. Daskow and Ange stood nearby, watching Nebaya and Anatellia talking quietly with Shamar and another elder about what would happen in the morning.

Ra'ah sighed. As expected, Cardaya looked to be their first success. But that was no surprise, as Cardaya had always been a village that tended toward the emotional and outrageous ideas that circulated the valley.

His thoughts drifted to the village where he had grown up. The people of Bato were far more reserved and guarded. Priding themselves in their knowledge of the Living God, they looked down on the people of Cardaya because of their lack of emotional maturity and control. He sighed softly at the thought of the exodus of Cardayans about to sweep through the Bato countryside on their way up river. Rumours of the message that he and his friends carried would surely go before them, and he wilted at the thought of having to face his family once they finally caught up with those rumours. The elders of Bato would have already made up their minds before they ever heard the warning from the messengers' lips.

"Hey you." Ange stroked his arm and smiled at him in concern when he looked down at her. "What's on your mind?"

"Bato," he admitted quietly with a small smile.

"Well, stop it," she chided gently, knowing him well enough to know what he was likely thinking.

"Yes, ma'am," he sighed, and looked back up at the stars.

The conversation with the elders wrapped up and the others came over to join them. Together they all stood quietly and looked up at the stars with him. It was something they did quite often in camp. It made Ra'ah feel connected and accepted in a way that transcended words. Finally Nebaya looked around and motioned to a low building nearby.

"My uncle has offered the community house to us to get some rest. There is currently no one staying in it. Apparently they've already set out food and water and bedding for us." Her voice spoke of her unhappiness with the attention and favour they were being paid.

"I did not know one of the elders of Cardaya is your uncle," Angelis commented quietly, probing.

"I have avoided him every time we come here, and he avoids me at my request. He is my uncle in name, but he has never really been my family." Nebaya's answer had a soft finality to it. For her, the subject was closed.

"Family or not, he helped our mission immensely," Anatellia pointed out as they made their way to the low-roofed community house.

"He serves the Living God." Nebaya clipped each word. "He prides himself in that."

At that the conversation ended and they stood in an open room with cots laid out near the hearth and tables with food and fresh water against the wall. Ange sighed happily and went for a bowl of fresh fruit while the others made themselves comfortable on the cots. Ra'ah had not realized how tired he was, but the cot under him convinced him to shut his eyes briefly before getting some food. The last thing he remembered was Daskow begging Ange to share an apple from her bowl.

6

Unexpected Signs

Ra'ah woke with the sun streaming through the cracks of a shuttered window and a sound like market day in Kathik just outside the door. He bolted upright in shock, realizing that he'd fallen asleep with everything but his pack on. At some point, one of his friends had covered him with a blanket. He rubbed the sleep from his eyes and took in the room. He heard a gentle chuckle and turned to see Nebaya toasting a slice of bread over the coals of the fire.

"Morning, sleepyhead," she teased. "Better freshen your hair and grab some food. The village has gathered for our story and I don't think we'll be staying much past the telling if Anatellia has any say."

"We're leaving so soon?" he mumbled as he got up and stretched.

"As soon as possible," Nebaya nodded. "We don't need to be here once they've got the warning. We've got nothing else to offer and we've still got a long road before our part is done."

"I guess so." He realized she was right. Their job was to give the warning and not organize the response.

"Sorry there's no real breakfast—our cook slept in." Nebaya shot him a crooked smile. She always reminded him of what an older sister would be like.

"Your toast is burning," he shot back casually as a tendril of smoke rose from one corner of the hunter's breakfast.

"Oh no!" She quickly flipped it, revealing a perfectly toasted side. "See what happens when you don't do your job?"

He smiled as he splashed water over his neck and head, realizing from the reflection in the basin that his hair was a little wild. With a practiced run of his fingers the spikes were flattened, and he turned his attention to the fruit and cream left behind by the others.

Outside he heard a voice that he recognized as Elder Shamar's rise above the milling of the large crowd, calling the meeting to order. With a sigh, he scooped up the breakfast plate he'd put together and went back to sit by the fire with Nebaya. If she wasn't in a hurry to go out there, neither was he.

She smiled as he sat down, and stole a berry from his plate. Together they enjoyed a quiet breakfast and listened to Ange retell their story again to the entire crowd of enthralled villagers.

"How many times will we have to retell that story before we're done?"

"More times than we really want to think about," Nebaya admitted.

The story progressed outside as they munched on fruit and toast. Ange was just finishing up the last part of the story with the Maylak's warning when a ruckus broke out some way off, obviously out of the village square. Shouting arose and rippled through the crowd outside. Ra'ah and Nebaya both stopped and listened for a moment before they jumped up and headed for the door. They stepped out just as a group of sheriffs entered the square, carrying something between them.

The village square was absolutely packed with people, and with all their heads in the way, Ra'ah was of too average a height to see what the taller sheriffs were carrying between them. But whatever it was caused a great stir among the crowd. He saw Ange raise her hand to her mouth in alarm from the raised dais, and Anatellia went white. The crowd parted for the sheriffs in a noisy wave, pushing back away from them and their trophy as they approached the stage where the elders stood with the rest of their friends.

"Come here!" Nebaya grabbed him by the collar and herded him along the front of the common house toward the nearest edge of the stage.

The group of sheriffs made it to the dais and set their prize on the ground in front of it. Nebaya and Ra'ah hopped onto the platform to stare down at what they had brought. Ra'ah's budding suspicions were confirmed when he looked down at the great body of another black beast. Its fur matted down and dirty black. Its tongue lolled out to the side of great jaws lined with great, jagged teeth. Its eyes dead and lifeless, no hint of red in the milky blackness. No hint of the dreadful intelligence he had seen just a night before last. From the great beast's scruff stuck a great shaft of white, the fletching dirtied by filth and ichor from the beast's wound.

The elders came forward to look down at the beast. Murmurs ran rampant through the crowd. Ra'ah thought he heard weeping. But he didn't take his eyes off of the white arrow—the second white arrow he'd seen in as many days.

He realized that Elder Shamar was talking, questioning the lead sheriff. "Where did you say you found it?"

"Off the highway," the sheriff repeated. "About three miles from the village. It had been dead awhile when we found it."

"Is that like the beast you five say you saw?" Shamar asked Anatellia and Ange.

"It is," Anatellia admitted as Ange simply nodded. "Right down to the arrow sticking out of it."

"Whose arrow is it?" Shamar asked the sheriff, who simply shrugged.

"None of us carry arrows like that," the tall man admitted. "And it's buried deep. It'll have to be cut out. None of us are particularly crazy about doing it, though. This thing is foul."

"It certainly is," the elder agreed. "It smells like it's been dead for a week. Get it out of here. Burn the carcass. But away from the village, mind you."

"Yes, Elder Shamar," the sheriff nodded, and motioned to his compatriots to pick the beast back up.

With quick strides Nebaya crossed the dais and grasped the shaft of the arrow. The sheriff moved to grab her hand, his head shaking. With determination she pulled on the missile, expecting it to be stuck, but it slid out of the carcass with ease. She staggered back and had to be caught by another sheriff, who stared at the arrow in her hand with consternation.

"Did none of you try that?" Elder Shamar asked with raised eyebrows.

The sheriff just looked bewildered as he made sure Nebaya had her feet under her. The ichor from the wound rolled off of the arrowhead as if repelled by it, leaving it much whiter than it ought to be. There was an unnatural look to it, like it was not meant to be used for such crass purposes.

"May I see that, child?" The elder reached down as Nebaya lifted the shaft to him.

The other elders crowded around him as he examined it with careful, almost reverent hands, running his fingers over the feathers of the fletching and down the length of the shaft. The arrow appeared completely unscathed by use. The dirt and blood came off to the touch. Everyone ignored the silent procession of sheriffs leaving with the beast as they watched the elder's examination.

"Well," he finally breathed out a held breath, "I'd say we've been given enough signs, wouldn't you all agree?" The others nodded in sombre agreement.

"People of Cardaya," Shamar's voice rose to carry over the square, "You've heard the account of the Five. You've heard the warning from the messenger of the Living God, the Maylak. You've seen with your own eyes the beast that terrorized us, slain with this arrow. An arrow that I can tell you is unlike anything made anywhere in the Valley. The other elders and I agree. We must obey the warning. We must seek the Mountain of God and trust that the One who warns will be the One who guides. Do we agree in this?"

"We do!" The assent of hundreds of voices rose as one in the village square.

"Very well," Elder Shamar nodded. "Leaders of houses shall meet in the banquet hall and we will form our plans."

The crowd broke into milling chaos as Shamar motioned the five companions to join the huddle of elders on the dais. The man's face was grave as he looked at each of them. It felt to Ra'ah that they were each being measured and weighed. Finally satisfied, he handed the great white arrow back to Nebaya.

"This belongs to you, sister's daughter. No one would be right to dispute it. And I sense it was meant to be in your hands." He reached out and took a leather satchel from Elder Breck and handed it to Anatellia. "Elder Deatre and I spent the early morning writing to various leaders in the other villages and also in Kathik regarding your charge and our assessment of its importance. I'm afraid the task before you is, well, monumental…" He shook his head before continuing. "You will need all the help we can give you and then some. But He who has given you this task will be with you, to help you see it through."

He then motioned to the side of the dais where Deacon stood, and the sheriff lifted a bundle from the corner and brought it over. Setting it on the ground, he held the edge and gave a push, unfurling a large cloak that had wrapped several unstrung bows with quivers of arrows and a half dozen daggers of varying size. They all stared down at the offering until the tall sheriff spoke through their confusion.

"These are for those of you that don't have one. Everyone who can shoot a bow should take one. Everyone without a blade should have at least one on them. I do not know what help they may be against one of those beasts, but they will be better than nothing." He picked up a small delicate blade and handed it to Ange. "And I do mean everyone."

"I can't," Ange put her hands behind her back. "I wouldn't know what to do with it."

"It's simple." He seized her hand from behind her back and placed the sheathed dagger in it. "Pointy end toward what scares you. Please, just take it for an old fan of your songs."

"Okay," she conceded, overwhelmed, "but I won't use it. I'm just as likely to cut myself."

"Then Ra'ah can patch you up," Deacon smiled. "He's well known for his healing skills."

"I am?" Ra'ah faltered as the sheriff handed him a bow and a blade of his own.

"Thought we didn't notice?" Deacon smiled. "Everyone knows you've got the heart of a shepherd—now protect your sheep."

Ra'ah nodded in bewilderment. A bow and a dagger were handed to Daskow, despite his protests, and the last bow went to Anatellia. She accepted it without a word. Shamar and the others watched silently through the whole process. The elder nodded once it was complete.

"The Valley is no longer safe," he said by way of explanation. "These gifts are for your defense only. You've already seen two beasts—it would be foolish to assume there are no others."

"While it is true that we have seen two beasts slain in as many days," Nebaya agreed, "it is also true that we have not had to raise our hand against either of them. The Living God has set a guard around us, and I wonder at the wisdom of thinking we could face the next one in our own strength."

"Do not assume the Enemy of the Living God has sent only one type of foe," Deacon admonished. "It is said he is crafty and wise in his own way. Be vigilant and cautious as you go down the valley. Assume the beasts are not alone."

Ra'ah realized in shock that he actually had made just the opposite assumption. Deacon's words sobered him up quickly—and not just him. His friends' faces all registered shock at the same realization.

"Will you not reconsider our offer of escort?" The sheriff directed the question at Anatellia.

"There was nothing in the Maylak's message that suggested we could bring others with us."

"There was nothing saying we couldn't," Ange protested.

"Think, Angelis." Anatellia turned to her friend. "Think about who we are. We don't belong to any village, yet we are welcome in all." She waited for Ange to nod in understanding. "What would happen if we came to the other villages with a group of Cardayans? They would listen to our story and look at who we brought with us and say it's all just a bunch of Cardayan overreaction."

"Not necessarily," Ange protested.

"I'm afraid she's right, young one," Elder Deatre interjected. "The most we can offer are the letters. We will go to all those settled in our area of influence to share your warning, but you must go to the other villages alone. Your best chance of being heard is in being unaffiliated with any one settlement."

"I've never understood the distrust between villages," Ange lamented. "Why can't you all just accept your differences as part of the great tapestry that the Living God has created?"

"Ah, young one"—a smile cracked across Deatre's face for the first time since they'd arrived—"if only everyone thought so little of those differences. Truly there is more that we can agree on than disagree on. But those disagreements are so old and our desire to be comfortably unchallenged is so great that we refuse to even make the overtures anymore. And it is a big enough valley for all."

"In four weeks it will be an empty valley," Daskow cut in.

"Indeed," Deatre nodded sadly but then brightened. "But look at what the five of you have been given: a chance to bring all of the valley back to unity under the Mountain of the Living God."

"What Elder Deatre says is right," Elder Shamar affirmed. "You five have been given a monumental task. We offer you whatever help you need. Provision up. Rest up as much as possible. And then depart with our blessing."

The next hours were hectic and centered around squeezing as much food as possible into five packs. Ra'ah took charge of sorting through the rations provided by the village, focusing on nuts, dried fruits, and meats. It had been pointed out to them almost immediately that they could not assume a warm reception at each village. They also couldn't rely on their regular pattern of trade and barter to get more food as they went. Hunting would be almost impossible with the pace they expected to set, especially as they intended to stay on the highways now. So each of them would have to take as much light, high-energy food as possible.

The idea that villages might reject them outright disturbed him. The pace of the past two days had kept him from thinking too much about the next weeks. He hadn't really considered what would happen if the warning was completely ignored. But as he filled their packs with food, he considered what it might mean to lose entire villages to war.

He realized suddenly that they were all going to lose their homes, at the very least. He'd left his home and the idea of staying in one spot years ago—what would it be like for those who did not get to choose, but were forced to give up their homes? To give up everything they had worked for? The weight of what they were asking people to believe and to do fell on him like a tree. Why were the Cardayans so willing to give up what they had built?

He caught himself as he was placing a wrapped bundle of dried meats in Ange's bag. With a smile, he swapped an equal amount of dried fruits and nuts out of his bag to pack into hers, taking the extra meat. It was far easier for him to accept the idea of fleeing the Valley because he had what was important to him. He had his friends. They were his family and his community. And he also realized that he was trying to save what mattered most about the valley: the people within it.

An argument at the door caught his attention. Nebaya was heatedly telling a group of young men to go back to their families. He looked over and realized they were armed and carrying packs.

"What is this?" Anatellia looked up from sorting the letters, obviously just noticing the altercation herself.

"They want to join us in going down-valley," Nebaya explained in exasperation. "They think they're going to war."

"No." The tall merchant shook her head as she tucked the letters into her pack next to the rations Ra'ah had set aside for her.

"That's what I said." The huntress gave the young men a withering look.

"We will go on our own if we have to," the leader of the group insisted.

"We cannot stop you from making your own choices," Nebaya admitted. "But we do refuse to endorse them. Chances are you will only succeed in dying if you choose to fight this enemy."

"Says who?" he pressed back.

"The Maylak, right after we asked her why we shouldn't just do what you're suggesting." Ra'ah's irritation poured into his words. "You'll get nothing for your cocky bravery but death. And you'll get everyone who follows you killed as well."

"We just want to do something besides run and hide!" The leader was taken aback by the abrupt rebuke, and Ra'ah realized he was younger than he had first thought.

"We are called to the Mountain of the Living God," he cut in in a gentler tone. "That is not running and hiding. If you want to be brave and also obedient, why don't you make it your mission to go to every surrounding hamlet, farm, and settlement to spread that message?"

"That would be far more helpful," Nebaya said as she motioned them out the door.

"And stay as a group," Anatellia added from her pages. "There are probably more of those black things out there."

The young men paled considerably as they were herded out. Ra'ah had to resist laughing. So brave and ready to go to war, and they hadn't even considered they might face one of the beasts on the way. The Valley had never known war. Their desire to join one was more romance than thought. He had to admit to the same feelings, though. Death in war wasn't something the people of the Valley thought about.

"How is packing going?" He looked up from his thoughts to see Anatellia looking at him.

"Pretty much done," he admitted while taking mental stock of what they now had. "I don't think I overpacked any of the packs. They're all a little heavier than normal, but they'll be normal weight by the time we reach Pethe."

"And we might be wishing they were heavier by the time we reach Bato," Nebaya said as she tested the weight of hers. "No, that's good, Ra'ah. You've done really well. Although—don't think I didn't notice Ange didn't get any meat in her pack this time."

Ra'ah just smiled as both women laughed.

— 7 —

Three Days to Pethe?

They ate a quiet lunch and then walked with the elders out of the village. A great many came out to see them off, including a substantial group of young men and women with packs who were waiting beside the highway that led down to Pethe and Kathik. Nebaya scowled at the young man who seemed to be their leader, the same young man they had chased out of the common house earlier that morning.

"We have decided to travel with you until the Kathik junction," the leader of the group announced. "Then we will take our leave and make our way back through the side roads and trails. We will be sure everyone we can reach will hear the warning."

"Just so long as you understand we will not slow down for you to keep up," Nebaya admonished.

"They have already been told not to impede you," Elder Shamar confirmed; then he gripped Nebaya's arm in farewell. "Safe journey, sister's daughter. You would make your mother proud. I am proud of you on her behalf.

"Safe journey to you all." He extended his arms out as if to encompass them all. "I regret we have nothing more to offer you to aid your journey. We will see you all again at the Mountain. May the Living God grant you favour and success."

"Thank you, Elder Shamar," Anatellia spoke for them. "And thank you everyone, for your help, and above all for listening to the warning that the Living God gave us. You have given us hope."

Without further comment she turned and set a pace down the highway. Ra'ah and the others quickly followed. He smiled to himself at the awkwardness of being escorted out of the village. It was much easier when they would pack up and leave without anyone watching. He also wondered if he was the only self-conscious one of the group. Looking over, he caught Ange looking at him. She rolled her eyes and then pretended to stumble, glancing back as she did to see if anyone watching them noticed. Obviously she was feeling similarly. He smiled and then settled into Anatellia's pace. At this speed they'd lose half of the young people walking with them by late afternoon.

"Did you want to just run for a while?" Daskow teased from behind them, noticing their leader's motives as well.

Anatellia glanced back with a half-smile.

"I hope they packed foot salve," she replied casually, getting a barking laugh from Nebaya as the huntress surveyed the already dispersed group behind them.

They had lost a full third of the young people before they reached the place they had met Deacon and his sheriffs just the day before. The romance of doing something important quickly faded for many and the more practical, less dedicated ones grouped up and branched off the main road to start spreading the news closer to home. Of those that remained, there wasn't a single one who didn't show some sign of strain and soreness. Ra'ah chuckled quietly as he remembered the first few months out on the road with Anatellia and the others. If you weren't used to travelling from place to place by foot, you simply could not be prepared for it.

Deacon and a small group of sheriffs were waiting for them by the same pond when they got there. The leader smiled broadly atop his mount as he quickly studied each of them.

"I'm glad you chose to keep them." He pointed to the unstrung bow and quiver on Ra'ah's back. "If nothing else, you're four times more likely to bring down a squirrel along the road. Although at the pace you set, you could just run one down."

"We didn't expect to see you again," Anatellia said.

"We were actually sent to divert your shadows." Deacon nodded to the footsore youths behind them. "The elder figured a few hours following you would make them more agreeable to instruction."

"No doubt," Anatellia agreed, and then turned her head to call out. "Deacon has an important new task for you all."

Deacon laughed and waved as the five passed. Then he called the youths to him, ignoring their protests. The voices fell behind them as Anatellia quickened her pace. After a few minutes Ra'ah smiled to himself as a new quiet finally settled over the road. He hadn't realized how loud the group had been.

"Can we maybe reduce the pace a bit?" Angelis grumbled as she jog-walked beside him.

Obligingly Anatellia slowed, forcing Ra'ah to come up even with her when he didn't anticipate the sudden speed change. He looked at her and saw her smiling, which he answered with a questioning brow.

"I wasn't going to spend a day and a half with those puppies following me. It was nice of the elder to anticipate the need."

"They meant well."

"We will make better time without them, whether they are well meaning or not."

"I'm surprised they didn't offer us horses," he said, pivoting on the subject.

"They did," she admitted, and then continued in explanation when he looked at her in shock. "People don't realize that horses wouldn't automatically make us faster. As far as I know, I'm the only one with riding experience of the five of us. Travelling by horseback isn't simply a matter of sitting on it and going, you know."

"It isn't?" he asked incredulously.

"No, it's not!" she laughed good-naturedly. "A person who rides in the saddle like a sack of potatoes all day would be laid up the next day. Your legs are far more involved than you realize. And on top of our riding inexperience, horses require tending and care and feeding. Which is expensive and limits where we can stop for the night. Since the horses being offered belong to the sheriffs and tend to be a lot more spirited than any nag you may have ridden when you were a kid, I also declined on safety grounds. The chance that at least one of you would get thrown before our first nightfall was really, really high. And I know you hate setting broken bones."

"Well, at least you didn't reject the offer of horses 'just because,'" he teased. "Still, the thought of getting to the villages at horse speed is appealing."

"Maybe someday we'll have the opportunity for me to teach you all to ride. But in the Valley, riding horses is a luxury that I don't see a need for."

"Except when racing ahead of unseen armies bent on the destruction of everything you love and hold dear," he finished sarcastically.

"You'll have to trust me that we'll make better time without them!"

"Without what?" Ange came up alongside them, sensing a conversation in progress that she was missing out on.

"Horses," Ra'ah stated flatly.

"Oh no," the short woman shook her head emphatically, "I don't get along with horses. They always try to throw me into trees or bodies of water. And my butt aches after riding one for any length of time."

Anatellia turned her head and gave him an "I told you so" look that would have been shouting if she'd expressed it in words. Ra'ah sighed in resignation. He had very little experience riding horses, he had to admit. His family had never needed one, and his friends' families never rode either. But the image of trotting down the road as he sat in the saddle still filled him with longing, and somehow knowing that they had been offered horses rankled him.

"I don't ride horses, either," Daskow chimed in from just behind them. "They make me sneeze."

Ra'ah remembered that. If the only place in a village they could find to sleep was a stable, Daskow would sleep in the woods. He'd gotten so good at avoiding stables and the like that most of them forgot the reason why he did so.

Ra'ah looked around for Nebaya to see if she wanted to weigh in, but she was walking some way off, lost in her own thoughts. "How about you, Neeba? What's your feeling on horses?"

"Pass," she responded flatly.

"Nebaya absolutely will not ride any animal more stubborn than herself," Anatellia laughed as she looked back at her friend.

"As a matter of principle, yes," Nebaya nodded with a frown. "I still remember that nag you put me on when we visited your parents. We were five miles from the stable when it decided to just go home."

"I have not forgotten," Anatellia admitted. "I followed your screaming all the way back. But you did good to hang on the entire way. Even my brother said so."

Nebaya glared at her until they both broke out laughing. Of the five, they were the oldest friends. In fact, they had been Two for unknown years before they took in Angelis, then Daskow, and finally him. Ra'ah didn't know how long they'd been friends, but many of their stories were shared.

"Okay," he concluded in resignation, "no horses, then."

"Sorry, kiddo," Anatellia said through soft giggles.

The road unfolded before them as they walked, seasoned travellers one and all. There wasn't anyone in the Valley with whom he would rather be doing this. He trusted these four and they trusted him. And the Living God had entrusted them all with His message. He pondered and wondered what it all meant as the miles passed around them.

They walked that first day until it was almost too dark to set up camp. They stopped at the edge of the highway between the road and the river and kept their fire well hidden. After a shared meal and almost no conversation, they all curled into their bedrolls and fell immediately asleep.

Ra'ah only woke once in the night, to a sound that he wasn't sure was real or in his dream. By the glow of the dying fire, he could see his four friends sleeping soundly around him. He lay still and listened for many minutes, but whatever the sound was, it did not repeat. So with a sigh he leaned over and added a few more pieces to the fire, and was back asleep almost as soon as his head hit his arm.

They all woke with the dawn the next morning, and after a quick breakfast they put out their fire and continued down the road. Normally they would have already been joining an assortment of travellers heading between the villages and Kathik, but like the day before, the road stayed extraordinarily quiet. There was not even a single farmer to be seen in the fields. They wondered at this quietly, and on Nebaya's suggestion the others strung their bows.

For the rest of the morning Nebaya gave instruction on the use of the weapons. Although at one time or another they had all tried their hands at it, they still listened to her intently. As she reiterated from the very beginning, having shot a bow does not mean you'd done it while on the move, or in a hurry. And the last thing she wanted to see was an arrow stuck in one of them because someone else wasn't paying attention.

Ra'ah found it difficult to be moving and handling a bow. Anatellia insisted they keep a good pace despite Nebaya's training. Several times he almost tripped himself or someone else as he practiced pulling the bow off his shoulder. This was before he even attempted to nock an arrow. He realized very quickly the value of what she was trying to teach them, so he set himself to learn.

By the time noon rolled around, the students had the motions down. Ra'ah doubted he'd be able to shoot accurately once he had the bow ready, but at least he wouldn't trip over it and dump his quiver all over the ground when he tried.

They stopped to rest and eat a quick lunch, and just as they got back on the road the rain started. It was just a gentle shower at first, but the sky darkened quickly and the wind started to pick up. They hurriedly drew covers over their packs and wrapped their cloaks around themselves. Bad weather was by no means new to them, but they were all a little shocked by how quickly it turned from a summer shower to full downpour.

They knew there was no real option to stop and find shelter, so they double-checked each other's packs, pulled their hoods over their heads, and pushed on.

They came upon the Crossroads quite suddenly in the driving rain. It announced its presence with the realization that the trees that had provided them shelter from the full force of the storm had disappeared to either side. The road opened up before them into a large cobblestone space that marked the joining of the Kathik highway with the Cardaya and Pethe highways. The monstrous shadow of an inn rose out of the rain to their left, and Anatellia immediately turned towards it despite their hurry.

"I think we could all do with something warm to drink," she spoke over the rain.

They all nodded eagerly for her to proceed, and they hurried under the great eaves of the stone inn. A sign swung wildly in the wind and made the name impossible to read. Ra'ah seemed to recall its name was the Wayward Ox or something like that. Daskow opened the door to the great room and they all piled in out of the rain.

The interior was more pleasant than he remembered. Lamps were lit along the walls and a fire burned in the great circular hearth in the centre of the room. There were tables throughout and a long oak counter on one side. The room was surprisingly empty for the time of day. A group of sheriffs with the livery of Kathik sat at a table on the far side of the hearth and stared at them with curiosity and a hint of suspicion. Several men sat on stools along the counter talking with the innkeeper, who looked up as they entered and motioned broadly to sit where they like.

"Welcome travellers! Sit where you like and hang your cloaks by the fire. I'll send the missus over to serve you."

They nodded in thanks and picked a broad table by the fire. They leaned their packs against the stone wall of the hearth and hung their cloaks on pegs. The innkeeper's wife came from the kitchen as they settled at the table and smiled at them in welcome.

"So good to see travellers out, even in this weather," she chattered. "I was surprised when I heard folks come in, but then I saw that it was you five and I said to myself, 'Well of course they'd still be out, what with having no homes to hide in.'"

"Such is the life of our little peddler troop," Anatellia smiled back at the woman. "But we tend to travel the high country between the villages. Why do people seem to be staying off the road?"

"Truly? Have you not heard?" The innkeeper's wife seemed more pleased than surprised at her question. "There are evil wolves suddenly infesting the valley. They say a whole pack of them crossed up into the valley from the forests downriver. Following the game, they say. The sheriffs from Pethe and Kathik have been patrolling up and down the highways keeping people safe. They say a stray one even killed a youngster and his entire flock up Cardaya way."

"A pack of evil wolves?" Anatellia feigned surprise. "Sounds like a job for hunters, not sheriffs."

"I said the same thing myself," the innkeeper's wife nodded. "But then there was that hunting party that got attacked by those same wolves two nights back. They thought they were hunting the wolves, but the wolves ended up hunting them. Killed all but one of those men, and he only survived by throwing himself into the river. They fished him out just over here at the bridge."

"That is terrifying," Ange admitted softly, glancing at the others.

"It's not safe out there," the wife agreed. "I'm scared for people who have to be out there with those monsters running around loose. Anyway, you're safe here. What can I get for you?"

"Mulled wines and broth for us, please," Anatellia requested.

"We've got rooms upstairs for you to stay as well," the innkeeper's wife assured them. "I'll speak to my husband about making you a good deal."

"Thank you, no," Anatellia declined. "We will be on our way after we've rested and warmed up."

"But, my dear, didn't you hear me?" She looked at Anatellia and then the others in confusion. "The wolves?"

"We will stick to the highway," Anatellia assured her, "but we have urgent business in Pethe and then Kathik and we cannot be delayed."

"Well, you know your business, I suppose." The woman's tone suggested she didn't believe her own words. "I'll get you that food and drink."

There was silence at the table until the innkeeper was out of earshot, and then Angelis turned on Anatellia, her voice low and angry.

"Shouldn't we be telling them? I mean, isn't it our responsibility to tell everyone we meet that they need to get out? That everyone needs to get to the Mountain before the month passes?"

"I know it seems like I'm picking and choosing here, but I don't know the wisdom of telling everyone we meet," Anatellia shot back. "I cannot explain it, but I feel like we should stick to the plan and our understanding of the charge given to us. We will warn the villages through the elders, and then the villages can send people throughout the Valley to warn each individual."

"It doesn't seem right to me," Ange shook her head. "It feels like we're not telling the truth."

"We are not lying to anyone," Anatellia bristled.

"I didn't say we were lying, I said we're not telling the truth."

They went silent abruptly as the innkeeper's wife brought a tray with bowls of broth and steaming bread and set them out in front of them. The innkeeper came over expertly carrying five flagons of mulled wine, and set them on the table with the broth. He seemed about to return to the bar when he stopped and looked at them with concern.

"My wife tells me you intend to keep travelling toward Pethe tonight." He regarded them from under bushy eyebrows. "May I suggest you stay with us till morning?"

Anatellia made to protest but he raised his hand and nodded toward the table of sheriffs across the fire from them.

"Those sheriffs there are waiting for another group coming up from Pethe, escorting a bunch of merchants that'll be returning to the city. They should be arriving this evening, and then the sheriffs from Pethe will be heading back tomorrow morning. You could travel with them and be in Pethe before tomorrow night. That way you won't have to be camping along the road in the rain tonight, and my wife won't be having nightmares about you nice folks being torn apart by wolves and keeping me up all hours. And I'd be willing to trade whatever useful skills you five possess to offset the room and board."

Anatellia looked at her friends, at a loss. Ra'ah could see her weighing his words against the loss of time, but the innkeeper's offer was both wise and incredibly generous. He just nodded when she looked at him. Nebaya shrugged. Daskow nodded. Ange all but looked at her like she would be crazy not to say yes. Finally she sighed and nodded in agreement.

"We accept your generous offer—thank you," she conceded, to the happy clapping of the innkeeper's wife who was listening from behind her husband.

"I would love the opportunity to perform for your patrons," Ange confessed. "I sing and dance and I have some wonderful stories that I'm sure are new."

"A bard's touch may be just what we need tonight," the innkeeper agreed.

"Excellent!" Ange ignored the suspicious look she was getting from Anatellia.

It only occurred afterward to Ra'ah that the women's argument was left unresolved.

They spent the rest of the afternoon helping around the inn. The couple who ran the place were short-staffed and more than happy for the help. By the time supper prep rolled around, Ra'ah found himself in the kitchen helping the innkeeper's wife roast a haunch of venison while she prepared vegetables for a stew. She was happily chattering away to him as he nodded and said "uh huh" in the right places. The woman was more sociable than Ange.

Daskow and Nebaya came through the door to the back courtyard with armloads of firewood to finish stacking against the walls around the hearth. He smiled at his friends, who had chosen to work out in the rain rather than be subjected to the woman's constant stories and questions.

Nebaya rolled her eyes at him as she stacked her armful and headed immediately for the door.

"Oh, my dear, that's enough. Why don't you sit here with me and help with the veggies?" The kindly woman motioned with the carrot she was cutting to an extra stool beside the high table.

"Oh, thank you, no." Nebaya's smile was quite forced. "I think I heard a group of riders come into the courtyard as we came in. I'll go see if the stableboy needs a hand. Daskow can help you."

Daskow blinked like a deer caught in the open mid-chew.

"Oh, I do hope that's the group up from Pethe," the innkeeper's wife worried. "It'll be dark soon, and it's not a night for travelling."

"I do hear a fair number of voices in the courtyard," Nebaya assured her as she exited.

"Maybe I should go help." Daskow motioned to follow.

"No, young man, I need you right here." She set another knife on the table beside the empty stool and patted the seat. "If that is the party from Pethe, then I'm behind and need the help."

Reluctantly Daskow acquiesced and hung his cloak alongside the others by the door. Sitting beside the matron, he picked up the knife and accepted the basket of potatoes she offered. With a sigh he started cutting, only to be firmly corrected and shown how to pare and chop them. Ra'ah chuckled to himself, hiding it under the guise of grabbing the buckets to fetch water from the well in the courtyard. He threw his own cloak on, gave Daskow a sidelong smirk, and stepped out into the soaked courtyard.

The sound of horse hooves and wagon wheels came clearly from the main courtyard that separated the inn from the stables. There was a great deal of general commotion that spoke of the size of the group that had just arrived. The matron had said there was a large group of merchants coming up from Pethe, and she hadn't exaggerated. He was tempted to leave the buckets at the well and look around the corner to see when Nebaya came around the corner with another cloaked figure, supporting a visibly injured man between them. He immediately left the buckets and went to help.

The injured man's leg was hanging uselessly, and a bloodied bandage was wrapped around his foot. He was visibly pale and in pain. Nebaya saw Ra'ah and motioned toward the kitchen door. He understood immediately and ran for the door, bursting into the kitchen to the surprise of both Daskow and the innkeeper's wife. Ignoring their protests, he cleared off a back counter and was on his way to the hearth for the kettle when Nebaya and the other man entered with the injured man between them. The matron immediately become all business.

"Okay," she nodded, wiping her hands on her apron and motioning to the counter that Ra'ah had just cleared. "Lay him there and we'll see what can be done. Young man, leave those potatoes and go back out to that woodpile and get us two of the straightest sticks you can find, and some of that rope in the stable."

Ra'ah grabbed an empty bowl and a cup. He saw clean rags on a shelf, but he needed his bag. First things first: he needed to know what he was dealing with. He handed the bowl to the matron, who raised her eyebrows but then took the kettle from him and filled the bowl as he regarded the man on the table.

"What happened?" he asked the man who had helped bring in the injured one.

"Horse spooked and threw him," the man snorted. "He'd have been fine but his ankle got caught in the stirrup and he didn't fall off clean."

"How long ago did this happen?" he asked as he gently unwrapped the ankle.

"This morning." The injured man gasped as Ra'ah gently examined the wounded leg. "About midmorning."

"This morning?" Ra'ah asked incredulously, looking first at the injured man and then at the other. "Was there no one in your group who knows about injuries?"

"We're sheriffs," the uninjured man stated pointedly.

"That must come with a different set of skills in Pethe than the other villages." Ra'ah shook his head and then looked apologetically at the injured man. "Your leg has swollen so much the pant leg is cutting off circulation. I hope these weren't your favourite pair."

"What do you mean?" the man asked, confused.

"He means they're going to have to cut them off, genius," his associate barked.

"Oh… isn't there a way you could maybe save them?" The man seemed genuinely concerned about his pants.

"I will try," Ra'ah sighed, "but I'm not a seamstress."

"Cooks must come with a different set of skills where you're from," the other man said pointedly.

Ra'ah smiled at the return shot. The wounded leg looked much worse than it was, he realized. His skills really did extend beyond cooking. If his mother had had her way, he would still be in Bato, training under one of the greatest healers and apothecaries in the Valley. But then he'd be missing this. And miss being chased by evil wolves out of ancient stories. He felt a brief homesickness, but let it pass. With an air of quiet confidence, he set about tending the injury.

8

Angelis Makes a Mess

With the arrival of the sheriffs and the merchants from Pethe, the common room of the inn was once again back to a normal level of busyness. Several dozen locals had joined them, braving the threat of wolves to come out and have a drink and conversation. After Ra'ah had splinted up the sheriff's ankle, he was suddenly beset by a stream of patrons who had various complaints—from frequent headaches to persistent corns to infected cuts and wounds. The innkeeper's wife seemed to be facilitating a steady stream of infirmities for him as she busied herself in the kitchen.

"I don't understand why so many people seem to have no idea how to look after themselves," he admitted at one point. "Who is your healer here?"

"Healers are for the villages and the city," she pointed out. "There has not been a healer-trained person living near the Crossroads for several years. Everyone has to travel to Kathik or Pethe for serious help."

"Oh." He felt slightly embarrassed that he didn't know that. "I guess I never thought about that. We usually trade in the villages, where my knowledge seems common."

"You are anything but common, young man," she noted in that matronly tone. "You could be one of the best, I deem. Why did you quit your training?"

"I don't know," he lied. "I guess I just never felt like it was for me."

"You mean the Call was stronger," she corrected, giving him a smile and a penetrating look.

"I guess." He flushed in embarrassment at how accurately she had seen through his lame excuse. "But I'm still trying to understand what that even means."

"You're young, and the Call isn't taught anymore in most village circles," she agreed. "And that is a loss we may all learn to regret."

"What do you know of the Call?" His curiosity peaked.

"The Call is the manifest presence of the Living God upon our destinies," she spoke as if from memory, shaking her paring knife at him. "The Call pushes us toward that which we were destined to be."

"I have never heard a teaching like that."

"I was a theologian's daughter," she laughed. "I was being trained up by my father to take my place in Kathik society. Then I heard the Call. I heard my place in it. Now I'm where that led me."

"Here?" he asked incredulously.

"Here," she said with such contentment and love that he was taken aback. "With the man I love, cooking and caring for people, laughing with them, sometimes crying with them. The Call is my lifestyle more than my destination. I daresay you understand that better than you think."

"I guess I do," he admitted after a long period of silence. "I love my four friends out there. And I know that the Living God has purposes for us. Especially now."

"Especially now?" She raised her eyebrows, catching something in his tone and choice of words that he hadn't intended to communicate.

"It's a long story," he admitted reluctantly, but then made a decision in his heart. "But I'll tell you about it after we've fed those people out there."

"I'll hold you to it, but first let me check on the girls. Mr. Willard can be a brute when things get busy." She set aside her dirty apron and went through the kitchen door to the common room.

Willard, Ra'ah thought to himself. *That's right, the name is Willard's Ox Inn.* He found it funny that they'd been there for the entire day and he didn't even know the innkeeper's name—or his wife's, for that matter. He was so used to facing a certain level of guardedness and mistrust in the villages towards them. As they were outsiders, few people knew or cared to know their names—at least so it seemed to him. But then he never asked people for their names, either.

His thoughts were interrupted by Anatellia coming through the door. She was wearing a serving apron and had an all-business look on her face. He was surprised to even see a little bit of spring in her step as she quickly took in the kitchen, looking for something. That something was him, apparently.

"There you are," she said matter-of-factly. "Matron Willard says it's time to start serving food."

"Yes, ma'am." He jumped up and started organizing the baskets of bread and small pots of stew that would be taken to the tables.

"Call me ma'am again and you'll find yourself waking up in a creek some cool fall morning. And what's this I hear about you offering healer services now?" she teased as she watched him prepare the trays. "I thought you said you weren't good enough to practice."

"Apparently the bar gets lower the farther from the villages you get."

"Or you're better and more knowledgeable at it than you let on!"

"Maybe we'll talk about that later." He lifted a large tray he had loaded with food and bowls and handed it to her. "Right after we talk about how gifted a server you are."

She stuck her tongue out at him and then balanced the tray on her shoulder and spun back out the door to the common room. Seconds later Ange came in, looking back over her shoulder.

"She's exceptionally good at that," she admitted in surprise.

"Isn't she?" he laughed, holding out the already prepared tray for her.

"We should think about acquiring ourselves an inn of our own!" Ange declared as she took the tray and carefully balanced it the way Anatellia had. "How does she do that so gracefully?"

"I don't know—but be careful with it; the stew is hot."

"Back in a flash." She flashed a smile at him as she pushed through the door.

The matron came in almost before the door closed, a happy flushed look on her face.

"You kids are a blessing, to be sure. We've got a full house tonight." She quickly switched aprons. "How's your baking skills?"

"Rusty but passable. My father was a baker."

"You are still full of surprises! I didn't bake enough bread this morning, so let's get busy baking something that doesn't need time to rise."

The supper rush seemed to last forever. Ra'ah whipped up one batch of biscuits, then another. The stew was gone; the venison, too. Ra'ah raided the inn's larder for ideas, and three meat pies topped off the evening with two trays of apple crumble that Daskow had been called in to peel and cut. The common room seemed to have become a place where current worries dissolved in a celebration of food and drink.

Ra'ah sat on a stool by the fire with his back to the hearth, a mug of mulled wine in his tired hands. Nebaya and Daskow were busy cleaning dishes and pans, a job neither of them complained about, as it kept them out of serving in the common room but let them contribute. Ange had switched from serving into the role of the bard, and he could hear her voice rising in song over the cheers and laughter of the patrons. He had not felt quite this content and happy in a very, very long time.

Anatellia came in with the last of the trays of bowls and empty baskets and plunked them down beside the two dishwashers.

"There is a table in the corner set aside for us if you want to join the common room. Ange is in rare form tonight."

"Is she taking requests?" Daskow asked as he scrubbed.

"The Loneliest Donkey?" She turned and gave him a wink.

"Oh, please, no!" Nebaya hung her head.

"Oh, yes please!" Daskow smiled and nodded exaggeratedly.

Ra'ah groan. That was Daskow's favourite song. But it was no secret that he liked it because it was the silliest song Ange knew. And it was a song that was notorious for getting stuck in a person's head.

He must have drifted to sleep sitting on the stool, because the next thing he knew the pots and pans were clean and the bowls and cups as well. His wine was lukewarm, and Daskow and Nebaya were staring at him with smiles on their faces.

"Did you hear me?" Nebaya asked.

"No, I wasn't listening."

"You were asleep," Daskow accused him.

"Maybe." He looked at his wine in sadness, not making eye contact with either of them.

"We're going out to sit down and listen to Ange if you want to come," Nebaya repeated.

"Ange is going to do my song," Daskow revealed excitedly as Nebaya rolled her eyes.

"I think I'm just going to enjoy the quiet of the kitchen," he said.

"Alright, but don't go to sleep again and fall off your stool into the fireplace!"

"Don't sing along so loud you wake me up," he shot back as they left through the door.

He got up and stretched. The nap had been a good one, he realized. He grabbed the fire poker from the side and set it in the coals of the fire. He needn't waste half a mug of mulled wine, he reasoned as he placed the hot metal into his mug. The sound of laughter rose from the common room, and over it he heard the telltale *"eeh haa eeh haa"* of Daskow's favourite song. Ra'ah secretly believed he loved it so much solely because it drove Nebaya crazy. With a sigh, he stepped out of the back door into the night air.

The rain had stopped during the supper service, and the sky had cleared except for ragged ribbons of rain cloud pushed against the distant peaks. The torches from the courtyard of the stable cast shadows around the corner of the inn but failed to bring any real illumination to the rear yard. He looked up at the stars that lay in all their scattered glory and took a deep drink from the reheated mug. For the longest time he stood there in the cool damp night, feeling content. The music and the laughter were muffled and distant out here, but could still be heard over the wind in the trees and the drip of water off of the eaves.

The song ended in a riot of laughter and one last *"eeh haa,"* and silence settled like a blanket over the courtyard. Off in the distance a new sound arose, indiscernible and infrequent at first, but growing louder every time it resounded—the sound of howling carried on the wind.

The thought of a pack of those evil creatures running in the night sent chills down his back. He turned to go back into the shelter of the inn when a movement in the trees caught his eye. Turning to look, he saw a pale white form walking through the edge of the forest that surrounded the inn. Clad in white armour under a white cloak with a great bow held before it, the Maylak turned to regard him at a distance and then turned and disappeared deeper into the forest. The glow quickly faded into the trees and was gone.

The sudden opening of the kitchen door made him jump and he turned to see who was there. Anatellia stood in the doorway holding two mugs and trying to see him as her eyes adjusted to the night. The door closed behind her and she handed him a mug even though he was already holding one.

"I know you're not used to wine, so I brought you a mug of hot cocoa. Willard's private stock, I'm told." Her smile lit up the dark as she took a long drink from her mug.

"Decadent," he murmured, and tasted the rich smelling liquid. He didn't tell her he'd never had cocoa before in his life. But as he took small sips, he realized it was probably one of the best drinks he'd ever tasted. He set the mug of wine on the ground beside him and leaned back against the inn wall.

"Do you hear that?" Anatellia whispered anxiously.

"Oh, you mean the wolves?" he asked casually between sips. Truly, hot cocoa was amazing.

"Yes." Anatellia nodded emphatically, looking at him like he was drunk. "Of course I mean the wolves."

"Yeah." The howling continued. "They're getting closer."

"You are drunk," she said matter-of-factly, shaking her head and shivering.

"Don't worry, Anna—the Maylak is closer."

"Really?" She sounded both excited and relieved. "You saw her?"

"Just before you came out," he admitted. "Although I cannot be sure it was the same Maylak. It looked different."

"Where did you see her?" she pressed, straining to look into the night.

"Out there just inside the treeline." He pointed. "It looked this way and then went deeper into the forest."

"Why do you keep calling her 'it'?" she asked testily, still straining her eyes for any sign of their holy guardian.

"Well—" He thought about it. "I honestly don't think they are hes or shes."

"The one we met certainly was," she insisted

"Was she?" he asked. Anna pointed at him as he realized what he had just done. "I think we attribute gender to the Maylak simply because we lack understanding. I've never heard of Maylak children or anything like that."

"Maybe you're right," she conceded. "I hadn't thought about it before."

"And from what I could tell at this distance, it was a 'he,'" Ra'ah added drolly.

"Ah," she nodded with a smile and leaned back with him against the inn.

With sadness he realized his mug was empty—the best drink he'd ever had, he decided.

The peace of the moment was broken by the door opening again. Nebaya's form was outlined in the light of the kitchen. She looked around for a few seconds until she saw them.

"Anatellia, we have a problem." Her tone was concerning even to Ra'ah, who recognized her "someone is doing something bad" tone.

"What?" Anatellia's voice rose in pitch.

"Ange is telling them everything." The frustration in the tall woman's voice was palpable.

"That woman!" Anatellia hissed in anger. "Why can't she listen when it matters!"

"Maybe she's right?" Ra'ah offered quietly. He decided not to add that he had already told the majority of their story to the innkeeper's wife in confidence.

"I don't know if she's right or not!" Anatellia turned on him in a low voice. "But none of you truly understands the politics of Kathik, and the last thing we want is to send rumours of our purpose ahead of ourselves into the city!"

"I'm afraid if that is your concern, it's too late now to stop it," Nebaya admitted quietly.

"Living God," Anatellia breathed a prayer, "I hope I'm wrong about this. I truly do."

Another shadow appeared behind Nebaya in the kitchen door. Nebaya stepped out into the night to allow the innkeeper's wife into the doorway.

"I'm not sure about the wisdom of sending those merchants ahead of you into the city with that kind of story," the matronly woman said.

Anatellia just extended her hands toward the woman, directing an exaggerated "I told you so" look back at Ra'ah.

They came into the common room to find Angelis surrounded by a concerned group of locals and sheriffs from Pethe. They were asking her questions about what the Maylak had actually said and what it meant. Some were asking for more information about Cardaya's plans. Everyone was clamouring to ask her their question, and she was doing her best to answer them as honestly as she could.

Daskow saw them come in from the kitchen and just shook his head in resignation.

Ra'ah noticed that the group of the sheriffs from Kathik and the two tables of merchants and their apprentices were staying out of the questioning. But they were listening intently, their eyes focused on the young bard. By tomorrow evening, the news of their story and their mission from the Living God would be circulating throughout the city. He had no small experience with the power of rumour from living in Bato. What kind of damage would the story do in the city?

"Do we help her sort this mess out?" he heard Nebaya whisper to Anatellia.

"She just told the entire room their homes, their way of life, maybe even their very lives are going to be destroyed in four weeks. How do you suppose we sort that out?" Anatellia asked dryly as they made their way to join Daskow.

Ange locked eyes with Anatellia from across the common room. She shrugged imperceptibly in apology. Ra'ah recognized that she realized her mistake. He wondered if she understood how big that mistake was, and he wondered when she'd had the epiphany. Judging by the questions she was being asked, it hadn't prevented her from sharing the entire story.

"I'm sorry," she said for the tenth time.

It was so very late when they finally moved in and apologized to the remaining patrons in the common room, pulling an exhausted Angelis away from answering the same questions people had been asking since she finished telling their story. They all wanted more than Ange could give them. More clarity. More information. More understanding of the threat to the Valley. She had fallen into repeating herself as they got more and more frustrated.

Now she stood in the middle of the room they had been given to sleep in, tears in her eyes, apologizing to Anatellia as the other woman just stared at her.

"I'm not sure sorry is going to help us," Anatellia finally said. "I wish you'd come to me with your plan before you followed through with it."

"I thought I was doing the right thing. I still don't really understand why telling them was so wrong," she repeated again for the tenth time.

"Those merchants and their sheriff escort are going back to Kathik tomorrow as we head to Pethe," Anatellia finally explained. "They will not keep this to themselves. They will tell their wives. They will tell their customers. They will tell everyone in their favourite taverns. The sheriffs will tell their superiors. Those superiors will tell their superiors. If it takes us a week to get to Kathik, how far will the story have gone? What kind of story will it be after so many tellings?"

"Isn't it a good thing to have it go ahead of us?" Ange argued. "Won't that mean we can just show up, confirm it as true, and our job will be done?"

"Ange, you can't be that naïve." Anatellia's sharp words made the bard flinch as if struck. "The message will be shredded beyond truth before we ever get there. We'll be faced with a hundred different stories birthed from the one you shared tonight, and none of them will help us complete our task."

"You don't know that. You can't know that."

"I can know," Anatellia corrected emphatically. "I've witnessed it. Countless rumours will be waiting for us when we arrive in Kathik, and our message will become one version of dozens. You've made our task infinitely more challenging. It would take a miracle to get the message out now."

"What do we do, then?" Daskow stepped in to take the heat off of Ange, who was finally wilting under the reality of what she had released. "Do we change the plan and go to Kathik first and then come back to Pethe?"

Anatellia became silent for a long minute, looking at each of them.

"No; I think we must still stick with our original plan," she sighed heavily. "And I do believe in miracles."

9

Rejection

They woke the next morning and broke fast in the kitchen of the inn. Anatellia's hope was that the group headed to Kathik might forget about the night before and the bard with the wild story of invasion. For their part, the merchants with their sheriff escort left just as dawn broke over the mountains. The other group of sheriffs bound for Pethe were delayed by the problem of their wounded comrade, whose leg would not allow him to ride. The innkeeper finally solved their problem by offering his wagon and team of horses to them, on the condition that they be sent back with Anatellia's group in the coming days.

This was agreeable to everyone, especially the Five, since it meant they could keep up with the mounted sheriffs and get to Pethe that much quicker. So they loaded up and said their goodbyes and were on the road before midmorning. The innkeeper and his wife thanked them for their help and promised them all beds when they came back through. Anatellia returned their thanks and promised to take good care of the horses and wagon.

They waved goodbye as the wagon rolled away, following the troop of sheriffs on their horses. Ra'ah felt like he was leaving family. The short time he'd spent in the Willard's Ox Inn had definitely left a mark and even a strange longing. It was the first time in as long as he could remember that he wanted to remain in a place. He could be happy in that inn.

The others seemed to be mulling over their own thoughts, so he turned to the injured sheriff sitting beside him with his foot propped between their packs and cloaks. The ankle hadn't looked badly broken when he had set it, and the swelling had gone down immensely since the night before. He made sure the leg was raised as much as the wagon and packs would allow, gripping the man's shoulder reassuringly when he saw his worried look.

"You'll be fine so long as you let the bones heal before you dance on it again!"

"Hope so," the man laughed. "I'm supposed to get married in a little over a month. How am I supposed to have my first dance with my wife?"

"I'll find you a crutch when we get to Pethe. Your village healer will have everything you need for a full recovery."

The man nodded, suddenly lost in his own thoughts. They both watched the trees pass on both sides of the road. There were only a few people on the road today, all of them travelling toward Pethe with the sheriffs. He noticed them waiting in farmyards and lanes for the party to pass, and then they would follow, using the sheriffs for protection against the new threat. He pondered where the beasts might lurk and how many of them there actually were. The howls came back to his mind from the night before. *It didn't sound like a chorus,* he thought. However many there were, he wasn't worried. The presence of the Maylak in the forest last night reminded him that the Living God would not let them face anything they could not handle. *But that doesn't mean everyone is safe,* he reminded himself.

"Is it true what the bard said last night?" The wounded man suddenly broke the silence of the wagon.

Ra'ah looked over to Ange, who was briskly walking by herself some way behind the wagon. She'd been uncharacteristically quiet all morning, evidently brooding. He felt bad for her, but couldn't shake Anatellia's dire prediction, either. He knew first-hand the power of rumours.

"Yes, it's true," he finally admitted.

"You saw a Maylak? You've seen one of those black wolves?"

"Yes." He didn't see a point in being evasive. "And the message is also true. We all heard it."

"So the Valley is going to be overrun?" The sheriff looked lost and confused. "Everyone and everything we know is lost."

"What?" Ra'ah was confused. "Where did you get that idea?"

"She told us the Maylak said the enemy was coming and would raze the Valley of Amatta to the ground!"

"But that's not the whole message at all," Ra'ah protested. "Didn't she tell you what the Maylak charged us with? We're supposed to tell everyone to come to the Mountain of the Living God. Leave behind whatever you can't carry with you and flee to the Mountain."

"But everyone knows the only way to the Mountain is through the Valley of Death." The man looked at him like he was simple.

"What?" Ra'ah asked again, perplexed.

"The holy texts clearly state that only those who pass through the Valley of Death can see the Mountain of the Living God. And the Valley of Death is, well, death."

"I always thought those passages to be more poetic than literal," Ra'ah admitted. "And we have a good idea where the mountain is, because Anatellia has seen it."

"Seen it?" the man asked, befuddled. "How could she have seen it?"

"I have seen it," Anatellia assured him as she dropped back beside the wagon from where she'd been eavesdropping. "And I guess in a way I did pass through the Valley of Death to get there. Maybe that's what the ancient writers meant."

"I don't understand," he said in confusion.

"Then let me tell you the story," she sighed, and then vaulted into the back of the wagon.

There was a small audience surreptitiously listening in around the wagon by the time Anatellia was done retelling her story. A few were sheriffs who had heard everything the night before, but some were travellers who had joined up as they passed. The young man sat in troubled contemplation as she finished.

"I will be honest, that is more than a little unbelievable." He locked eyes with her. "More than a few people I know would outright call you a liar, or say you dreamed it or were deceived."

"I've been called worse," she admitted, never breaking eye contact with him. "But I know what I remember. I am not a liar. And none of the other accusations make sense."

"The people of Pethe don't allow for open interpretation of the holy texts," he smiled sadly. "You're going to have a very rough go convincing any of us that what you're saying is true."

"That may be true, but we have to try."

He nodded. "If only you had been given proof."

"What is your name?" she asked gently.

"Thomas," he said quietly.

"What proof could change your mind. Thomas?" she asked him. "How many people walk the highways claiming to have seen a Maylak? How many people have you spoken to who claim to have a message from the Living God?"

"These are all words," he insisted. "Words are easily forged. I've heard that the people of Cardaya say they hear from the Living God all the time. How much farther is it to say you've heard this message from Him?"

"Why would we make this story up?" she pressed.

"I'm sure I don't know. You'd be cast out from the Valley if you did. No one would want you among them."

"Exactly! There is no gain for us. One witness might be touched in the head. Two are unlikely. But five of us? There is nothing for us to gain in spreading false stories. As you said, we'd be outcasts in all the villages. We'd likely be arrested and imprisoned in Kathik."

"You still might. You'd be wiser to forget this quest of yours. All of you would be wiser."

"We can't," she stated flatly. "And neither could you if you'd been there in our camp four nights ago."

"I don't know… you speak with a conviction that is hard to dismiss. But this is so far outside of Doctrine. And like I said, words are easily forged."

"But Doctrine allows for the Living God to speak to us," Ra'ah pointed out.

"Yes, through the holy texts, which is the Word of the Living God," Thomas replied. "That is how He speaks to the Valley."

"Even the texts tell us He has spoken directly to us in the past. And through His messengers, the Maylak," Ra'ah insisted.

"But the holy texts clearly state that He would not always speak so. That form of communication became unnecessary with the completion of the holy texts. Now the Word of the Living God comes through them and not by Maylak."

Ra'ah shook his head and looked across the wounded man to Anatellia. He hadn't realized how deeply the Pethen people were committed to literal interpretation of the holy texts. He had always thought of them like the people of Bato. But this conversation revealed a deep stubbornness and commitment to literalism. He started to wonder what they would do if Pethe refused to listen to them.

"Thomas," he said, "what if we are telling the truth? What if we did encounter a Maylak in the high country four days ago? What if that Maylak did give us the warning for everyone to flee up the Valley in search of the Mountain of the Living God? What if there really is an army coming to the Valley to kill everyone they find and destroy everything they see?"

"We will trust in the Living God," Thomas stated flatly. "We will trust in the Word of the Living God as is given by the holy texts."

"Do you not see the conflict?" Ra'ah asked in frustration.

"The Living God would not contradict Himself," the man stated stubbornly.

"No," Ra'ah sighed, "but He very well might contradict our interpretations."

They had picked up over threescore more travellers by the time they stopped to rest and water the horses and have some lunch. These people were for the most part locals that often made their way to and from the villages selling the various crafts and products of rural life. The way they clustered close to the armed party made the road seem crowded. But even with such a crowd, there was very little chatter between them. A murmur rose and fell in the wind as the members of each little group talked amongst themselves, but there was little communication between the groups. There was an almost palpable cloud of fear over everyone that kept them in their own loose-knit groups and away from others.

One exception was the cluster of little groups that were drawn to the wagon where Ra'ah and Thomas continued to spar over Doctrine and holy texts. Although they were loath to speak into the conversation, they seemed drawn to it like moths to flame. The two men argued themselves to a standstill numerous times, lapsing into a silence that was surrounded by the murmuring of small conversations around them.

Ra'ah hopped out of the wagon when they stopped and refilled the water skins they had drained. Daskow joined him and placed a hand on his shoulder. When he looked into the tutor's eyes, he saw concerned humour.

"You two have argued each other in circles all morning."

"He just can't see past the interpretation of the texts that he's been taught," Ra'ah said in exasperation.

"He has been taught all his life that those interpretations are correct. To him they are life. To him they are salvific." Daskow shook his head. "You are asking him to question his very relationship with the Living God."

"But if they're all like him in Pethe, they aren't going to listen to us," Ra'ah worried. "And we have no signs and wonders to offer."

"That may be true, but on the other hand, it's not our message to defend."

"I don't understand."

"It's the Living God's message through us, Ra'ah," Daskow admonished. "It's not up to us to defend that message or prove that message. That is between the Living God and the people of Pethe."

"That's frustrating."

"I can imagine you are not the first messenger of the Living God to get frustrated, my friend." Daskow smiled and gave his shoulder a squeeze. "But never lose sight that we are just the children of a greater Father. His plans are not ours, and we rarely see the end from the beginning."

"You should be the one talking to Thomas."

"Thomas doesn't want to learn at this point." Daskow shrugged. "You've planted an idea in his head that threatens to bring down his entire understanding of his life in the Valley and the Living God. He's struggling just to keep those walls from falling."

Ra'ah sighed. Yes, he could see what Daskow meant. In fact, he'd experienced that very thing before leaving Bato. He remembered so clearly when the Living God had invaded his carefully built walls of Doctrine and belief—when his desire for the One caused the destruction of the other. Now he walked through life in a far more open world.

After the lead sheriff called out for his troop to mount up, he hurriedly capped the water skin and went back to the wagon. Thomas was being helped back himself, and was thankful for Ra'ah's aid in getting his leg situated again. A quick check confirmed that the limb hadn't changed much on the trip so far, which was a good thing.

"I've been thinking," Thomas ventured, "that if you even had one physical piece of proof of your story, it might be more believable."

"Like a black wolf pelt around my neck?" Ra'ah suggested ironically.

"Well, it would have to be more than a common-looking wolf pelt!"

"Wait…"—the realization hit Ra'ah when he saw Nebaya walking nearby—"maybe we can test this theory of yours. "Nebaya," he called, motioning her over to the wagon.

"Don't get me involved in your little argument," she warned affably. "I have little patience for that kind of discussion."

"I won't drag you in," he assured her. "I just need what's in your quiver."

She shrugged with a smile and handed him her quiver from off her shoulder. The feathered shaft of the white arrow stuck out past all of the others and he carefully caught hold of it and pulled it free, being careful not to spill the other arrows in the process. Nebaya had cleaned it before putting it away, and it gleamed bright white in the sunlight.

"What is that arrow painted with?" Thomas asked in surprise. "I've never seen a white like that!"

"It's not painted," Ra'ah assured him. "This arrow was removed from the creature that was killed in Cardaya. It's the arrow of a Maylak."

"Come on," Thomas scoffed, reaching out for the arrow to prove him wrong.

Ra'ah handed him the arrow. He immediately scraped at the shaft to remove what he thought was paint. Whatever the shaft was made of didn't even mark under his scratching. He turned the arrow over and over. He rubbed the silver arrowhead and tested it with his nails. He ran his fingers over the white feathers, a look of wonder crossing over his face.

"I've never seen craftsmanship like this put into anything as simple as an arrow," he admitted.

"There is more to it than that. The wood of the shaft, the metal in the arrowhead, even the feathers of the fletching aren't of a quality we can reproduce."

"The world is a larger place than the Valley," Thomas countered, but his eyes were shadowed in doubt.

Ra'ah took the arrow back from Thomas. The sunlight disappeared behind a cloud, but the arrow still threw light from its shaft and feathers. He handed it back to Nebaya amidst the murmuring of fellow travellers who watched the arrow, mesmerized.

"That was one physical piece of proof from our story, Thomas." He watched the other man slouch into silence, his face reflecting nothing of what he was thinking.

The mob of travellers arrived in Pethe by mid-afternoon, slowly dissipating into the busy streets until only the Five remained with the sheriffs. The plan was to leave the wagon and horse team at the village stables until they were ready to return to the Crossroads. The sheriffs were polite enough, but Ra'ah got the impression they wanted to be rid of his troop. Anatellia, who had remained uncharacteristically silent since her conversation with Thomas, seemed eager to oblige them.

"Do you know where we would find Elder Sophia at this time of day?" she asked Thomas.

"Sophia?" He seemed surprised she would know the name. "She would be in the library during the day. She is our chief librarian."

"The library? Where is that?"

"By the House of the Living God." He pointed toward a hill opposite the river. "Over there. That stone belltower."

"Perfect—thank you," she said as she looked at her friends. "Let's get about our mission."

"Be careful," Thomas warned. "We aren't Cardayans here."

"A fact I am too painfully aware of." Her tone did not match the smile she gave him.

Thanking the sheriffs, they collected their packs and cloaks from the wagon, and after Ra'ah readjusted Thomas's leg, they departed from their escort and made off down a connecting side street towards the stone building rising over the village a dozen blocks away. Looking back, he saw the lead sheriff watch them go and lean over to speak to a subordinate, who rode off quickly ahead of the troop.

Feeling somehow lighter being away from the sheriffs, they walked in amiable silence. Next to Kathik, Pethe was the oldest settlement. Its buildings were of stone and its streets were paved. The people who lived here could trace their families back to the village founders. There was a sense of history almost matching that of the city in depth.

Ra'ah wondered what the library of Pethe would be like. They almost never entered the older section of the village when they came to trade, finding the business that suited them on the fringes of the village proper. He felt the village's age weigh on him as they went deeper, a sense that they didn't belong there. The people they passed looked at them as if they were out of place. He couldn't ever recall feeling so unwelcome.

"Who is this Elder Sophia we're going to find?" he asked just loudly enough for Anatellia to hear him.

"Hers is one of the letters Elder Shamar gave us," she explained. "I've never heard of her myself. But to be honest, Pethe is not my favourite village, so I know almost nothing about its leaders."

"I just thought we avoided Pethe because there was so little business here," he mused quietly, being careful not to be heard by the residents they passed.

"Are you kidding?" She laughed softly. "Pethe is easily one of the richest villages in the Valley, second only to Kathik herself. But it's got a stuffy, unfriendly feeling to it. Can't you feel it?"

"I thought it was just me."

"No," she sighed, "Pethe tends to be the family member you avoid visiting. Almost all major trade is done with the city, and all of us entertainers, peddlers, and tinkers stay on the fringes with the other riffraff."

"I've seen that," Ra'ah acknowledged, "but I don't understand why."

"That's because you've got a good heart." She smiled warmly at him. "You always want to connect with everyone at that heart level."

"You don't?" he asked, surprised.

"She can't," Ange interjected from right beside him, making him start.

"No I can't," Anatellia nodded, giving Ange an unreadable look.

"It's not that she doesn't want to," Ange continued, seeming to understand the look she had been given. "But Anatellia sees things on a different level. Up here…" She made a move above her own head with her hand.

"It's true," Anatellia admitted, looking around them to get her bearings. "But I sometimes forget that people who connect at that heart level can't help themselves. They have to believe for the best in every encounter."

"You have a good heart as well, Anatellia," Ra'ah affirmed, troubled that she might think otherwise.

"Maybe so," she agreed distractedly.

He looked away from her face to realize they had entered a large square that fronted the great stone House of the Living God. The buildings here were the largest he'd seen outside of the walls of Kathik.

Which one of these is the library? he wondered.

Finding the library turned out to be as easy as asking. The first group of students they asked pointed to a large building to the right of the House.

Upon entering through the great doors, however, they realized that it wouldn't all be so easy.

The main room of the library was row upon row of tables and bookshelves. Rooms branched off of the main room, and through the doors more bookshelves could be seen. People were sitting at the tables reading and writing. Librarians moved around the tables and shelves with determined purpose, keeping the books and scrolls in regimented order.

The first person Anatellia approached asking for Elder Sophia was seated at one of the nearby tables. She simply shushed her and went back to studying the scroll she had unrolled in front of her. Anatellia shrugged helplessly at her friends. Daskow shook his head with a smile and walked toward one of the librarians. Waiting for his attention, he leaned in and whispered a question. The man shook his head and pointed through far double doors to the next room. He then looked over at the other four huddled by the front tables and said something else to Daskow that Ra'ah assumed was uncomplimentary. Pointing to one of the doors to the side of the main entrance, he then said something that definitely carried a sense of finality to it, because Daskow turned on his heel and returned to where they were waiting.

"Charming," was all he muttered as he led them to the door the librarian had indicated.

The door revealed a hallway with alcoves along either side. Many had curtains drawn across them, but those that didn't revealed booths where people could sit and study in relative solitude. Daskow led them to the end of the hall and through a door that opened into a comfortable study. Plush chairs lined a table in the centre of the room. An unlit fireplace sat at the far end and several couches lined the walls. They all filed in and he closed the door behind them all.

"He probably didn't mean this room, but I don't really care," Daskow muttered. "You three stay here and wait for us. Apparently the librarians take a dim view of 'campers' traipsing through the halls. Leave your gear here, Anatellia, and we'll go find Sophia."

"Always knew one day we'd find ourselves in a situation where your skills would be the difference between success and failure," Anatellia chuckled as she set her pack to the side. "I've got the letters—let's go."

The two left, closing the door behind them. Nebaya leaned her pack and bow against the wall, kicked off her boots, and flopped on a couch. Ange and Ra'ah watched her in shock for a long minute before settling onto their own couches.

"How much trouble could we get in if we're caught like this?" Ange giggled.

"They won't survive the smell of our feet long enough to kick us out," Nebaya said sleepily.

"This will not give a good first impression," Ra'ah concluded.

Time passed slowly in the study, and all three of them eventually dropped off to sleep. The sound of the latch was their only warning that someone had found them. All three sat bolt upright as the door swung open, revealing a familiar figure. Daskow stood in the doorway and just stared at them.

"Comfortable?" His tone dripped sarcasm.

"Quite," Nebaya admitted as she reached for a boot. "Until you opened the door without knocking."

"Well, forgive me!" He bowed slightly. "Your presences have been requested."

They gathered up their things, including Anatellia's, and followed Daskow out the door. The afternoon sun that had lit the hall through high windows when they entered the study was gone, replaced by the pale light of dusk. Ra'ah wondered what had happened with Elder Sophia. He felt like events had passed him while they napped.

"Did you find Elder Sophia?" he finally asked as they made their way down another hall that led farther into the library's interior.

"We did," Daskow nodded.

"So will we be brought before the elders?"

"We will not." Daskow shook his head in exaggerated slowness.

The other three exchanged looks behind Daskow's back.

"I don't need to see those looks to know those looks," the tutor commented dryly without turning. "I'm not going to get into it until we're in Elder Sophia's chambers."

"Is it something I did?" Ange's voice was downcast.

"No, not really, Little Sister," Daskow assured her. "Pethe was always going to be a tough sell."

"Tough sell," Ra'ah muttered. "Their village is going to get burned around their ears."

"According to five simple peddlers from the forest," Daskow finished.

"The Maylak gave this message to the wrong people, then," Ra'ah shot back hotly, regretting how loud his voice sounded almost immediately.

"The Maylak didn't make a mistake, Ra'ah," Nebaya assured him quietly. "The Living God chooses exactly the people He means to."

"But why us?" He let his frustration pour out. "Why not a group the villages will respect and listen to?"

"He uses the meek to confound the proud," Daskow quoted as he opened a door and motioned them through.

The door opened into a small entryway with hooks lining one wall. He motioned for them to leave their gear and cloaks there. Two doors led off the entryway, and after they had set down their packs and hung their cloaks, he knocked softly on the one opposite. A muffled reply came back to them, and he opened the door and ushered them into the study of the chief librarian.

The walls of the room were covered in bookshelves. Every possible square foot of space seemed dedicated to the storage of books and other artifacts. The room was warmly lit by enclosed lamps spaced around the room. A desk sat across the room from the door, and sitting in a high-backed chair behind it was a tall, elderly woman regarding them with icy blue eyes. Anatellia sat on a long sofa angled to face the desk with a cup of tea in her hand. Across from her on their own sofa sat two elderly gentlemen with stern faces. They had obviously been interrupted and resolutely ignored the entry of the four, keeping their stoney gazes on the woman behind the desk.

"Please, sit." The woman in the chair gestured in front of her desk. "Elder Paradis was just telling me about the stir you have caused in coming to town."

They quickly found seats around Anatellia as the two men now glared at them. Ra'ah felt like he'd been brought into a meeting with his father and tutor about his conduct, and immediately found a spot on the edge of the sofa opposite the men. Nebaya found a chair in the back corner and returned their looks with one of her own. Ange tried smiling for a second, but quickly lowered her eyes and sat on the sofa with Anatellia. Daskow simply stood with his arms crossed beside the door. The woman behind the desk raised her eyebrows at him, but continued gracefully. "Elder Paradis, if you would continue."

"There is not much more to be said," the elderly gentleman huffed. "And I will not repeat myself for the sake of the tardy. These vagrants are spreading rumour and false teaching and when we came to you to warn you, we find them here."

"Elder Paradis"—the woman's smile did not reach her eyes—"as we've already established, these five are not 'vagrants.' As our contemporary Elder Shamar has outlined in his letter, these are perilous times and they come claiming a message from the Living God."

"Blasphemous!" the man beside Paradis snorted. "That is heresy."

"Brother Shaquar, you are Elder Paradis's guest here, but in my study outbursts are not tolerated. Nor is slander." She raised her hand to forestall another outburst. "Comply with my expectations or leave."

"What Brother Shaquar is so inelegantly trying to convey"—Paradis paused to glared at his associate before continuing—"is that there are forms that are not being observed if this is actually a warning that comes from the Living God Himself. And a messenger of the Living God would know this.

"Now I suspect our 'contemporary' from Cardaya would choose to ignore these forms and conventions. Cardayans are not known for their devotion and adherence to sound Doctrine after all. But we will not simply ignore our own understanding to hear unsubstantiated fear-mongering from a pack of tinkers from the forest."

"I'm sorry; we were not given a manual when the Maylak gave us our message," Nebaya's brittle, barely restrained voice floated from the back of the room.

Brother Shaquar half turned in his seat to retort hotly, but the slap of Elder Sophia's hand on her desk shut his mouth tight. Nebaya returned glare for glare and the room settled into awkward silence.

"I fear we may be so sure of the mind of the Living God contained in holy texts that we might miss even the simplest of messages spoken in an unfamiliar way," Elder Sophia spoke softly into the silence her hand had created. "I am unwilling to ignore Miss Anatellia and her friends simply because they don't come with the pomp and ceremony you expect from such messengers. And frankly, Elder Paradis, I trust Elder Shamar's connection with the Living God more than yours.

"It is unfortunate that rumour has gone ahead of them," she continued. "Rumour is rarely truth's ally. But you have not even heard their story and the message they carry. That is as foolish as judging someone based solely on rumour alone. For my part, I have listened to what Miss Anatellia has to say and although I have my own personal doubts, I do not doubt she believes what she and her friends have heard and seen. And you know me better than to question my ability to judge character. I believe that at the very least they should have the opportunity to tell their story to the elders."

"I disagree." Elder Paradis shook his head. "And I have the support of the Brotherhood in that respect. You may be respected among the elders, Sophia, but you will not force your will onto the elder council in this. I came here to dissuade you from supporting these… messengers."

"*Elder* Paradis, have you given consideration to what your arrogance could cost Pethe and its people?"

"I serve the Living God," he said through clenched teeth. "I will keep the truth of the holy texts and Doctrine in all things. The forms are very clear and established regarding how messages are sent and received. Do you reject the purity and sufficiency of the holy texts?"

"I am the chief librarian," she reminded him hotly. "I, more than you, understand that where ancient text meets modern interpretation there is always need for grace in interpretation. And that is not blasphemy, that is wisdom."

"You would not be the first to confuse the two," Paradis returned. "I would rather Pethe stand strong in Doctrine and risk utter destruction than to run away somewhere and sacrifice our dignity to false prophecy. And the other elders will agree with me."

"We will bring this to them," Sophia declared, rising from her seat.

"I already have," Paradis sneered. "And I have the support of the majority, as you may already realize. As I have already said, you are respected amongst the elders. This is my olive branch to you. Don't lose that respect by forcing this issue."

Silence settled over the librarian's study as the two elders stared at one another across her desk. Ra'ah couldn't believe what he was hearing. The request to speak to the council was going to be refused. He didn't much understand politics, but he recognized the forces at play. That Elder Paradis would be so blatant and open with them made the young man's blood boil. He felt something rise up inside him in response.

"Elder Paradis," his voice sounded with barely concealed emotion, "You're risking all the lives of Pethe in political games. You claim to serve the Living God, but you only serve yourself and your ambitions. The Living God will hold you to account for the lives lost by your actions."

"Silence, boy!" Brother Shaquar slammed his hand onto the arm of the sofa.

"Silence yourself!" Ra'ah turned savagely at the robed man. "You are worse than him! You claim knowledge of what you have not seen and do not understand. You look in the faces of those who have seen and call them liars! Well, I have seen, so let the Living God judge between you and me who is right!"

"Peace!" Elder Sophia's voice boomed over them all.

Silence fell over the room again. Brother Shaquar's face was livid with rage. Elder Paradis sat still as stone, regarding his counterpart across the desk. The others just stared at Ra'ah with a comical mixture of surprise and approval. For his part, he felt the weight of the lives of Pethe that hung in the balance.

"I think this meeting is concluded," Elder Paradis declared. "You will not bring these children before the Elder Council."

"I fear the young man is correct." Elder Sophia shook her head sadly. "And my heart breaks."

"As to that," Paradis concluded, "I will send sheriffs to collect them. They will have to answer for the public nuisance they have caused."

The five looked at each other in shock. Nebaya looked ready to fly across the room and strangle the elder where he sat. Never in all Ra'ah's thinking did the idea that they would be punished for the message occur to him.

Elder Sophia's quiet voice broke through all their chaotic thoughts. "No," she said simply. "They will not."

"Sophia—" The rebuke was cut short again by a sharp raise of her hand.

"You will not use these youths for your sick political machinations, Paradis," she insisted in a voice that silenced him completely. "I will see them escorted out of Pethe at first light. I will not allow them to be punished for the virtues of honesty and sincerity any more than they unfortunately already have been. And you and your brotherhood lap dogs will allow this."

"And if I don't?" he asked hotly.

"Then you will know and understand what it means when I say I will commit myself wholly and completely to your political conflagration." Her smile was not reflected in her icy eyes.

"Very well." His composure temporarily cracked under her stare. "If they are not gone by noon tomorrow, they will be arrested. And if they ever return to Pethe, they will be arrested."

"Elder Paradis, if they are truly messengers of the Living God, there will not be a Pethe to return to by the new moon," she responded coolly.

"Bah!" He stood up abruptly. "You have not heard the last of this."

"To be sure." She motioned to the door. "You can see yourself out."

The two men stormed out of the study, all but slamming the door behind them. Elder Sophia sat behind her desk in silence and waited in distaste until a second, more muffled slam signalled their complete departure from her apartments.

"Do not feel this is your fault. I doubt Elder Paradis would have accepted your message if you'd brought the Maylak herself. Men such as he are lost in their own ambition. Unfortunately the Brotherhood has become little different."

"What can we do?" Angelis moaned. "How will we get the message out to Pethe?"

"You must leave that to me," Sophia said. "For better or worse, your message is delivered."

She leaned back to the wall and pulled a cord set against it. From somewhere outside the room a bell rang.

"Since you must leave in the morning, let's get this message down clearly tonight."

10

Detoured

They spent the rest of the evening giving account of the events of the last four days. Scribes were assigned to each of them, men and women whose skill seemed to be to specifically draw out details that the five didn't even realize they had not expressed. Sophia explained to them that while Paradis may have had the ear of a majority of the elders, there were still a few who would listen. Once the scribes had dutifully dug out everyone's full recollection of events, they would form them into a single, comprehensive narrative that would be distributed throughout Pethe to spread the message.

"Will there be enough time?" Ra'ah caught himself asking after she explained the plan.

"We've been given three weeks warning thanks to you five," Sophia assured him, and then held up the letter from Elder Shamar. "Cardaya has promised support for everyone heading up the valley. They will have checkpoints to guide groups moving up the highway to Cardaya and then across the river toward Bato. I suspect that everyone who wishes to heed the warning will be on their way up river within two weeks. Well ahead of whatever monstrosity follows on the new moon."

"I had no idea about Cardaya's plans," Ra'ah admitted. "I just kind of imagined everyone racing up the Valley to Gellah."

"Not very practical or wise," Elder Sophia smiled. "But it wasn't your responsibility to plan the logistics of obedience, was it?"

"I guess not," he smiled back.

"We all serve the Living God," she declared. "We will obey with the gifts we've been given, according to the tasks at hand."

"Why send everyone up to Cardaya before crossing the river?" Angelis asked from the chair where she had been eavesdropping. "Why not cross at Kathik where's there is a bridge?"

"Because your message has not come to Kathik yet, nor to Bato," the elder explained patiently. "The road will be unguarded and the city and village unprepared for refugees. Remember, our enemy has already come into the valley and in numbers we still do not know. The black beasts have surely been sent ahead to prevent this retreat."

"I hadn't thought of that," Ange admitted with a shiver.

"Once we get to Kathik, we will be able to mobilize the sheriffs and the Guard," Ra'ah assured her. "Then they can secure the roads and hunt the creatures out there."

"I wouldn't hold too tightly to that hope," Elder Sophia lamented. "The politics of the city make our little political world in Pethe seem unremarkable."

Ra'ah woke to a hand shaking his shoulder. He opened sand-filled eyes to see the blurry form of Nebaya standing over him. She smiled apologetically and held out his pack. With unintelligible groaning he uncurled from the chair where he had fallen asleep, stood up, and stretched. They had retired back to the meeting room sometime in the early hours to get a little sleep before they departed back to the Crossroads. A faint light filled the hallway beyond the door, revealing that sunrise was already upon them.

"I feel like I didn't even sleep," he muttered as he took the pack from her.

"Well, you did. Although with your snoring it's unlikely anyone else was able to."

"I know *you* slept," he shot back. "You woke me up at least twice with your snorting. How far is it to the stables?"

"You can thank Elder Sophia for the extra sleep. She felt it better if her man went and retrieved the wagon for us. It's waiting in the square out front."

Ra'ah was relieved. Pethe had lost any sense of friendliness it may have had since their arrival the evening before. Ange came over to join them, her hair a tangled mess that was a signature of hers when she'd just been woken up. Smiling, she gave Ra'ah's arm a squeeze and then walked out the door. Smiling back at her silent encouragement, he and Nebaya followed her out into the hall and down to the front entry.

The wagon was sitting there, the horses fresh and watered. A man of about fifty sat on the seat, holding the reins loosely in one hand. The other hand ruffled the scruff of a large wolfhound lying across the seat beside him, its great head resting on the man's lap. The hound opened its eyes to regard them as they came out the door and, deeming them no real threat, closed its eyes with a huff. The man regarded them with casual interest and then returned to scanning the courtyard watchfully. He was dressed in a well-used travel cloak and boots that looked out of place in the village.

Elder Sophia stood by the wagon with two other well-dressed people that Ra'ah had not seen before. They were talking with Anatellia but finished up as the three approached. The new man and woman were of a similar age to Sophia, dressed in the fine fabrics of the merchant class. They regarded the newcomers with neutral stares, nodding as Sophia made introductions.

"Elders Ako and Peith, this is Ra'ah, Nebaya, and Angelis." She gestured to each as they bowed slightly in respect. "And here comes Daskow, back from the errand I sent him on."

Daskow bowed at the waist awkwardly as he hurried down the steps behind them, a leather scroll tube tucked under his arm. The two elders regarded each of them in turn, unconcerned about any discomfort they might be causing.

"The elders share my concern for Pethe and the Maylak's message to us all. They will help me guide as many as possible toward understanding and obedience, though it will cost us our seats on the council."

"I'm sorry," Ange blurted.

"Why?" Elder Ako, a tall, slender woman with intense eyes, asked her. "If we valued our positions more than truth and the lives of those we are in authority over, we would be unworthy of those positions. I am an elder by Calling, not by popular vote."

"I just meant I was sorry that we're causing so much trouble," Ange replied sheepishly.

"Do not apologize for the Living God," the elder named Peith chastised her gently. "How can the messenger do anything but faithfully deliver the message of her Master?"

"Thank you," was all she could think of to say at that point, wishing she were invisible.

"I've tasked Amon here with escorting you out of Pethe." Elder Sophia motioned to the man and dog sitting on the wagon. "He is not bound to you beyond the Crossroads, though he may be of his own mind as to where he goes from there."

The man simply nodded to them in greeting.

"Take the lessons you've learned here to heart," she admonished them all. "Kathik will be anything but predictable. Use wisdom in both what you say and whom you say it to. By no means assume your task will be quick or easy there. I've added letters of my own to the letters of Elder Shamar, and we will send what further help we can once we've done all we can here."

They all thanked her and climbed up into the wagon. With a soft call, Amon started the team of horses and set off at a brisk trot out of the square. The wolfhound, disturbed from his slumber on the wagon seat, quickly hopped down into the wagon bed with them. With a good-natured stretch, he allowed Angelis to scratch his ears and then proceeded to inspect every inch of them and their bags.

"What's your dog's name?" Ange asked the stoic man driving the wagon.

"Pestos."

"Hello, Pestos." She scratched the dog's scruff as he dutifully continued his exploration.

They were out of the village proper in short order and were on the highway before Ra'ah really realized it. Pestos had thoroughly gone over each of them, eliciting small treats from each of them as they secretly made offerings of friendship to the affable hound. As he scratched the dog's neck, he suddenly noticed they were no longer within the confines of buildings; rather, the trees of the highway surrounded them on either side. With stiff legs, he climbed up into the seat beside the driver. Amon acknowledged him with a nod and then returned to scanning the road and forest ahead.

The highway was all but empty of travellers even though the sun was shining over the mountains. The few people they did encounter were heading into the village with furtive glances into the fields and copses on either side of the road. The fear and tension were palpable.

"Has something happened since yesterday?" Ra'ah asked Amon.

"Black wolves," the man nodded. "They've been attacking people without the sense to travel in large groups. Three or four separate incidents yesterday. But they know enough to avoid large groups or armed travellers. And they won't come anywhere near Pestos without him letting us know about it, so you needn't worry."

"I doubt they will come near us for more than that reason," Ra'ah said casually, remembering the Maylak in the woods just the night before last.

Amon just snorted and nodded. His eyes were bright and never stopped scanning the road and land in front of them. Ra'ah doubted black wolves could sneak up on either him or his dog. He looked over to where the man's bow and quiver rested within easy reach of the seat. Even though they looked worn with use, the craftsmanship was evident.

"What kind of work do you do for Elder Sophia?"

"Whatever she requires of me." He gave the young man a sidelong look before continuing. "She's got a deep affinity for the forest and mountains. Always curious. Always needing to study what she doesn't understand herself. Books don't satisfy that curiosity. I'm her guide and companion outside of civilized circles."

"You're *that* Amon," Nebaya murmured from the back of the wagon.

"I'm sure I don't know what you mean by that." Amon looked back at the tall huntress. "But I've travelled the length and breadth of the Valley and the mountains beyond since before any of you were born."

"I meant no disrespect," Nebaya responded apologetically. "It's just that I believe you knew my parents."

"Oh? Who are your parents?" The man returned to scanning the road ahead.

"Their names were Breck and Amaya," Nebaya answered quietly. "They lived in a small cabin high on the slopes above Cardaya."

There was silence for so long that Ra'ah wondered if the man hadn't heard her. Nebaya never mentioned her parents. He had never even heard her speak their names in all the time they'd travelled together. Amon's eyes seemed focused on something in the far distance. Finally, with a soft sigh, he turned to regard her from under his thick eyebrows, as if studying her.

"Yes, I knew Breck and Amaya. I also knew their spirited daughter, although she does not remember much of me." He continued to stare at her. "It was a sad day among the Called the day they died."

"A sad day all around," she agreed softly.

"I'm not surprised to find you wandering the wilderness," he continued gently. "You heard the Call at a younger age than anyone I've known. I told that uncle of yours that very fact, when we brought you down to Cardaya."

"What?" Nebaya's eyes were haunted as she jerked around to fully face the man in the front of the wagon.

"It was the old apothecary and I who found you in the cistern of that burnt-out cabin after the fire. You were barely alive when we found you, shivering and fevered and lungs full of smoke. We took you down to the village healers and your uncle said you were home now. I warned him you wouldn't stay put for long. Looks like I was right."

"That was you?" she whispered roughly.

"Aye, that was me," he nodded, turning back to the road. "It's a small Valley, isn't it?"

The wagon rattled on to the beat of the horses' hooves as Nebaya regarded the back of the now silent Amon. To Ra'ah's surprise, he saw silent tears rolled down her cheeks. Angelis noticed them too, and laid her hand tentatively on Nebaya's knee. Nebaya smiled sadly at her, and then in a move that surprised everyone pulled Angelis close and buried her face in her shoulder, her body betraying the weeping she suddenly let free.

The morning rolled past them in the form of sunny fields and tranquil tree groves. No one travelled the road with them, and the few people they saw along the way were wary and stayed close to their homes. Some time after midmorning Nebaya broke the silence and started telling Ange about her parents. Ra'ah and the others sat quietly and listened as she poured out her memories—almost for the first time, it seemed.

From her sobbing rambling they learned that her mother and father were a bit of a scandal in Cardaya. Her mother was the daughter of a village elder and a gifted orator in her own right. It was assumed that she would one day take her father's place on the council. But she fell in love with a young traveller named Breck, and they ran off together to follow the Call. They became renowned throughout the valley for their ability to interpret dreams and provide timely wisdom. They eventually settled in a cabin up the slope from Cardaya when Amaya became pregnant with Nebaya.

She had fond memories of the cabin where her father taught her to shoot the bow and snare their suppers. She talked for a long time about the creek nearby and the forest that surrounded their home on all sides. She talked herself quiet and then simply sat for a long time. A cloud passed over the sun briefly, and as if on cue she started talking about the day the fire came.

She didn't remember much, she admitted. She looked at Amon's back, but when he didn't immediately offer his version of events she continued with her broken memories of that awful day. She remembered how dry that summer had been. Her father had dug the cistern after the creek had started to dry up. The sky at night was full of dry lightning, but no rain. The wind had picked up that morning and was blowing hard up the valley by noontime. She remembered she was eating her lunch when her father burst into the cabin. Behind him the clear morning had turned to a rolling grey white. She remembered the fear in his eyes.

The rest of her recollection was jumbled, pieced together like the fragments of a broken vase. Incomplete, like the vase had been smashed into a thousand pieces. She recalled their initial flight to the edge of the dell. Her father looked down in horror at the rolling smoke and flame all around their cabin. He realized that the fire had surrounded them. They ran back to the cabin. There was a roaring sound all around them, louder than Gellah Falls in flood. She remembered the heat. Her parents lowered her into the cistern. The water was only up to her knees. She remembered her mother's scream, and her father slammed the stone lid of the cistern down. She remembered the roaring, the terrible roaring. The cistern filled with so much smoke that she struggled to breathe. She sat down in the water and cried.

Tears in her eyes again, she remembered waking up to voices and a light above her. She did not know how long she'd been down there. She felt cold and removed from her body. Her lungs hurt. Arms picked her up and she was lifted out of the cistern. She thought she had woken up in hell. The dell that they had lived in all her life was a blackened, burnt bowl. The trees were blasted spears of black. The cabin was gone. Her parents were gone. Her heart crawled deep inside her and hid.

She remembered waking up again in the Healer's House in Cardaya. Her uncle introduced himself and told her she would be coming to live with them. She refused. She would go back up into the forest and find her parents. She tried sneaking out of the house so many times they eventually had to lock her in her room at night. She didn't remember exactly when the reality hit her that her parents were really and truly dead, but she remembered the last words she spoke to her uncle in that house. She was twelve, and had gathered all of her belongings in a pack she had secretly bought the day before. She was met at the gate by her uncle, who told her she was being foolish. He warned her that he wouldn't stop her this time and if she left, she was on her own. She said she was fine with that. She said a great deal more than that, pouring out a hurt-filled litany against the man who had become the focal point of all of her pain. And then she left, never to return to that house.

"I owe that man an apology," she concluded softly as the wagon rolled on.

They made only a brief stop to water the horses and take a quick lunch, and then they were back on the move. Keeping that pace, they arrived at the Crossroads mid-afternoon and pulled up to a stop in the side courtyard of the Willard's Ox. The yard and stable looked all but deserted until they found the stable boy sleeping soundly in the loft.

The women left the men to help the sleepy-eyed stable hand unhitch the team from the wagon and put it away. Pestos gave a quick glance at Amon and then followed Ange and the others around the corner to the entrance. Ra'ah suspected the sudden friendship between the woman and the hound had to do with the treats she had been sneaking him since they'd eaten lunch. Amon just shook his head at the dog.

They unhitched the team of horses from the wagon and helped the boy stow the gear in the tack room inside the barn. The stalls were empty of guest horses, which explained the stable hand's ability to take a nap. The boy led the horses to their stalls, and the men went around to the front entrance and entered the common room.

The room was empty except for their friends talking to the Willards at a table. Matron Willard waved them over as soon as she saw them. The innkeeper went back to the bar and retrieved three more mugs and another jug of cider.

"You all made better time than you should have," the kind woman noted as they sat down. "The girls were catching us up on what happened. Self-righteous fools."

"Now, mother," the innkeeper scolded, "that is not very gracious."

"There is a time for being gracious and there is a time for telling the truth!" she insisted, and then realized there was a sixth member of their group. "Oh, but forgive me, I spoke crossly and meant no real harm."

"No harm has been done, Abigail," Amon laughed as he lowered the dusty hood of his travel cloak. "I find blunt honesty refreshing when I can find it."

"Why, Amon!" The matron's face lit up in recognition. "Look, Bill, it's Amon come to visit."

"I recognized him by his mutt." The innkeeper nodded to the dog as he poured cider. "And you would have too, but Miss Ange has him wrapped around her finger with those treats she's sneaking him."

"Pestos and I have developed an understanding." Ange froze in mid-slip and Pestos nudged her hand to release the treat. Amon shook his head at the dog.

"He's a fickle friend," he admitted ruefully to her. "He'll follow whomever has the treats and then abandon them once the treats are gone. You've been warned. And it's a good thing we're walking from here, or he'd become too fat to be of use on the road."

"You aren't going back to Pethe this afternoon, are you?" the innkeeper's wife worried. "At least stay the night here with us before you return."

"I will stay the night," Amon conceded. "But I will not be returning directly to Pethe. I've got errands to run up-Valley."

"That employer of yours should have sent sheriffs with you," she scolded. "It's growing positively unsafe in the open country."

"It will take more than black wolves to hinder Pestos and me. And Sophia needs every sheriff loyal to her right now."

"We were just getting into that with the ladies here," Abigail agreed. "Have a seat and let's hear the full story of the last twenty-four hours."

"Pethe as a whole has always valued their traditions and interpretations of holy texts more than actually seeking beyond the words to the One the texts speak about," Abigail lamented after they told them the whole story. "Could be why so few from that village actually hear the Call."

"There will be people who hear this one," Amon assured her. "Elder Sophia will be sure of that. You'll be seeing movement up the highway within the week."

"I take it that's why you're going up-Valley?" She got up and made for the kitchen door. "Join me in the kitchen, Ra'ah. I've got to check my stew, and you're going to show me what you did to those biscuits the other night. There's something in your recipe that puts mine to shame."

"Coming." Ra'ah stretched his knotted back as he stood. He should have walked a little and not ridden in the wagon all day. "How far is it to Kathik from here?"

"We'll be at the gates just before noon tomorrow," Daskow confirmed. "Assuming we get on the road before the sun clears the mountains."

"I'm looking forward to finally seeing it again," he confessed as he followed Abigail into the kitchen.

"I'm not," Anatellia's voice followed him through the door.

Ra'ah spent the rest of the afternoon baking with Abigail in the kitchen. He showed her some of the spices he liked to use, and explained what worked with what dishes. She smiled and nodded, offering suggestions of her own when opportunity arose.

"A healer and gifted cook?" she teased him. "How has no woman convinced you to marry her yet?"

"I guess I'm good at hiding those skills." His face flushed in embarrassment. "And the thought of settling down in the villages doesn't appeal to me right now. Although I could get used to this."

"Master Willard and I were never able to have kids," Abigail lamented, although she smiled at his discomfort simultaneously. "Maybe we can combine our talents when all of this is over? Maybe even find you a wife?"

"Maybe," he laughed nervously, his face now burning. "But that seems far off and unlikely at this point, doesn't it?"

"Life continues, even in terrible times," she murmured, smiling to herself.

Life continues. His mind raced at the realization that they really had no idea how all this was going to end. He still vacillated between disbelief, despair, and blind trust regarding their mission and what it actually meant for the Valley. The realization that the villages, the city, and even this inn were all in danger of being destroyed. Destroyed by an army from beyond the Valley.

He knew there were lands beyond the Valley, of course. The holy texts told the story of the first people who, following the Call and fleeing persecution, came to the valley so many generations ago. Here they had set up a society where they could serve the Living God in peace. Here they were free. Free of the persecution and death of those distant lands.

And now an enemy approached, an enemy from those distant lands, coming to bring persecution and death to the descendants of those who escaped them so many years before. There was little teaching of who that enemy was. Servants of a greater Enemy, holy texts would say. The memory of the beast that had attacked them almost a week before flashed into his mind. That creature served a greater Enemy.

His thoughts were interrupted by a commotion at the back door. A young boy burst into the kitchen, panting and exhausted. His eyes darted wildly around the room until they fell on the innkeeper's wife. With a look of relief, he ran over and grabbed her hand and started pulling toward the door.

"Mistress Willard, Mom's hurt!" he panted, continuing to pull at her hand. "Dad sent me down to fetch you to help!"

"Goodness, Ethan, calm down," Abigail gently turned him around. "Now sit down a moment, and I'll get you some stew and you can tell me the whole story."

"But I've got to bring you back to Mom!" Ethan insisted. "She's real sick!"

"Ethan, I'm going to help, but do as I say." She led the boy to the back table and motioned for Ra'ah to bring a bowl of stew.

Reluctantly the boy sat down and took the spoon he was offered as Ra'ah set a small bowl and a biscuit in front of him. He looked to be about ten; his clothes were dirty and very rural. He took several quick bites and realized he was very hungry. With renewed vigour, he started shovelling the stew into his mouth.

"Slow down—you won't help your mother choking on stew," the matronly woman admonished.

"Mom's hurt," he began with a mouthful of stew, but stopped when Abigail gave him a withering look. He chewed, swallowed, and began again.

"Mom's hurt," he repeated more clearly. "She and Dad were checking the snare lines yesterday when they came upon a wolf. Dad said it was crazed or sick or something. Anyway, this wolf charged at mom and Dad stuck it with, like, six arrows. The thing was possessed or something, Dad said. Anyway, this great big wolf grabbed Mom by the leg and that's when she stabbed it with her knife. *Bam!* Right through the eye, Dad said."

"Your dad told you all of this?" Ra'ah asked in wonder.

"Well, no," Ethan admitted. "Dad sent me outside when he was tending her leg, and I heard them talking about it. But he was just trying to protect me from being scared. He seemed pretty impressed she got that wolf right in the eye, though. Said so himself."

"Ethan," Abigail refocused his attention, "finish your story. Why isn't your father here looking for help? Or better still, why didn't all of you come down here for help?"

"Well, that wolf bite got nasty infected in the night, and this morning Mom was in pretty bad shape. Dad says she's got a bad fever and he's done everything he can do. He sent me here to fetch you while he looked after Mom, because he didn't think I could. She's awfully strong and the fever makes her thrash around." He looked from one listener to the other to see if they understood.

"You were very brave to come down alone, Ethan," Abigail said. "And we'll get your mom the help she needs. Now finish that stew."

"Ra'ah"—she turned to him, and he knew what she was about to ask—"would you be willing to go? It's about an hour to their cabin."

"I'll get my things and see who will come with me," he agreed quickly. "I may need some supplies I don't normally carry."

"I have everything you'll need. An innkeeper is forced to be prepared, as you already know."

It took only a short time to get everything organized. Everyone agreed that Nebaya and Amon would go with him—the latter all but insisted. They had enough light to get to the cabin, but not if they got lost, Amon pointed out. He and Pestos could get them there safely and then get them back to the road so they could catch up with the others who would depart for Kathik first thing in the morning. They would have to spend the night with Ethan's family, however.

Ra'ah packed the supplies that Abigail set out for them and they ate a quick meal before heading out the back kitchen door and into the forest behind the inn. The other three stood with the innkeepers and waved as they disappeared into the trees. Ethan bounded ahead of them, eager to complete his mission. Amon suggested he stay a little closer in case another wolf was about and the boy's eagerness became tempered, his eyes glancing uneasily from side to side as they followed the trail up the slope of the valley.

There was little doubt the wolf that had attacked Ethan's mother was one of the black beasts prowling the Valley. Nebaya was particularly disturbed to hear that the beast had taken six arrows and still came on. Amon was also disturbed by that part of the story, but even more so because he knew the father and his skill with a bow.

"In the time it took to fire half that many, the beast should have been dead." He shook his head. "We need to hear this story first hand."

"I'm just happy to have you go with us. None of the others can handle a bow under pressure," Nebaya said.

"They shouldn't need to on the road to Kathik," he assured her. "Once our young healer here has done what he can for Emily, I'll get you back to the highway."

The tall huntress nodded, warily scanning the forest.

The hour it took them to get to the cabin was uneventful, and they arrived as dusk settled in. Ethan ran ahead as they reached familiar territory, ignoring Amon's earlier warning. Ethan's father, Mark, was waiting for them in the doorway when they entered the clearing.

"Mark," Amon called, "how's Em?"

"Fighting," Mark said shortly, the strain on his face revealing more about her condition, even to the two strangers, than his word and tone conveyed.

"This is Ra'ah," Amon introduced the young healer. "Abigail speaks quite highly of him."

"A healer?" Mark regarded the younger Ra'ah with mild suspicion.

"Healer-trained," Ra'ah assured him. "I've brought bandages, salves, and some tea for the fever."

"Come, please," He stepped aside and let them into the cabin, following closely behind.

The cabin was lit by a fire in the hearth. The main room was spacious with two rooms off the back—obviously bedrooms. On a makeshift bed by the fire lay Emily. She didn't look up as they entered, but lay staring at the roof shivering. Mark hurried over to her as Ra'ah immediately got to business. He gave soft orders to Nebaya, who moved to follow his direction. Amon stood with Ethan, keeping the boy out of the way with an expert hand on the lad's shoulder.

"Help is here, Em," Mark assured her, taking up a cloth that had fallen off of her forehead and rewetting it in a bowl of cool water beside the bed. Gently he dabbed her face, concern written on his brow.

"I need to look at her leg," Ra'ah explained apologetically as he pulled back the blanket that covered the wound.

The jagged marks of a great jaw were outlined on her calf, which was swollen impossibly large. It looked much like a wound he'd seen on a trapper who had caught his leg in a bear trap some years before, before he'd left Bato. He examined the leg carefully, gently touching the swollen flesh and the pus-filled tooth punctures. She cried out in pain and he apologized softly as he continued. The wound was obviously infected—but there was something else, something about one puncture in particular.

"You cleaned the bite?" he asked the man.

"Yes," Mark nodded. "It wasn't much of a bite, really. It bit down on her and she stabbed it through the eye so quick, it didn't have time to savage the leg. Just punctured the skin through her pants. But I had to pry that cursed thing's jaws open."

"Did you check its teeth after?" Ra'ah probed one puncture carefully, wincing as Emily cried out.

"What?" Mark looked confused. "Why? No, I pried the jaws from her leg, washed it with our canteens and helped her back here where we cleaned it up properly and bandaged it. She was fine when we went to sleep last night, and when I woke up this morning she was fevered and incoherent."

"I think there is something in this puncture." Ra'ah motioned for a candle on a nearby table.

Nebaya grabbed the candle, lit it in the fire, and handed it to him. He held the light to the woman's leg and leaned in. With a shudder, he handed it back to Nebaya and drew a narrow knife from the sheath that he kept at his side.

"There is something in the wound," he confirmed. "I think it's a tooth."

"Let me see." Mark took the candle from Nebaya and held it to the spot that Ra'ah had just examined. He stared for a long moment. "It can't be a tooth—it looks black."

"Nevertheless"—Ra'ah pulled a small flask of alcohol out of his pack and motioned for a bowl on the table nearby—"that looks like a tooth."

He took the bowl that Nebaya handed him and poured the contents of the flask over the blade of his dagger, catching the runoff in the bowl. He felt a tremor pass through his hand at the thought of what he had to do next. He looked up at Nebaya and she immediately nodded in understanding.

"We need to hold her down," she told the husband quietly, and then looked to Amon. "I need you to hold her other leg while I hold the wounded one. Ra'ah needs to cut out whatever is festering in that leg."

Everyone is moving too efficiently, Ra'ah realized. He was barely ready. He hated this part of healing—causing pain to bring a cure always seemed such a contradiction. He looked over to Ethan, who had taken a seat at the far end of the room with Pestos. The hound rested his head on the boy's lap and regarded Ra'ah with unreadable eyes. *Everyone knows their job even better than me,* he mused. He motioned to Amon to take the candle from Mark, and the man took it after a moment of juggling, leaning on the Emily's good leg to free up his hand.

Ra'ah took a deep breath and turned the wounded leg so that the puncture in question was fully in the candlelight. The jagged edges of something black and ugly could be plainly seen sticking out of the wound, the woman's body rejecting its presence even as it killed her. He placed his hand on the leg and brought the point of the dagger to the edge of the wound.

"Hold her," he breathed, and then added to the almost comatose woman, "I'm sorry."

The echo of her scream carried out into the night.

The jagged black tooth was a horror to behold. Mark and Amon were busy examining it by the light of the fire, but neither of them felt inclined to touch it. Nebaya helped Ra'ah dress the now cleaned wound, applying salve to the punctures after he cleaned each one. He took extra care in cleaning the puncture from which the tooth had been removed. The tooth itself had been oddly serrated and rotten at its root. He thanked the Living God he'd been careful and not just tried to pull it straight out, or it might have broken apart and poisoned the woman further.

"This isn't a tooth from the wolf that attacked us," Mark insisted. "Those teeth were white."

"I believe you," Ra'ah assured him. "I also believe that it came from that wolf."

"I've never seen a wolf with a tooth rotted like this," Amon added. "In fact, I've never seen any tooth as rotten as this. Look, I think it's rotted more since it was removed."

"I think it started to rot after it broke off," Ra'ah offered. "There is something foul and unnatural about these things."

"It was like no wolf I've seen, and certainly not like the wolves that wander into the Valley from time to time," Mark confirmed. "Its fur was black and matted. And its eyes…"

"Malevolent," Ra'ah muttered. "Yes, we've encountered one before."

"So it was one of the beasts terrorizing the villages," Amon nodded to himself. "You were fortunate it was alone."

"There are more of them?" Mark's face furrowed in concern. "Where are they coming from?"

"From outside of the Valley," Nebaya responded cryptically. "We'll explain further when your wife is looked after."

"How is she?" The man looked at his wife's drawn face in concern.

"She's strong," Ra'ah nodded as he worked. "These salves will help deal with the infected wounds, and I've got some herbs and teas that will help her body fight off any infection in her blood. It's too early to predict anything about her recovery, but she hasn't gotten worse since I removed the tooth."

"It's a good thing you were at the inn," Mark sighed in relief. "Thank you."

Ra'ah nodded.

Emily regained consciousness as they finished wrapping her leg in bandages. Her eyes fluttered open and she called out her husband's name. Mark came over and took her hand.

"Hey, you," he whispered, smiling down at her.

"Oh, Mark," she murmured. "I've been having the most terrible dreams."

"I bet. How are you feeling?" Mark tenderly replaced the damp rag on her forehead.

"Like I just woke up from a nightmare," she admitted, and then her focus shifted to the others surrounding her. "You two…" she murmured, "you were in my dream."

"Do you think you can take a little tea?" Ra'ah asked as he crushed dried leaves into a cup and added water from the kettle by the fire.

"I am quite thirsty," she smiled wanly. "How long have I been sleeping?"

"It's been a day since you were attacked," Mark explained.

"Attacked?" Her face clouded in panic. "I thought that was a dream, too. Where is Ethan?"

"I'm right here, Mom," Ethan called from the table.

"Oh, thank the Living God," she breathed. "That, at least, was still a dream."

Ra'ah offered the cup to Mark, who helped his wife to drink. She drank greedily, draining the cup before Ra'ah could encourage her to drink more slowly. She regarded him with a recognition that made him uncomfortable. Taking back the cup, he crushed another bunch of leaves into it and added water again. Handing it back to Mark, she took careful sips this time, never taking her eyes from Ra'ah.

"Have we met before?" she finally asked when she was done with the second cup.

"No."

"Strange ..."

Ra'ah felt her head and cheeks with the back of his hand, trying steadfastly to ignore her penetrating gaze.

"You are still fevered. That's to be expected. But you seem to have more of your wits about you, which is a good sign."

"You were in my nightmare," she accused softly.

"You were delirious when we arrived. The mind plays some wild tricks on us when fever gets too high."

"Except that I remember you arriving." She stared into his eyes, looking for something. "That wasn't my nightmare. You woke me up from my nightmare."

"As I said," he soothed, "the mind plays tricks when a fever gets too high."

She shook her head and tried to sit up, looking around the room for something out of her sight. Mark pushed her gently back onto the makeshift cot. Confused, she looked from face to face, as if to remember who each of them were. Her eyelids drooped heavily as the tea started to take effect.

"I don't understand," she murmured. "Where are the other three?"

Icy fingers crawled over Ra'ah's flesh causing goosebumps to rise. He looked at Nebaya, who was sitting on the floor on the other side of the cot. She was staring at the now sleeping woman.

He looked over at Amon, and found the other man staring at the small bowl where they had placed the black tooth. There was an odd, unsettling expression on his face. Feeling Ra'ah's eyes on him, he looked up and locked eyes, and then offered the bowl without explanation. Curious, the young man reached for it and stopped short. He felt a knot in his stomach as he looked down at the lump of black ash at the bottom of the bowl.

"Living God," he breathed, "what have we found ourselves in the middle of?"

"What?" Nebaya started out of her own contemplation.

Amon showed her the bowl.

"What is that?" She screwed up her nose in disgust.

"That," Amon stated pointedly, "is what is left of the tooth."

Mark stood up and looked into the bowl. His face grew so white Ra'ah feared he was going to faint and reach out to steady him.

"What poison is this?" he whispered hoarsely, looking back at his sleeping wife in concern.

"I do not know," Ra'ah admitted. "Whatever it is, it's unnatural. These things have been sent here."

"Sent? By whom?" Mark demanded in confusion

"Let's sit down and we'll tell you what we know," he offered as he led the man to a chair. "But first we need to find something to put this tooth in."

They sat around the table in silence. The fire had burned low and the candle gave off a solitary point of light, shining on the glass apothecary jar that Ra'ah had found to secure the remains of the tooth in. They had each taken turns, sharing first the story of the Maylak and the warning they had been charged with, as well as about Cardaya and the black wolf and Pethe and their ignoble reception. They answered every question Mark threw at them with hushed voices deep into the night.

Mark then shared about their encounter with the wolf the day before. They had not been taken by surprise—being experienced hunters, they were wary when they found their snares emptied. They came upon the thief raiding another snare and Mark put an arrow into it before it even knew they were there. The bolt drove the creature mad and it charged them. Five more arrows had found their marks, and the beast still came on, lunging around him to attack Emily. She'd somehow been ready for it, and struck the beast through the eye even as they locked together.

"I have only ever heard of such madness from old trappers," he said. "When sometimes the sickness takes an animal and it loses all sense of fear."

Silence descended around the table, broken only by the snoring of the old hound sleeping soundly on Ethan's bed in the next room. Ra'ah stared at the sealed jar of dissolved tooth in the centre of the table. He knew they should all get some sleep, but sleep seemed to have forsaken these four. He decided to get up and check on his patient.

Emily's fever had reduced again. She still felt overly warm to his touch, but colour was returning to her face. He gently lifted the blanket that covered the wounded leg and saw that the swelling had gone down considerably. Relief flooded over him as he went to the fire to add wood and check the kettle.

"How many of you are there?" Although his back was turned to Mark, he heard the confusion in his voice.

"There are five of us," Nebaya answered sleepily. "The others stayed at the inn. We'll catch up in Kathik tomorrow night."

"Three others?" Mark pressed.

"Yes," she answered, becoming slightly confused herself. "Why?"

"Emily knew there were three more of you. She asked where the other three were."

Ra'ah's goosebumps returned. "Yes, she did."

"Has she ever had prescient dreams before?" Nebaya asked pointedly.

"Prescient dreams?" Mark shook his head in confusion. "Those are old wives' tales. Stories straight out of holy texts."

"Has she ever had a dream about something that came true?"

"Yes, I suppose," Mark admitted. "But they were always about things we'd already been talking about."

"What are you thinking, Nebaya?" Ra'ah had caught the edge in her tone.

"Prescient dreams are real," Nebaya declared flatly. "And they happen today, and not just in 'old wives' tales.' And I believe that Emily may have the gift."

"What makes you think that?" Mark scoffed.

"Because I have the gift myself. And the gift recognizes like gifting. And the way she spoke to Ra'ah stirred something in me, a warning deep in the Call. It was like an echo."

"Hopefully she still remembers it when she wakes up," Ra'ah said.

"This is all a little too crazy for me," Mark admitted. "I suggest we all try to get some sleep and pick up this conversation in the morning."

They all agreed, and Mark offered them the other bedroom, making a place for himself to sleep beside his wife's cot. Amon chose to slip outside, preferring the open sky to being indoors. Nebaya made her way to the offered bedroom, and Ra'ah simply laid his head on the table and drifted off into a fitful sleep.

He awoke with a start. The cabin was dark; the fire had fallen to a bed of coals in the hearth. He felt his heart beating in his chest and he sat up in the chair, listening for what had woken him up. The soft breathing of the people in the cabin was the only sound that came back.

He groped across the table and found the candle they had used the night before. Getting up as quietly as he could, he shuffled softly to the hearth and set the wick to the coals. He blew softly and the wick caught, shedding the candle's light into the room. He stood and looked toward the cot with the injured woman. Mark slept soundly on the other side of it, his deep, even breathing proving that he was asleep. He brought the candle closer to the woman in the cot and jumped. Her eyes were open and bright, and she stared at him with anxiety.

"My goodness," he whispered, "you scared me. Are you alright?"

"I had a dream," she whispered so low the breathing of her husband almost drowned it out.

"Do you want to talk about it?" He knelt down beside her, feeling her forehead. "Your fever has broken. The dreams should go away."

"No." She shook her head as tears formed in her eyes. "No they won't, Ra'ah."

"Hey now, it's okay. They are just dreams."

"No, they aren't," she whispered forcefully. "They are warnings."

"Warnings of what?" He felt his skin begin to crawl. When had she been told his name?

"You know," she insisted. "I saw you there, with the others. When that thing attacked you and the Maylak killed it. The same thing that attacked me. That was no wolf. I heard its voice in my dreams—I heard words."

"Emily…" Ra'ah faltered, overcome by the overpowering rise of the Call within him. He'd never felt the Call like this, insistent, demanding that he pay attention. "Go on, tell me the dream."

"I wake up in my dream in a forest by a stream. I hear voices nearby and see a fire, so I walk over to join them. I see you and four others in a clearing, but you don't see me. And then things happened so quickly and I see the black wolf burst into the clearing. I can't help you—I can't do anything. But I see the Maylak, although no one else does at first. She draws back this great bow as she steps out of the forest and shoots the creature even as it leaps at you. Then you all see her. She tells you about the army that is coming to destroy the Valley and gives you the charge to warn everyone.

"She then reaches down and the wolf ignites in blinding fire at her touch. She looks up right into my eyes at this point and the forest just melts around us. She walks over to me and takes my hand and leads me into darkness without a word. We come to the edge of a cliff overlooking a blasted valley of rock, and she motions for me to look down. I obey, and below us filling the valley are thousands upon thousands of soldiers marching in blackened armour. Amongst them are the black beasts like the ones that attacked you and me. Before I can react, a loud shout echoes across the valley, and the soldiers bend down and release collars from around the beasts' necks, and the horde of them run down the valley ahead of the army.

"Then the Maylak takes my hand again, and the scene melts away and I find myself standing on the balcony of a tall building. All around me I recognize the city of Kathik, although I have only been there once. I hear a shout from the streets below me, and when I look down I recognize three of the people from the clearing at the beginning of my dream being led in chains by the Guard up into the city.

"Once again everything melts away around me and I am here, except the Maylak is gone and there are the howls of black wolves all around the cabin. You are here, with Amon the hunter and his dog and the tall woman from the clearing. Mark and Ethan are here as well. The wolves start tearing their way into the cabin, rending the timbers like they are parchment. They break into the cabin and everything is chaos. A great beast jumps at me and then I wake up."

Ra'ah sat back on his heels, silently looking at the distraught woman in front of him. She returned his look with a look of her own, waiting for him to deny what she had seen. Expecting him to deny it. His emotions tumbled inside him in waves of alternating urgency, panic, and despair. Above all, he had a keen fear that what she saw was the truth.

"Your dream is accurate regarding what happened in the clearing," he finally admitted. "And I'm horrified by your vision of Kathik, to be quite honest."

"So your friends were arrested?" she confirmed.

"Not yet." He shook his head. "They're still at the Willard's Ox. They leave for Kathik in the morning. What you saw hasn't happened yet."

"Well"—she swallowed as a fearful realization dawned on her—"that means neither has the wolf attack on the cabin."

"No, it hasn't," he agreed, feeling oddly calm in the face of what should have been debilitating fear.

11

ATTACKED!

Ra'ah sat beside the cot in silence, expecting at any moment to hear the howl of hundreds of wolves outside the cabin. The only sound was the steady breathing of the sleepers spread throughout. Outside, not a sound could be heard—no wind, no night noises.

A sudden realization struck him and he got up and set the candle on the table.

"Amon is outside," he whispered to Emily. "I've got to warn him to come in."

He walked softly to the door and lifted the latch; the door swung silently into the room, revealing a black hole into the moonless night. Ra'ah stepped into the doorframe and tried to peer into the dark. The stars covered the heavens in a soft blanket of bright points that did nothing to illuminate the forest. The candlelight behind him threw dancing shadows into the darkness.

He opened his mouth to call Amon's name and felt a hand clamp tightly over his mouth.

"Quiet," the barely audible whisper hissed in his ear.

He nodded, and the hand slipped from his mouth. He looked over and saw Amon outlined in the candlelight, nocking an arrow on the string, his face pointed away into the forest on their right. Ra'ah strained his eyes, seeing nothing but barely discernible shades of black. Something almost imperceptible moved directly across the clearing from the cabin door, and his head jerked forward. From the indiscernible depths of the trees, two points of candlelight were reflected back at him. A pair of eyes.

His stomach went ice cold. Amon backed slowly into him, forcing him back through the doorway as two more reflections appeared beside the first. Amon, never taking his hands off the bow, hooked the edge of the door with his foot and carefully closed it, leaning on it so the latch fell into place.

A growl from behind them almost made Ra'ah cry out; a moment later, he realized it was Pestos in Ethan's bedroom. Recognizing he was holding his breath, he let out a slow stream of air, watching Amon for cues as the older man leaned heavily against the door.

Something struck the door from the outside with enough force to bounce the hunter off of it. The door shivered but held, a testament to the quality of its workmanship.

At the sound of the heavy crack against the door, Emily screamed in terror, and then the interior of the cabin turned to bedlam. Mark jumped up from a dead sleep, hand groping for a knife at his belt. Ethan shouted for his parents. And from the second bedroom a wild-haired Nebaya appeared, white arrow nocked firmly in her bow. Pestos stood in Ethan's doorway, hackles raised and teeth bared, looking every hair as frightening as the black beasts who were assailing them.

"They're going to get in," Emily wept. "They're going to get in and kill us all."

"No." Amon shook his head, his voice steady and defiant. "No, they're not."

"But my dream…" She looked at Ra'ah for confirmation, but he just shook his head.

"Prescient dreams don't work that way," Nebaya said calmly as she crossed the room to a shuttered window.

"What do you mean? What do you know of my dreams?" She shook in fear as Mark knelt down to hold her.

"I know the kind of dreams you've been having," Nebaya explained, listening at the window. "They are given as warnings, as confirmations. They aren't meant to be taken completely literally."

"But how do you know?" Emily begged through uncontrolled tears.

"Because I've had them all my life."

Another blow hit the door.

Amon looked between the two women and shook his head.

"I think we're past debating the basic theology of prescient dreams. The real question at hand is what we're going to do with the half dozen wolves currently outside this cabin."

"Half dozen?" Ra'ah shook his head in disbelief. "I counted two."

"No disrespect, young man," Amon replied sarcastically as another blow bounced him on the door, "but I don't think you counted all of them."

"That door is not going to hold," Mark pointed out. "Not if they keep hitting it like that."

Nebaya nodded. "We need a plan. A way to keep them from swarming us."

"Agreed," Amon nodded. "Ra'ah, get the fire going. Make sure to arrange the wood so the ends can be grabbed. We'll hope they don't like fire."

"That's a plan?" Nebaya countered with an edge of panic. "Burn the cabin down on top of us?"

"No, girl," he retorted hotly. "But it's going to get ticklish in here once we let a few of them in. It's important to have all options available."

"You're insane, old man." She shook her head.

"Daddy, something's outside my window." Ethan stood blurry eyed in the doorway to his room.

"Come here and sit next to your mom on the cot," Ra'ah encouraged.

"Shh…" Amon held a finger to his lips. "Listen."

They all become still as stones. All around the cabin they could hear the scraping of claws against wood and the snuffling of great noses against seams. Amon motioned for Mark to shut the bedroom doors, which he did. The fire sparked up, hot coals catching the new wood greedily.

The noises outside suddenly stilled.

"What are they doing?" Nebaya mouthed to Amon.

Amon shrugged broadly as silence fell over the cabin, both inside and out, accented by the crackling of the fire. Minutes passed and nothing could be heard.

Amon finally shook his head. "These things are not regular creatures," he hissed angrily.

"No," Mark agreed. "I've never seen animals do this."

"What are they doing?" Ra'ah looked to each of them in turn.

With that, Amon stated the obvious. "They appear to be waiting."

"Waiting for what?"

"I don't know…" The older man shook his head in frustration at the question. "Maybe for us to accept the invitation to come out? Do you want to open the door and ask?"

"They aren't behaving like wild animals," Nebaya explained. "They tested the cabin and then just… backed off."

"Oh." Ra'ah felt sick. "I think I would have preferred if they were wild animals driven mad. What are we going to do?"

"We're going to wait them out," Amon said. "At least until sunrise."

"We haven't got long to wait," Nebaya pointed out as she stared through the cracks in the shutters. "The eastern sky is lightening."

"Get as comfortable as you can, bows in hand," Amon advised as he tested the weight of the table. "Mark, help me with this."

They tipped the table and used it to screen Emily and Ethan from the door. Mark handed Emily the dagger that she had used to kill the beast that had wounded her. Amon directed Pestos, who had been busy exploring the edges of the main cabin with low growls, to lay on the floor behind the cot beside Ethan. Ethan was the best-protected person in the room, Amon assured his parents.

Ra'ah picked up his bow, and then when Nebaya gave him a deep look of concern bordering on fear, decided better of it. Instead, he took the knife that he used for butchering game and set it beside the fireplace poker in easy reach. Sitting with his back against the stone hearth, he joined with the others in waiting. Closing tired eyes, he wondered how they were going to get out of this.

He must have drifted off, because when he opened his eyes there was sunlight pouring through the cracks in the shutters and under the door. He looked around the room and found the others dozing as well. The fire, which had burned untended, was almost out. With a sigh, he placed more wood on the smouldering pieces, fanning life back into it.

He heard Nebaya stand up across the room and turned his head to look at her.

"How long were we asleep?" she asked quietly, peering through a crack.

"Based on the light coming in, it's about an hour past dawn," Mark confirmed sleepily.

"Are they still out there?" Ra'ah asked Nebaya anxiously.

"I can't see anything. There's nothing in the clearing."

"Cover me with that arrow," Amon offered as he stood up and reached for the latch.

Everyone tensed. Nebaya nocked the white arrow and stood at ready. Amon lifted the latch and peered carefully out the door. Ra'ah counted three long breaths, and then three more. Finally, Amon opened the door fully and stared out into the morning. Nothing stirred outside. None of them dared move.

Amon stepped out of the door onto the veranda, and with a snort Pestos got up and followed him. Nothing stirred in the forest. Amon looked down at Pestos, who stretched luxuriously and sat down beside his master. The old man scratched the hound's head and then shook his own.

"This doesn't add up," he grumbled.

"Where are they?" Ra'ah got up and looked out the door, expecting to see wolves suddenly dash out of the depths of the forest.

"I don't know," Amon shook his head again, "but they aren't here. Pestos would know if they were nearby."

"Would he?" Ra'ah looked doubtfully down at the wolfhound.

Amon gave him a look of flat rebuke. "Yes."

"Now what do we do?" Ra'ah felt the anxiety rise in him, along with the realization that Daskow, Ange, and Anatellia were heading to Kathik ahead of them. "They may already be on the road."

"Who?" Mark asked in confusion.

"His friends," Emily responded. "His friends are going to Kathik today. They are going to be arrested."

"What!?" Nebaya looked from the woman on the cot to Ra'ah.

"It's part of her dream," Ra'ah explained.

"I need you to catch me up quickly," Nebaya said.

Ra'ah quickly outlined Emily's dream in its four parts. Nebaya stared blankly as he finished and then closed her eyes and shook her head. "Living God," she whispered. "This is too much."

Amon came back in the cabin, his face set in determination.

"We need to get back to the inn. And I think you should bring your family down with us, Mark." He looked at each in turn. "We can't stay here."

"We certainly can!" Mark corrected. "It's a lot safer in the cabin than in the open. We'll get two hundred strides down the path and get ripped apart in the open."

"I can only tell you what I think is best," Amon said. "Most of the attacks I have heard about happened at night, your situation aside. And we cannot hide here indefinitely. The three of us cannot stay, at the very least."

"It's suicide," Mark insisted as Emily touched his arm. He looked down at her with love. "I will not risk everything we've built together trying to outrun wolves to the river."

"I think we must eventually, my love." Emily returned his loving gaze. "There is more to this than you understand. We need to listen."

"Then explain it to me, Em."

"We'll leave you two to decide." Amon motioned to the other two. "We're going to check the forest."

"We are?" Ra'ah asked incredulously.

"We are," Amon nodded shortly, handing him his pack. "Don't worry—Pestos will protect you."

"She's going to need a crutch," Amon told Ra'ah once they were outside. "We are going to need to move quickly."

"She's still recovering from the poison of the tooth," Ra'ah pointed out in frustration. "It would be better if they waited until help could be sent."

"And what will they do if those things come back?" Amon demanded as he searched for a suitable branch.

"I don't think they will," Ra'ah replied.

"Oh really? And what are you basing that on?" Amon asked hotly.

"A feeling," Ra'ah admitted. "A feeling that these things are acting out a purpose. And whatever that purpose, it hasn't been wholesale destruction. I mean, think about it—all of the attacks we've heard about are attacks of opportunity, out in the open forest."

"Except last night they wanted to get into the cabin," Amon insisted stubbornly.

"Did they, though?" Nebaya joined in, her brow creased in thought. "They didn't try very hard. I mean, from what I've seen and heard, they could have eventually torn that cabin down."

"Ack!" The older hunter threw his hands up in frustration. "None of this makes sense! Those things out there make no sense!"

"The fact is," Ra'ah reasoned, "we need to get down to the Crossroads, and Emily cannot keep up with us. You can organize a group to come back up here and escort them down once we are on our way to Kathik."

Amon made to protest and then lowered his head, nodding in concession. Ra'ah didn't know why, but he felt sure the small family would be safe enough once they were gone. And then they could be collected with the other refugees inevitably headed up valley to Gellah.

"I'll go tell Mark and Emily." Amon made his way back to the cabin.

"You think those things are hunting us?" Nebaya gave him a penetrating stare when the older man had left.

"I do," he admitted. "But what I don't understand is why they didn't just tear the cabin apart last night."

Nebaya shrugged. "Maybe they figured we'd come out in the morning and run out into the open for them."

"That's not a comforting thought!"

"No, it's not," she admitted in resignation. "But we've got to continue running the race set before us."

They said quick farewells to the small family. Ra'ah left fresh dressings for Emily's leg after checking it one more time and Amon warned them not to wander far until he either sent an escort or returned himself. Emily had told Mark about her dream, and he agreed to wait no longer than a week before they would try to head up the valley alone.

Ra'ah looked back and waved as their cabin disappeared among the trees, and then they were off down-slope, following the trail at a loping pace. None of them wanted to be out any longer than was necessary.

Amon took the lead with Pestos darting ahead through the trees. The forest was quiet, and although it was still early morning the heat was rising, making the air feel heavy. They made good time for the first twenty minutes, and then Amon stopped dead, holding his hand up for stillness.

Ra'ah stood as still as he could, his breath screaming to come out in heavy pants. The forest remained still, without breeze or the call of birds. He felt his flesh suddenly crawl as a noise floated down from the trail behind them, still quite distant but clear. The howl of wolves. He let himself feel hope that they were on the move and had chosen to pursue the three of them and not stay at the cabin. That, and they were behind them. He clung to that faint sense of relief until they heard distinctly the return call of another wolf, this time down the trail in front of them.

"Curse them—they're in front of us," Amon hissed.

"What can we do?" Nebaya kept her eyes back up the trail. "They're coming down from the direction of the cabin as well."

"The only thing we can do." Amon pointed up-Valley. "We have to try to go around them and come down on the Cardayan highway."

"How far out of the way will we have to go?" Ra'ah chafed at any delay.

"I don't know," Amon admitted in frustration as he left the trail, heading parallel with where the highway would be some forty minutes further down-slope. "But we need to move."

They moved as quickly as they could through the forest, the sound of the wolves growing slowly but steadily louder. Every time Amon tried to turn them downhill closer to the highway, new howls would break out down-slope. In frustration, they were forced further away from the

Crossroads, and slowly they were climbing away from even the Cardayan highway.

Finally, as the sun reached midday, the sound of wolves broke directly behind them. With a sharp command, Amon sent Pestos to be their rear guard, the great hound dashing at the beasts, but with his greater speed keeping away from them. Ra'ah glanced back as they all ran, seeing the wolves matching their pace, working their way down slope and running parallel to prevent them from breaking that way. Something about their behaviour immediately stuck in his mind.

"They're herding us!" he shouted to his friends, his mind racing.

"Yes?" Amon shouted back through gasping breaths. "You think so?"

"Stop!" Realization cut through him like a bolt of lightning, and he stopped and turned to face the pack of wolves coming up behind them.

"Ra'ah!" Nebaya screamed as she skidded to a stop and turned to hopelessly defend her friend.

"What are you doing, you fool?" Amon circled around, preparing for a final desperate stand. "There's too many of them."

Nebaya and Amon, more harsh words already forming on their lips, suddenly stood aghast as Ra'ah slowly and deliberately approached the suddenly stalled pack of hate-filled black creatures. The animals, far from leaping to tear him apart, seemed afraid of him, backing away as he approached. They were desperate to keep their distance from him.

"What in the name of the Living God is happening?" Amon breathed, his wary eyes on the circling ring of wolves.

"I just realized," Ra'ah called back breathlessly. "All this time and I just realized."

"Realized what, Ra'ah? How are you doing this?" Nebaya came up behind him with the white arrow ready, watching the ring close around them but come no closer.

"Something the Maylak said to us in the clearing," Ra'ah replied. "She said the Living God would not let us face anything we could not handle."

"Ra'ah," Nebaya whispered, "there are no Maylak here. And we still can't handle these things."

Ra'ah laughed suddenly, realization bringing joy into the crazy situation they were in. His laughter drove the wolves madder, and they snarled and snapped—but still they remained at a distance. Slowly Ra'ah started downhill, walking toward the wall of wolves. The beasts became enraged, but backed off as he approached, steadfastly staying a predetermined distance from him. He recognized now what they were trying to do: they were trying to keep them from the road. They were trying to keep them from their mission. He felt anger rise up in him.

"There is something else that I just realized I haven't shared with you," he admitted to Nebaya as he quickened his pace toward the dark wave of beasts desperately trying to part in front of him. "I don't think the Maylak ever left us."

Suddenly the pack stopped retreating. Worked into a frenzy of frustration and anger, they finally realized their prey was not going to return to their control. With a great snarling chorus they turned and attacked.

The forest was suddenly lit with glorious, blinding light. As if from nowhere, a host of Maylak stepped into the rush of death. Ra'ah felt the wave of light strike his chest like a physical force, and the forest erupted in a celebration of destruction as he fell to his knees. He heard Nebaya shout in ecstatic joy as she shot the white arrow into the head of one great beast. The force of light on his soul was too intense and he swooned, falling on his face against the forest floor.

12

An Unwelcome Reunion

Anatellia, Angelis, and Daskow left the inn about an hour after sunrise. They had half-expected the others to join them as they set out, but Ra'ah's patient must have required extra attention. The innkeeper and his wife stood on the front veranda and waved goodbye.

The road to Kathik from the Crossroads was broad and paved, built to accommodate the regular traffic from that entire side of the Valley. They reached the bridge within fifteen minutes and crossed the great stone span with the sun in their faces. The day promised to be beautiful. They looked out from the top of the span to the city in the distance, sitting on the opposite side of the Valley—still a four-hour walk away.

The river swept in a great loop that made this part of the Valley fruitful and well-watered. Spring floods were controlled by ancient water gates that would fill the hundreds of reservoirs dotting the Valley floor and irrigate the farmland in even the driest of summers. This was the fertile centre of the Valley, and the city of Kathik was the jewel on the crown.

They walked in silence, slowly being joined by local farmers and merchants, craftsmen and tradesmen. The fear that hung over the villages barely touched the land surrounding Kathik, if at all.

Ange walked between the other two, singing softly to herself and enjoying the warm summer morning. They tended to avoid the city proper in their travels. Both Anatellia and Daskow always got a little morose when they got close to their hometown. She really missed having

Ra'ah and Nebaya with them to talk to. It felt strange to be separated for any length of time

"Who do we contact when we get to the city?" she finally asked, preferring short, clipped conversation to none at all.

"Governor Taman, and I'm not sure who the other letter is for. Daskow, who was the letter that Elder Sophia gave us addressed to?" Anatellia's disinterested regard for the countryside hid a growing tension that was definitely in her tone.

"It's addressed to the Head of the Silk Merchants Guild," Daskow recalled.

"Hmm." The tension on Anatellia's face increased. "I wonder if that's still Master Egland."

"No, it was a Lady So-and-so." Daskow shook his head, trying to recall the name. "Lady Rapha, or Rachel…"

"Raphael?" Anatallia's voice dropped in dread.

"Yes," Daskow nodded in confirmation. "Lady Raphael, Head of the Silk Merchant's Guild."

"Do you know her?" Ange asked suspiciously.

"Yes," Anatellia nodded, her face turning white.

"Is she a friend of your family? I know they're silk merchants."

"She isn't a *friend* of the family." Anatellia looked at her friend in frustration. "She *is* the family."

"Oh…" Realization struck Ange. "Oh no. Lady Raphael is your mother?"

"Wait…" Daskow stopped in the road in shock. "You're telling me your mother is now the head of the Silk Merchant's Guild? How could you not have known that all this time?"

Anatellia turned back toward him. "First, I'm not telling you anything. And second, it doesn't matter. We've all left lives behind to be out there, in the Call. Are you telling me we know everything about who you were before you left? And what's happened since you did?"

"Well—I guess not; no…" he stammered, flustered in the face of her aggression. "But seriously, your mother is the head of one of the strongest guilds in Kathik!"

"A fact that she will never let me forget," Anatellia snapped, and resumed her march to the city.

Angelis and Daskow exchanged looks as they sped up after her.

"If I find out you're related to the High Minister I'm gonna lose it," he muttered to Angelis.

"No worries," she smiled. "I'm just a farm girl who sings."

They entered the outer market that stretched in front of the city walls. This was as close as Ange had ever been to being inside the city proper. She always loved the bustle of Kathik's market, but there was something off with it today. Everyone seemed more restrained and uneasy. City guards patrolled the stalls in much larger numbers than she remembered. They didn't pause to talk to the merchants and entertainers they passed; Anatellia simply pushed on to the gate.

Just before the gate, Anatellia brought them up and looked intently behind them. Shaking her head, she drew them in close.

"Nebaya and Ra'ah have not caught up with us. I don't know what that means, but I don't think we should delay in waiting for them."

"I assume there was a plan for this possibility?" Daskow looked around as strangers flowed past them, wishing two of those strangers would turn out to be their friends.

"There was. We were to go to the Dancing Dove and wait for them."

"But you're not going to do that," Daskow inferred.

"I feel time pressing," she admitted. "And I want to face my mother on my own terms as soon as possible. There is something off with the market today, and I feel like it has something to do with us, or our mission."

Ange and Daskow looked around the market, catching her uneasiness.

"One of us can come down tonight and meet them," she decided. "But I need to deliver Sophia's letter now."

They both nodded, accepting her lead. Satisfied, she turned and led them on.

There were many city guards at the gate as well, stopping those trying to enter. One captain saw the three of them and motioned them over. He looked them over before addressing them tersely. "How many of you are there and what's your purpose in Kathik today?"

"There are three of us—and when has this ever been required?" Anatellia shot back with a terseness of her own.

"There have been troublemakers about." The captain eyed her crossly. "Riffraff from the forest looking to stir up trouble, from what I've been told. The city elders are limiting the access of village peddlers and the like to the market"—he pointed back behind them—"that way."

"I see," she said icily, matching his glare with a calculating stare of her own.

"I suggest you go back to the market, miss," he declared pointedly when she didn't turn around and leave, "because you are not getting into the city to do business today."

"Come on, let's go back to the market." Ange took hold of Anatellia's arm gently and tried to turn her away.

"Captain"—Anatellia made up her mind about something, a look of steel in her eyes—"my name is Anatellia Beth-Raphael. I have been travelling with my friends here and wish to enter the city. I really don't have time to destroy the careers of overzealous city guards. Now let us pass."

The man regarded her with surprise and suspicion, and then turned his attention to Ange and Daskow.

"And who are your friends?" he pressed stubbornly.

"This is Daskow, a university-trained tutor, and Angelis his betrothed." She moved to regain his attention. "And my name should be more than enough for you to let us pass."

"You are the daughter of the Lady Raphael?" he almost sneered. "I heard you haven't been in your mother's favour for many years."

"Barrack gossip is a dangerous source for career choices, captain."

"Truly." He bowed, his demeanour suddenly shifting, and he gave her a small bow. "Forgive me. It has been a trying couple of days, and the manner of your arrival caught me off guard. Shall I send for your horses?"

"We have no horses," she admitted. "As to your apology, delay me no longer and all is forgotten."

"By all means." He smiled coldly, turned, and motioned to a young sergeant standing nearby. "Please escort Miss Anatellia Beth-Raphael and her two guests to her mother's estate in the silk district. See that she is not further delayed."

"Sir." The man saluted sharply.

"Report back to me when all is well," he assured the man, and then turned back to Anatellia.

"Miss Anatellia, sorry for the delay." He nodded to Daskow and Ange, who was blushing a rose shade of pink. "Congratulations."

They followed the sergeant briskly through the gate and into the city.

"It feels like you just told someone I was marrying my brother," Ange hissed at Anatellia's back.

The sergeant was a sure guide, and he led them through the streets of Kathik at a brisk pace. No one hindered them as they went; merchants and hawkers got out of the way as the man approached with his charges. Before long they passed out of the business district and into a part of the city where the merchants and aristocracy lived. Lavish houses and estates lined the broad lane that they walked up, until the man turned into the open gate of a particularly large estate house.

Anatellia stopped suddenly and turned to her friends. She had a hard look about her, like she was preparing for something she found distasteful and extremely uncomfortable.

"Listen, both of you," she spoke quickly and quietly. "Speak only when spoken to. Speak only the bare minimum to answer any question. Daskow, answer for Ange whenever possible."

"Will do," Daskow nodded.

"Now wait a minute," Ange began, but Anatellia simply turned and quickly went through the gate after the guard.

Daskow caught her arm before she followed and turned her to face him. "Ange, please do what she says. You aren't used to these types of people. This is a world of false smiles and insincere words. One misspoken word could literally mean disaster for us."

"Seriously?" She was already tired of this place.

"Dead serious," he assured her as he put his arm around her shoulder and moved her toward the gateway. "Kathik is not a good place. Don't mistake it for the market outside."

They found themselves in a spacious courtyard before a large mansion with stables on one side. A groomsman led a horse out of the stable door as the sergeant approached the stairs to the house. He glanced at the city guardsman only briefly before fixing his disapproving stare on the woman who followed. His disapproval changed quickly to uncertainty and then full recognition, and his face lit up with a warm smile.

"Lady Anatellia!" he called to her. "The Living God bless me, it is you, isn't it."

"Hello, Geran." She turned and returned his smile. "It has been a long time."

"Not so long that I'd forget my favourite riding prodigy," he assured her. He made to say more, but a movement from the top of the stairs silenced him and he returned his attention to the horse he was leading with a sheepish glance at her.

"It's not enough that you have to treat all the servants like your family"—a tall man looked down on them from the doorway—"but you disappear for six years and return looking like one of them. What are you doing here, sister?"

"Hello, Edward." She looked up coldly at the man.

"'Hello, Edward,'" he mimicked, and shook his head as he slowly descended the stairs. "Serious, Anatellia, what are you doing coming back here?"

"Am I no longer a member of this family?" she asked coldly. "I was not aware that this was your decision to make."

"Do you think Mother's reception will be any warmer, Little Sister?" He looked down at her with contempt. "You're not her pet project anymore. You burned that bridge when you ran away. And who are… these?" He all but sneered as he noticed Ange and Daskow.

"These are my friends Daskow and Angelis," she introduced them. "Guys, this is my middle brother, Edward."

Edward just shook his head and took the reins from the groomsman. He dismissed the sergeant with a curt nod to the gate, and then mounted in one fluid motion. The horse stamped as he returned his gaze to his sister.

"You always were a spoiled, privileged brat," he said. "Mother is in the house. I'd pay good coin to stay and watch this, but I have family business to attend to."

"Love you, too," she whispered.

He ignored her and jerked the horse's reins. Daskow and Ange dodged as the horse and rider departed the gate, leaving them with the groomsman.

"That boy always lacked the warmth you'd normally find in a snake," Geran smiled at her sadly. "But I know better of you."

She moved into his outstretched arms and he hugged her warmly.

"Ah, girl," he held her out and rubbed a tear from her cheek, "he's right about one thing—you should have stayed far away from this place. Your heart is too good for this family."

"Why are you still here then, Geran?" she accused playfully, wiping another tear from her cheek.

"Someone's got to protect those horses from your brothers."

"Seriously…" She looked at him fondly. "I'm surprised someone hasn't caught you speaking ill of the family."

"I still know who and where my friends are," he assured her.

"I guess I should go in and present myself to Mother," she sighed.

"You can still escape." He held his hand out toward the gate.

"I'm bound by the Call and a charge I cannot set aside," she declared softly and formally.

"Sounds serious." He nodded and stepped out of the way. "If you get a chance, I've got someone in the stable who would still love to see you."

"Storm?" Her eyes lit up in happiness. "I was sure Mother would have sold him out of spite when I left."

"She almost did, but I think she thought you'd return one day. And your mother is ever the strategist."

"Yes, she is." Anatellia turned and started up the stairs with Ange and Daskow in tow.

The front hall was huge, with doors on every side and a great double staircase sweeping up to the second floor. Anatellia stopped just inside and took it all in. A servant approached with a withering look and the obvious intention of removing them like the vermin they so obviously were. She squared off and gave him such an imperious look that he faltered.

"I do not know you," she stated bluntly. "Please tell Lady Raphael that her daughter is here to see her."

The man came to a dead stop. He opened his mouth and closed it. He looked her up and down. He looked at the two that were with her. He opened his mouth again but just closed it after nothing came out. Finally Anatellia lost patience with him.

"Where is the door warden?" she demanded in disgust. "Or Benjamin the butler? Surely there is someone less inept at this than you."

"I'm sorry," he finally composed himself. "I am the temporary door warden. Who did you say you were?"

"I am Anatellia, Lady Raphael's daughter," she insisted curtly.

"I have been under the employ of the lady for three years," the warden insisted. "And in all that time I have never heard mention of the Lady having a daughter. You really should do your research before you run a swindle such as this."

"Swindle?" Anatellia asked incredulously. "You little toad, I am her daughter. Find someone with more experience and wisdom and we will settle this."

He scoffed loudly. "I was going to let you slink back out with your friends, but now you've got a date with the city guard."

"Anna!" A loud shout carried from the top of the stairs.

"David!" Her countenance changed in a heartbeat as she saw the tall young man bounding down the stairs toward them.

The man all but barrelled into her, picking her up in strong arms and spinning her around—pack, unstrung bow and all—in a great bear hug. Ange and Daskow looked at each other in shock. The door warden looked absolutely perplexed and then wilted as she laughingly shouted, "Brother, put me down.".

"Fine, but don't tell me I'll muss you, Sis," he laughed as he set her back on her feet. "You're already mussed."

She glanced at the door warden and whispered "go" while waving three fingers toward the side door. The man all but ran.

"I don't have the same access to warm baths that I used to have," she admitted with a sigh.

"Serious, Anna, what are you doing here?" He looked at her with genuine concern.

"I need to see Mother," she confessed. "It's a matter beyond family."

"Well it would almost have to be." He shook his head in wonder. "I hoped I'd see you again one day, but honestly, not here."

"I'm not the same girl that ran away all those years ago."

"Well, she's still Mother. And time has only made her more so," he warned.

A commotion interrupted their reunion as the door warden came back into the front entry in the shadow of a slender man with hard eyes and hawk-like nose. He stopped in the centre of the hall and regarded the small group in disapproving silence. Anatellia stepped around her brother and smiled coldly at the man.

"Hello, Benjamin," she greeted him. "I'm here to speak with Mother."

"Indeed." He regarded her with barely veiled contempt. "Your mother requests you come immediately to her study. The warden can find a place for your… companions… to await your return."

"I'll look after them, Sis," David assured her, his eyes filled with sympathetic understanding. "We'll catch up when she's done with you."

"Thank you," she sighed. "Daskow, I need the letter."

Daskow took out one of the scroll cases he had picked up in Pethe and produced the sealed letter. David's eyebrows shot up, but he just motioned for Daskow and Ange to follow him. Anatellia watched them as they departed for what she assumed would be the kitchen. David introduced himself on the way, and her friends did likewise. In seconds they were gone, and she felt horribly alone and vulnerable.

"The Lady should not be kept waiting," Benjamin noted tersely as he led her away.

"I doubt I can foul her mood more than it already is," Anatellia shot back as she followed the rigid man across the room.

"You've always underestimated each other," the man responded shortly.

Lady Raphael's study was opulent and cold. She had remodelled it extensively after the death of her husband. Gone was any sense of warmth or welcome. The room was a calculated statement about the woman that visitors were about to face. The Lady herself sat in a great high-backed chair behind the large oak desk and stared at the girl turned woman in front of her.

Anatellia, for her part, returned the stare. She had taken in the room when she was delivered into it. It hadn't really changed much since the day she left. More opulence, but the same feel. The five people who sat on couches in front of the desk were testament to the meeting her arrival had obviously interrupted. She placed herself squarely before the desk and set the letter on the desk in front of her mother. Then she took a step back and waited in rigid silence.

"You dress like a vagrant," the woman behind the desk lamented as she reached for the sealed letter. "If I had known how little you resembled my actual daughter I would have had you bathed and properly dressed before allowing you to be seen."

"My business is pressing, Mother," she stated flatly.

"Indeed." Her mother glanced up from her study of the letter's seals. "If this is business, then Lady Raphael would be a more appropriate salutation."

"You always taught me that Mother was the greater title," she cut back as her mother opened the letter and started to read.

Silence fell on the room again, her mother ignoring her barb as she perused Elder Sophia's letter. Anatellia became aware of the four men and the woman on the couches to her right and left. She resisted the urge to gaze around the room like a star struck girl. It had been years since she left, but her mother's training was still there. *Stay still under scrutiny. Stand straight and tall. Stay focused on your goal. And never reveal what you're actually thinking and feeling. That's how you will one day run this family and its business,* she'd been taught.

A rustle of parchment brought her attention back to her mother. The hand that held the letter was barely restrained from crushing it as the elder woman stared daggers at her from over the edge of the paper.

"I don't see you for ten years, and then you bring this and lay it on my doorstep," she almost hissed. "Foolish girl—I ought to finally disown you here and now."

Anatellia simply stared at her. She hadn't really known what to expect from her mother, but it wasn't this kind of rage. She wondered what was actually going on here. She held her mother's stare, fighting down the panic created by how badly she had misread the situation.

A stocky man seated beside her cleared his throat in the awkward silence. "Perhaps we should take our business up later."

"No need," the woman behind the desk breathed out heavily. "My daughter has blundered in with our answers."

"My Lady?" the man queried, confused.

"Benjamin, where are my daughter's companions?" The woman ignored the man's confusion.

"Miss Anatellia's travelling companions are with Master David. In the kitchen, I would presume." The gaunt man confirmed from the back of the room.

"There are four, I presume?" she confirmed wearily.

"No, my Lady, there are two."

"Mother?" Anatellia felt her composer crumble. "Mother, what are you doing?"

"Cleaning up the mess you brought me." She regarded her coldly.

"Captain Naimon, go to my kitchen and take the two vagrants you find there into custody. The other two must be somewhere nearby, I expect." She paused in consideration. "I would prefer to hold them here."

The stocky captain got up immediately with another man and exited the room with a short bow. Anatellia felt the room spinning around her. Something was going terribly wrong. She heard her warning to Ange just two days prior ringing in her head.

"What is it, my Lady?" the woman on the couch asked in shock.

Lady Raphael extended the letter to the woman, never taking her eyes off of her daughter. Anatellia could see the gears of her mother's cunning mind churning out solutions to her current problem. The woman stood and took the letter, reading quickly to herself. She looked up in shock at the woman behind the desk.

"Yes." Anatellia's mother nodded coldly. "My daughter and her friends are the ones spreading chaos across the valley."

13

Late to the Party

The chaos around Ra'ah was in sharp contrast to the weight of peace that lay heavy on him like a blanket. He looked up from where he had fallen and watched as the small host of Maylak destroyed the pack of black wolves with mighty swings of swords and twangs of great bows. He marvelled at the deadly efficiency of the Maylak, reducing the once fear-inducing creatures to nothing. The presence that accompanied the servants of the Living God lifted slightly and he pushed himself up, looking around.

As quickly as the Maylak had appeared, they disappeared. One by one they vanished into the forest, leaving behind nothing but the stir of the summer breeze and the distant howls of the few beasts who survived to run panicked into the trees. Finally, only one remained, standing patiently before him.

"Thank you," he whispered.

"Why did you let this enemy deceive you for so long?" the Maylak asked in apparent curiosity.

"I didn't understand at first."

"Mankind is… often baffling." The Maylak looked around at the others. "So full of the image of the Living God, and yet so cluttered with dead thinking."

Ra'ah struggled with a sense that the Maylak's words meant more than he understood—like there were meanings under the actual words. "I guess so. But the Living God continues to redeem us from our dead thinking."

"Yes!" The Maylak's face lit up in wonder. "That is the mystery that we all long to see. The completed redemption of the children of the Living God.

"But now you must get up. What the Enemy intended for evil, the Living God has used for His purposes. Your friends have their task ahead of them, and now you have yours."

"What do you mean?" Ra'ah was confused. "We all have the same purpose—we have to catch up with the others."

"You will follow them to the city," the Maylak assured him, "but the Living God has another task for you, shepherd."

"What do you mean? What task?" he asked helplessly, confused by the strange title with which the Maylak had addressed him, but the being had already turned to regard Nebaya as she approached them.

"Daughter of the Living God, I have been commanded to give you this." He handed her a great quiver of white arrows. "The Living God has given you power over your enemies, to speak His judgements against those who would oppose you."

"I will." She took the quiver with a firm grip. "Although as the enemies increase, I may need more arrows."

"Each arrow has a purpose." The Maylak regarded her quizzically. "Do not use them for your own purposes."

"I will not," she stammered, unsure what to make of the warning.

The Maylak looked behind them to the old hunter, who stood a bit apart. "Amon, beloved of the Living God, I bear a message for you as well."

"Speak it," the man responded gruffly.

"He awaits you eagerly at the Mountain, Son of Thunder; He has not forgotten his promise to you." The Maylak turned and walked toward the forest.

"And I have not forgotten mine," the old hunter murmured back.

The Maylak nodded to them, passed behind a tree and was gone, leaving them to the now-silent forest and their own stirred-up thoughts.

"If you two can make it down to the road on your own, I'd like to get about my other business." Amon turned and started off without waiting for a reply.

"Thank you, Amon," Ra'ah called out as he and Pestos disappeared among the trees. "We'll see you again soon."

"By the will of the Living God," he called back.

"What do you think the Maylak meant about the others?" Ra'ah asked Nebaya as she helped him stand up.

"I'm still trying to grasp what just happened," she admitted as she swept leaves and twigs off of him. "What you did was colossally stupid. How did you know that was going to work out the way it did? What deception was the Maylak talking about?"

"I just suddenly knew," Ra'ah shrugged, trying to understand his own reasoning. "I realized that these creatures aren't our problem. From the beginning they haven't been our problem. And when I saw that they weren't attacking us but driving us out of our way with fear, that's when I realized that they knew they couldn't attack us. That if they did the Maylak would intervene."

Nebaya shook her head in wonder. "Ra'ah, you risked a lot on that hunch."

"But that's just it!" He shook his head and smiled at her. "In that moment I knew. Deep down in the core of me, I knew I was right. Like the Living God was right there telling me it was true. And I knew I had to stop running away from our friends and our mission. I had to make a stand based on what I believed in that moment."

"You've grown so much in the Call in the last week," she marvelled. "You won't be able to say you don't hear it as well as the rest of us anymore. I don't know many who stake their life on what they believe like you just did."

"I think you all would have done the same." Her praise made him feel uncomfortable. "But now that the wolves are dealt with, what can we do about the others?"

"Emily's dream seemed pretty clear," the tall huntress pointed out after a brief silence. "And if they have been arrested somehow, we may be on our own."

"Maybe they're still waiting for us at the Crossroads?" he offered hopefully.

She shook her head, "No—Anatellia would have gotten an early start. They'll be almost to Kathik by now. We can't prevent what is going to happen, what may have already happened."

"So what will we do?"

"Follow the plan," she stated simply. "If we didn't catch up to them before we got to Kathik, we were to meet them at the Dancing Dove. If we hurry, we can be there before it's completely dark."

"Let's go." He brushed the remaining leaves and twigs off of himself as he started downhill.

"By the way, you're a real lightweight when it comes to the Presence," she teased him gently as she followed. "I take it you've never felt that before."

"No," he admitted, remembering the powerful, heavy presence of light when the Maylak had appeared. "Have you?"

"Yes," she nodded, lost in a memory of her own. "A long time ago."

They found the Cardayan highway within an hour and struck out back toward the Crossroads. Ra'ah chafed at how far they had let the creatures drive them, and he forced his legs to maintain a hard pace. Nebaya had no problem matching him with her longer strides, but she grabbed his arm when they reached the Crossroads and pulled him toward the inn.

"We need a quick rest and some food. We'll still be on track if we stop for a bit."

"We can still catch up with them," he insisted feebly.

"No way." She continued to drag him toward the front door. "You're dreaming if you think they haven't already arrived."

He gave up resisting and they entered the common room. The Willards welcomed them and immediately brought out food and drink, and they shared the events of the previous night and morning. Abigail gasped to hear of the wolves' attack on the cabin and then jumped up with a shout as they recounted their amazing deliverance from the pack.

"Praise the Living God!" she shouted, dancing around. "That is magnificent news!"

"Calm yourself, dear." The innkeeper stared at his wife in embarrassment.

"I will not, Master Willard," she teased him, her joy infectious. "Didn't you hear? Miraculous things are afoot in the valley."

"Didn't you hear," he jabbed back, "that there's an army coming to destroy us all?"

"I'll choose which report to put my fear in and which report to put my hope in, thank you very much." She danced over to the counter and picked up a fresh pie she'd brought out for them. "Eat some pie and then you should be on your way."

They smiled at her antics as they accepted the pie. They finished quickly and thanked the Willards before donning their packs again. The white quiver on Nebaya's back shone even in the lamplight of the inn, reminding Ra'ah of everything the Maylak had said. Innkeeper Willard regarded it with amazement and just shook his head.

"I might be inclined to think you dreamed that whole story if it wasn't for that thing on your back."

They took their leave and headed down the Kathik highway, crossing the bridge the other three had crossed half a day before. They saw the city in the distance and wondered how their friends were. The thought that they might even now be in shackles in some barracks made Ra'ah anxious.

The highway grew busier the closer they got to the city, and they found themselves clustered in a small army of farmers and peddlers making their way to the market as the day waned. Everyone seemed to secretly desire the companionship of others as they walked together in their separate groups, a quiet murmur of dozens of conversations overshadowing the group as a whole.

A curious number of city guards travelled the road against the flow, stopping couples every so often to question them. The practice seemed unusual to Ra'ah, and at one point he asked Nebaya about it. She nodded when he asked if she had noticed, anxiety on her face.

"Let's move a little closer to that group of tinkers," she suggested cryptically. "Act like we're with them."

"Why?" He suddenly felt anxiety rise.

"Because they're stopping groups of two who are walking by themselves."

"They're looking for two people..." he realized out loud, "...and you think they're looking for us."

"Yes," she whispered flatly, "I do."

"What are we going to do?" He lowered his voice and whispered back as a group of guards looked their group over from across the road.

"We're going to trust in the One who sent us. And we are going to get to the Dancing Dove and trust that our next move will become apparent to us."

"This is not how I saw this whole mission unfolding," he confessed quietly, and smiled as one of the tinkers looked over and nodded to them with a welcoming grin.

The sun had set and the stars were out as they made their way through the bustling outer market of Kathik. Many of the market stalls had closed, and those that were open lit lamps that shed light across the streets and cast dancing shadows all around them. Music could be heard from the myriad of taverns and common rooms that made up the bulk of permanent buildings.

They had avoided any questioning by the bands of city guards that roamed the highway and the streets of the market itself by staying close to different groups of travellers, blending in with them. They witnessed many couples being questioned along the way and some being escorted back to the city. It was unnerving to think that it was actually the two of them the guards were looking for.

In this way they arrived in front of the Dancing Dove without incident, and Ra'ah stared up at the sign depicting a rather animated bird dancing with musical notes all around it. This was Ange's favourite inn, and they always stayed here when they passed through the city. Or rather the edge of the city, Ra'ah realized. In all of the time he'd been part of the group, they had never actually passed through the gates.

They entered the busy common room, and a blast of scents and music surrounded them. A young group of singers were on stage, their harmonies intertwining around a melody that was hauntingly familiar. Nebaya swung her pack off and pointed to an empty table toward the back of the room, to which they made their way. He noted she was careful to shield the white quiver between her pack and her body.

"It would have been easier if we had a room to put our gear in before settling in," she said. "But I'm not sure where we are going to spend the night yet."

"Agreed," he nodded curtly, as he guided his own pack through the crowd of people surrounding the tables at the centre of the room.

One of the servers came around as they settled at the table and took their orders. Ra'ah recognized her as one of the women that worked there regularly and took the opportunity to ask her about their friends.

"Angelis?" the woman repeated. "No, they haven't been in in a couple of months. Is she in the city? I hope she stops by—she always inspires good tips."

Ra'ah shrugged at Nebaya as the woman took their coins and scurried off to get their drinks. He tried not to be offended that Angelis was the one that everyone knew. It was probably better that they weren't as recognizable, given the likelihood that they were wanted by the city guard.

"It's going to be harder to get information without Ange," Nebaya lamented in sync with his own thoughts.

"I half expected that server to tell us they'd been arrested," he admitted quietly, leaning in so she could hear him. "You'd think that would be the talk in every pub and common room in the city."

"Unless someone wanted that knowledge to be kept quiet," Nebaya replied as she watched the door.

"Who?" He was genuinely confused by the idea. "Who would actively try to keep it a secret? Why not do what the Elders of Pethe did and just treat us like frauds and troublemakers? Maybe they just arrested Anatellia and the others and ran them out of the city?"

"You don't understand much of politics, Ra'ah." She glanced at him with a raised eyebrow before returning her attention to the door. "And this city worships politics and power at least on par with the Living God. They wouldn't simply let any of us go and risk us spreading trouble in the market or in the other villages."

"But surely they have to listen to the warning, right?" he insisted. "They still serve the Living God."

"Oh, that is what they say." Nebaya shook her head. "They've served like their forefathers served. Their lives are full of the ritual of service. But you can tell what a person truly values most by threatening to take that thing away from them."

"I don't understand," he replied lamely.

She smiled at him again. "I know you don't, and that is something that makes you special to all four of us. You have an innocence of trust and belief that is unaffected by the reality of the Valley around you. But trust me when I say that it wouldn't be the removal of their ability to serve the Living God that would make many in Kathik rise up."

Ra'ah shook his head, and then smiled at the server as she set down ciders in front of them. He thanked her and she gave him a wink. He looked away sheepishly as a tall young man entered the common room from the courtyard outside. There was something oddly familiar about him, but he knew immediately he'd never seen the man before. Dressed in the expensive clothes of a merchant, he was an odd sight in any establishment outside the walls.

"That man doesn't belong here." Nebaya read his thoughts.

"Why does he look so familiar?" Ra'ah asked as he watched the man scan the room.

"You're about to find out," she muttered as she took a drink of cider to avoid the man's eyes, which were suddenly fixed on them.

"Crap," Ra'ah cursed softly as he watched the man make his way to their table.

"Excuse me," the tall man addressed him politely before turning his attention to Nebaya. "Hello, Nebaya."

"David." She gave the man a wary glare. "I didn't think you would remember me."

"We never forget our first love," he confessed deadpan.

"You know this man?" Ra'ah finally asked in shock.

"Ra'ah, meet David," Nebaya introduced them as she set down her cider. "You know his sister."

"Sister?" He looked up at the tall man incredulously, and then he saw it. "You're Anatellia's brother?"

"Guilty as charged. May I join you?" He sat down beside Nebaya without waiting for an answer and waved at the server to bring more drinks.

"What are you doing slumming in the market pubs?" Nebaya gave him a critical look.

He looked wounded. "Oh, that's not gracious. There are no slums in the Valley."

"You know what I meant," she insisted. "This isn't the normal scene for a silk merchant's son."

"Have you seen Anatellia?" Ra'ah interrupted.

"This one is direct and to the point, I see," the tall man smiled at him. "That's refreshing. Is he competition for your hand?"

"No!" they both uttered pointedly.

"Seriously, David," Nebaya continued, "answer his question."

"Yes," he nodded in exaggeration, "I've seen my sister. I left her just this evening to come looking for you two."

"Is she alright?" Ra'ah asked softly, scared of the answer.

David paused to take the three mugs from the server and give her some coins. He set two of the mugs in front of them and took a great pull from his own. He regarded each of them before he chose to speak again.

"Anatellia is under house arrest. As well as your two other friends."

"Under whose authority?" Nebaya asked quietly.

"Our mother's, of course," he answered flippantly. "Anna came to visit earlier today, and Mother locked her in her old rooms and locked your friends in the cellar quicker than I can down a good cider."

"So why are you here?" Nebaya asked pointedly, her eyes focused on the door again.

"Not to turn you in, if that's what you're thinking." He waved his hand to break her focus. "I snuck in to see Anna this afternoon and she told me your whole crazy story. Frankly it's more unbelievable than any you'll find in the pubs around here."

"So," Nebaya pressed, "why are you *here*?"

"I only recall one other time I've heard her tell a comparably crazy story," he continued. "But she's told you about that one, too. Anyway, I love my sister and even if I have a hard time believing her I don't agree with what our mother is doing to her or your friends. So when she asked me to come meet you both here, I agreed to come. And it gave me a chance to rekindle that old spark."

"You are as delusional now as you were then," Nebaya retorted. "What is your message from her?"

"Ah, well, it was worth the shot," he lamented as he pulled a bundle of papers from his shirt. "She said you two will have to continue to Meletsa and Bato without them."

"What?" Ra'ah's outburst caught the attention of nearby patrons and he moderated his tone before continuing. "We can't leave without them."

David regarded him with amusement. "Oh? And what will you do? Dash into the city, storm my mother's estate, and break your friends out? That would be an amusing tale for a few weeks around here. But know this—if you did that, your quest would be over. You'd be arrested and detained as well. And if Anna's story is true, the city will come down around your ears in about a month's time."

"Thank you for delivering this." Nebaya took the papers from David's hand. "She always said you were her favourite brother."

"Oh, now the flattery." He smiled at her before his face got serious. "Don't worry about my sister and your other friends. If it comes down to it, I'll sneak them out myself. But Anna says she needs to see this quest through on her end, and in her mind that means spreading the word through the city. And to be honest, that will be worth seeing and maybe participating in."

Nebaya gave him an earnest look. "Look after them for me."

"You know I will." He took another drink and then asked casually. "Can I see the arrow?"

"What arrow?" she asked innocently.

"The one you pulled out of the dead wolf in Cardaya. Like I said, she told me the whole story."

"I used it this morning to kill another one," she admitted. "It's lost."

"That's too bad. I would have loved to see something crafted by the supernatural. It's a shame you couldn't recover it."

"I couldn't, but that's okay…." She gave him a coy look and slipped the quiver from behind her pack. "…because I was given these instead."

"Living God," David breathed as he ran his eyes over the white leather and bundle of feathered ends. "That is truly unbelievable workmanship."

"Isn't it?" She partially drew out one of the arrows and presented the quiver to him, admiring it herself.

"This isn't wood from any tree I've seen," he admitted as he studied it. "Neither are the feathers."

"Feathers aren't from trees," she teased.

"Would you like me to leave you two alone?" Ra'ah asked as he watched them.

"Anyway"—Nebaya's cheeks flushed as she shot him a glare—"the Maylak gave me this this morning."

"He's better than a brother at chaperoning," David nodded toward Ra'ah, but he kept his eyes on the arrow and his brow furrowed. "This goes a long way toward confirming Anna's story."

"I'm not happy about going on without them, David," Nebaya admitted.

"Even if I could get the other two out of the house, I couldn't do it right away. And Anatellia felt you had no time to spare. But if you were to stop here on your way back through, I could be persuaded to help reunite you with them."

"We're actually going to leave them here?" Ra'ah asked Nebaya as she returned the arrow and quiver to its hiding place behind her pack.

"I think we have to." She stared at him for a moment. "Think about it: this is the other task that the Maylak spoke of."

"But we cannot just leave our friends!"

"Remember what I said about what you value most?" She waited for him to nod. "Don't make us that thing you value more than obeying the Living God."

"You're right," he admitted with difficulty. "But we'll be back for them."

David smacked the table gently. "Good. Now that that is settled, tell me how you got that quiver. That sounds like another unbelievable chapter in this whole affair."

14

Hard Choices

They woke up just as dawn was lightening the eastern sky. David had warned them that the city guard was actively searching for them, a confirmation of what they had suspected. He suggested the longer they stayed in the area, the more likely it was that they would be caught and taken for questioning. They agreed that they could not afford the delay if they were all being held, and it did not take the two of them long to realize they could not help their friends. So the only course of action left was to trust the Living God and continue with the mission.

The market was almost deserted as they left the Dancing Dove and made for the Meletsa highway. Meletsa was the village that lay at the base of the Koreb Pass, the only passable route into and out of the lower valley to the lands beyond. The Valley River itself entered a narrow gorge at the base of the pass and made travel by water all but impossible. The secretive merchant guilds sent their caravans up and through the pass to the lands beyond, bringing a great amount of wealth to the Amatta Valley, and specifically to the city of Kathik. Ra'ah had once thought he'd like to join one of the guilds. The idea of seeing the lands beyond sent a thrill through him. But after Anatellia had explained their strict vows of silence regarding all things outside of the Valley, he decided it wouldn't really be worth it. What good would it be to see wonders and not be able to share them with the people back home?

They quickly found they were not the only travellers seeking an early start, and they tucked themselves in behind a merchant caravan leaving for the pass. The merchant guard paid them little heed, marking them as two peddlers simply looking to share the afforded protection of a large group. One valuable piece of gossip they had picked up the night before was that news of roving bands of wolves had reached everywhere.

The road to Meletsa was remarkably well-built and maintained. Built for the heavy traffic of merchant wagons, it was well paved with smooth stone cut from quarries that could be seen at intervals in the steep slopes of the valley wall. There was little in the way of the great sweeping forest on this side of the river, the timber long harvested and the land long turned into fields for the crops that fed the city. This part of the Valley was long established and civilized, and Ra'ah found it made him feel uncomfortable.

"This never feels like part of the Valley," he admitted to Nebaya as they walked behind the last wagon.

"No." She shook her head. "I much prefer the upper Valley. This feels more like the lands and cities you read about in the Holy Texts. Where man wrestled with nature and crushed it, putting his own creation over top of it."

Ra'ah nodded and stared out over the farmlands to the river in the distance and the treeline across it that marked the road to Pethe. The slope on their right rose steeply up to the high country and bare rock above. The trees were few, and herds of goats grazed in and around them, keeping the grass shorn like the lawns of the rich.

"Do you suppose the enemy army will be coming down from there?" He pointed ahead to where the road out of Meletsa snaked up into the pass above the river gorge.

"Unless they're flying or climbing like goats," she teased gently. "There are really only two ways into the valley otherwise. No one has ever come back from a trip down the river. And there is nothing but mountains and wilderness up river."

"And the Mountain of the Living God," Ra'ah added. "But we're assuming the enemy will come down out of the Koreb and not out of the Shaar Pass."

"Why would the Living God send everyone toward the Mountain, which is up river, if the enemy they are fleeing before is coming from that direction?" She looked at him like he was being silly. "Our ancestors came here out of the Koreb. There isn't anything but wilderness and mountains beyond the Shaar."

He was silent for a long while. "In the last week, haven't you ever questioned what we're doing? Haven't you wondered if we've got it right? If maybe we've misinterpreted something or made the wrong assumptions?"

"No," she admitted after a short while. "I haven't really questioned it again since that night. And everything that has happened since then has only served to reinforce my conviction in our course."

He sighed. "I'm jealous. I'm constantly doubting and wondering. Even this decision to leave the others in Kathik and push on alone to Meletsa. I don't know for sure if this is the right choice."

"It is!" She put her arm around his shoulders. "I'll lend you my confidence in that. And I won't tell you not to question or wonder. You did yesterday, and it gave us a great victory over those wolves. We need each other in this. I don't like leaving the others behind, either. But I also believe and trust in the One who leads us, that He will stand in the gap for us."

"Will we be enough to convince Meletsa to hear the message?" Ra'ah spoke his most recent doubt out loud.

"What did I just say?" She laughed softly, and then thought for a moment before continuing. "I think you and I are the bare minimum needed to complete this part of the task. And it's not like we've been all that successful as a group of five, either."

"I guess not," he admitted as he went over the last week. "The Cardayans were always going to be the easiest to convince, I think. And Pethe was a disaster. Kathik, well, that's in the hands of the others and they're under house arrest."

"Exactly!" She laughed again. "You see? The Living God just needs willing vessels. Cardaya is on the move. The message got to Pethe and those who will listen will also move. And don't count Anatellia and the others out yet, although I'm betting they will have a rougher time than us."

"I haven't had a lot of interaction with Meletsans," Ra'ah noted. "I tended to just tag along behind you all when we've been here."

"Meletsans have a different view of life and theology than you're used to," she warned. "Don't be surprised if they take the warning in a direction you don't expect."

"Like Pethe?" he asked bitterly.

"No, it'll be different than Pethe," she assured him. "I cannot say for sure, but I try to avoid religious discussions with them. We'll find the recipients of these letters and then we'll move as we see opportunity."

"What will we do if we ever come to the point of no opportunities?"

"We'll turn around and figure out how we so badly missed the path that He has laid before us." She squeezed him close as they walked. "And that's hard to do if you're sincerely looking, little brother."

As they walked, the end of the Valley grew steadily closer, and with it the village that lay at the foot of the pass. They rested only when the merchant wagons did, and enjoyed a brisk pace when they were moving.

Mountain streams cascaded down to flow under the road through stone culverts, and the road passed through great culverts—tunnels—of its own in places where avalanche paths would have sent the road to far out onto the Valley floor. Here like nowhere else in the Valley, the citizens of Amatta contended with nature and forced it to submit to them.

The setting sun was resting on the mountain peaks when they looked up to realize that they had finally reached the outskirts of Meletsa. Kathik and Pethe may have been the oldest settlements in the valley, but Meletsa felt older than either of them. It had started out as nothing more than a barracks of sorts, an ancient guard post set up to watch over the only path to and from the Valley. The idea that the forefathers had fled oppression so many centuries ago was imprinted deep in the psyche of the Valley residents. Everyone agreed that the path back to those oppressors should be guarded somehow, but no one had wanted to live that close to the Koreb pass and under the shadow of that memory.

It wasn't until trade started many centuries later that the village actually took shape and grew. Over time, the village had sprawled across the lower end of the rapidly narrowed Valley. Every building was made of stone, wood being a luxury compared to the one resource that was still close and plentiful. Terraced gardens graced every home from the lowest to the greatest, and the village was a vibrant testimony to the values of home, family, and pride in one's labours that held in all of the other villages of the Amatta. But Meletsa was still very much a village set apart from the others.

The highway had drifted away from the steeper sides of the Valley to where it could plunge straight through the centre of the village. In the dying light of the day, they started looking around for a place to spend the night. Nebaya's knowledge of the inns was not great—they usually let Angelis find them lodging, sometimes in inns, but often with various entertainers that made their livings in Kathik and Meletsa. And without her they were stuck searching for a suitable inn.

"There was an inn that was quite nice on the river side of the village," Nebaya recalled. "Off the main road a ways."

"Do you remember how to get there?" Ra'ah looked around him in the dimming light.

"I think so," she nodded hesitantly. "I remember it had a donkey on the sign."

"Really?" Ra'ah almost laughed out loud.

"What?"

"I'm just wondering how many requests Ange got for 'The Loneliest Donkey' in that inn."

"Ah!" She smiled knowingly. "She was forbidden to sing that song in that inn. I remember that quite distinctly."

They left the merchant caravan and turned down a side street. Lamplighters were out, tending to the lamps that lit the villagers' paths. After some time, they found themselves on a road built atop a stone causeway that paralleled the river and provided access to the waterfront properties. The sound of the river came up to their ears, warning of swift water as it narrowed and prepared to plunge into the gorge at the far end of the village.

They walked for only a short distance before they saw the inn on the river side of the causeway. The bright painting of the saddest-looking donkey he'd ever seen swung above the entrance with bright letters advertising the inn's name.

"Oh my!" Ra'ah laughed.

"Right?" Nebaya nodded in the growing darkness, eyeing the sign in victory.

"Well, it's my mission tonight to get the story behind that," he declared as they climbed the veranda and entered the warmly-lit common room of the Loneliest Donkey Inn.

15

Harder Choices

Anatellia glared at her reflection in the mirror. She hated dresses. She most especially hated *this* dress. Silk and lace and so tight she wondered how she could breathe. The collar felt like it was going to cut off whatever air she could draw in. She almost hit the woman helping her "into" it. The lady-in-waiting was obviously one of her mother's, and the woman took great joy in working out the tomboyish problem before her. Anatellia by no means dressed like a boy, but she had absolutely raged when her mother demanded she wear a dress to dinner "like a proper Lady of Kathik."

The lady-in-waiting made a clicking sound of disapproval at something she saw and attempted to adjust the dress, but Anatellia slapped her hand away. They glared at each other for several long seconds before the servant huffed and backed away.

"Suit yourself," she muttered. "I've done everything I can."

"Feel free to return to your Lady's den," Anatellia dismissed the woman. "The she-wolf will be looking for a report."

"I will return to my Lady's chambers," the woman bowed her head stiffly. "And politer company."

"Good luck with that," Anatellia snorted in a most unladylike fashion.

The woman backed away and exited the room without another look. Anatellia returned to the mirror, fuming as she pulled on the collar. If she hadn't needed to consider her friends in the cellar below, she might have chosen open warfare with her mother over this. But her mother had seen the threads of her daughter's soul and pulled on them like she always did, manipulating the young woman to her will with promises of compromise and concession. Anatellia felt sixteen again as she seethed at her own reflection.

"We'll see who wins this exchange, Mother," she vowed.

Her only moment of solace since being unceremoniously escorted from her mother's study had been David's visit late in the afternoon. She'd poured everything out to him as he sat in the drawing room chair, sharing every minute of the last six days like they hadn't been apart for a decade. David always had been her favourite brother, the youngest of three and least like their mother. In him she confided all of her hope for the success of their mission.

And in true David fashion, he agreed to help. She didn't care if it was because he believed in the cause or because he simply took every opportunity to be the thorn in their mother's saddle. He promised to be the go-between for her and the other two in the cellars below the estate. He also promised to go meet Ra'ah and Nebaya at the Dancing Dove—a little too eagerly. He'd only met Nebaya briefly in the weeks before she had run off, but he had been smitten from their first meeting.

A knock at her door revealed the face of the skinny kitchen girl her mother had promoted as her daughter's own lady-in-waiting. The poor thing was clueless, she realized. And she would be replaced by someone better trained in the morning. She waved to the girl to come in.

"My Lady." The girl performed an awkward curtsy. "Your mother requests your attendance at dinner."

"I know," Anatellia murmured.

The girl looked between the door and the woman she was supposed to be serving. It was obvious that Mother had sent someone to escort her down. The man was probably waiting impatiently in the outer room, expecting her to appear on command. Anatellia was not going to play the compliant daughter tonight. They could wait a bit. She waved the girl out.

"Tell him I'll be out when I'm ready."

The poor girl curtsied again and left, pulling the door shut behind her. After a brief pause, a man's voice rose in anger from the other room and the door burst open. The man in the doorway was immediately recognizable to her, even though she hadn't seen him in ten years.

"Malik." She turned her back on him even as she spoke. "I was wondering when I'd be graced by your presence."

"Anatellia," he seethed, "Mother requests your presence at dinner."

"I know. I guess I shouldn't be surprised that she sends her firstborn to summon me. What wise words do you have for me, big brother?"

"I will not lie," he snarled softly, "I had hoped you would have had the common sense to stay away, Little Sister."

"Oh, don't worry." She felt her anger slipping as old feelings rose up. "I'm not going to stay any longer than I have to. You can have the role of favourite, for what it's worth."

"I will never be her favourite," he admitted candidly. "Her favourite will always be the one who ran away. The spoiled little brat who rejected the gift others would have given everything to have."

She snorted softly. "Gift? It's no gift. I would have given it to you if I could have."

"Please, Anatellia…" He composed himself and started again. "Come to dinner."

She nodded and checked herself one more time before walking to the door.

"Sincerely, Malik," she said quietly but forcefully, "I am not back, and first chance I get, I'm gone again.

"Then why are you back at all?" he asked just as quietly as they left her apartments.

"I'm surprised she didn't tell you," she said as they went down the hall.

Daskow and Angelis sat on cots set on opposite sides of the small apartment in the cellar of Lady Raphael's estate house. The room smelled musty, and the thick layer of dust within it was proof that it had rarely been used—possibly never for its current purpose. The guard that locked them in had surveyed the room in horror, returned with water and food and a handful of candles, and then left without a word, shutting the heavy oak door behind him.

They had passed the hours talking to each other, until the door opened to allow David in. He apologized profusely until Daskow told him flat out that he had nothing to apologize for. As he had promised when the guard had come to arrest them in the estate kitchen, he had discovered the reason for the arrest. He told them of Anatellia's predicament and his agreement to help.

"And so I came here to ask for the letters. I've got to go meet Nebaya and your other friend at the Dancing Dove."

"We have little choice but to trust you." Daskow separated out the letters for Bato and Meletsa and gave them to David. "You could have simply taken our packs from us when we were thrown in here."

"Yes…" David's brow furrowed. "That is strange, isn't it? Shows they aren't concerned with what you carry, only with you."

"Can you get us out of here, David?" Ange burst out.

"Yes," David nodded after thinking for a moment. "Although I wouldn't recommend escaping tonight—they'd just scoop you back up. And Anna seems to have some kind of plan, although I doubt it has a chance with Mother involved."

"If you can sneak us out, I may still have friends at the university that can help us," Daskow offered.

"Let me go see your friends at the Dancing Dove, and then we can work out something." He stuffed the letters into his shirt and knocked twice on the door. "Don't worry. Mother is many things, but she's not one to make people disappear."

"That"—Ange's face contorted in thought—"is absolutely no comfort at all."

"Sorry," David's voice floated around the door as it closed.

Ange looked at her friend. "What was that supposed to mean?"

"Don't worry." The tutor leaned back against the wall. "Trust that the Living God has a plan."

"Be nice if He could share it," she muttered, and then sighed softly. "I hope the others are alright."

Dinner at Lady Raphael's table was marked by a quiet tension, like a mountain clearing before the avalanche swept everything away. Everyone was already seated when Anatellia and Malik walked into the room. Edward and a sharp-nosed woman sat on one side of the table. An empty chair sat between them and another woman that Anatellia immediately recognized as the woman Malik had been courting before she'd left. She noted that there was no extra seat for her on that side. Even David's seat had been removed, although she knew he wouldn't be attending in advance.

On the other side of the table sat the woman from her mother's study and a man that was apparently her husband, judging by how close and handsy he was. There was another man beside them, a well-dressed man who held himself like a politician and eyed her with open curiosity. There was no empty seat on that side of the table, either.

She looked in discomfort at the seat being held out at the end of the table, down the length of which sat her mother, still staring daggers at her. Being relegated to the "foot" of the table, as they used to call it, was like being sat in the witness stand at your own trial. She forced herself to follow the protocols that had been drilled into her for most of the first sixteen years of her life. With a curtsy, she apologized for her tardiness.

"Some grace must be extended." Her mother had the ability to say the exact opposite of her words' meaning.

She moved as gracefully as she could to the chair being held out for her, but before she could sit her mother introduced her.

"This is my intemperate daughter, Anatellia," she announced to the table. "Anatellia, this is Governor Taman and his wife. I thought since you'd been so kind to bring him his letter from Cardaya, we might enjoy his company for dinner. This is Helen, my assistant, whom you met earlier today, and her husband. And of course you should know your own family." She waved her hand along the other side of the table, her meaning clear.

"Governor Taman." She nodded to the man closest to her as she sat. "Eldar Shammar sends his best regards."

"Indeed." The man gave her a meaningful look as he lifted the letter she had brought from his jacket pocket. "I'd be interested to hear your side of this tale."

"My daughter is weary from her travels," Lady Raphael broke in crisply. "I'm sure she can make time in the coming days to regale us all with her tawdry travels. Shall we eat?"

Anatellia felt heat rise in her cheeks, but was saved by the young woman beside Edward.

"I'm delighted to meet you, Anatellia." The woman's high-pitched voice was a little too shrill to be beautiful. "I've heard so much about you. I'm Edward's wife, Margaret."

"Margaret, dear," the matriarchal voice came down the table like a hammer on the anvil, "please don't disturb our meal with your chatter."

"Yes, Lady Raphael; I'm sorry."

Anatellia glared down the length of the table at her mother. Ten years and she hadn't changed. In fact, she'd only grown into a stronger version of herself. *Well,* Anatellia decided, *so have I, Mother, so have I.* She felt a fire ignite in the depth of her soul.

"Let's begin." She smiled coldly. "I've worked up an appetite."

All but three sets of eyes lowered to their plates as servants served the meal. The gazes of Anatellia and her mother remained locked, each refusing the other's demand to break contact. And between them Governor Taman watched them both with faint amusement.

"You set a wonderful table," he complimented his host politely.

16

Do Your Part

Nebaya and Ra'ah sat in the warm light of the common room of the Loneliest Donkey Inn drinking mulled wine. They had stowed their packs in their room and come down to enjoy what food and entertainment might be available. The innkeeper was a large man with laughing eyes and an impeccable memory. He recognized Nebaya almost immediately, and asked eagerly if Miss Angelis would be joining them tonight. Ra'ah saw the man's face fall when they had to explain that no, she was currently visiting Kathik. But he perked up almost immediately and found them a clean table in a quieter corner of the room.

Nebaya laid down the two letters they had been given for Meletsa, one from Elder Shamar and the other from Elder Sophia. The letters were battered and a little worse for wear, no thanks to David's treatment of them, but the names were still clear. One letter was addressed to Elders Eman and Timao, and the other was addressed to a Master Dunhamai. When the innkeeper passed by, she waved him over.

"We have to deliver these letters; can you help us?" She gave him a hopeful smile.

He looked at the names in flowing script and nodded enthusiastically. "Certainly, miss. The elders are regulars here. They should be around before too long. I'll introduce you to them if you like. And Master Dunhamai's house is just inside the Pass Gate. If you go up there in the morning, anyone can point you to it."

"Thank you." Nebaya offered him a coin for his trouble. "We'd appreciate the introduction as well."

"No need to tip me for that," he laughed—but kept the coin. "I'll bring you both some more wine while you wait."

Nebaya thanked him again and leaned back in the chair. She gave Ra'ah a significant look and took a sip.

"See, little brother? The Living God makes a way."

"Yes." He nodded and took a drink. "But let's hope these people are willing to hear our story."

"Of course they will," she assured him. "Why else would Sophia and my uncle have written letters to them?"

The elders arrived a short time later and the innkeeper, true to his word, motioned Ra'ah and Nebaya over to their booth once they were settled. Elder Eman was the older of the two, with deep sunken eyes and wispy white hair. Elder Timao was taller than her companion by a head with striking blue-grey eyes and a full head of long hair tied with leather straps and draped over her left shoulder. They extended their hands as the innkeeper introduced the two of them.

Motioning to the innkeeper, the tall woman immediately said, "Bradley tells us you have a letter addressed to us both."

"Yes." Nebaya produced the battered letter and handed it to her.

"It's quite travelled," the elder smiled as she took it.

"That's polite," Elder Eman barked hoarsely. "It looks like they used it as a pillow."

Elder Timao looked at the script and the seal before handing it to her companion. She turned her gaze back to the two of them. Ra'ah shifted uncomfortably, realizing how scruffy they must look.

"Join us," she finally offered. "Tell us why our sister from Pethe would send us a joint message through the likes of you two."

They politely accepted the invitation and sat in the booth across from the two elders. The innkeeper had their beverages from the other table brought over before they were even settled. Elder Timao slid two coins to him and ordered ciders, and then returned her patient stare to the two peddlers across from her. Elder Eman ignored them both as he cracked the seal on the letter and proceeded to read, his lips moving as he did.

"So," Timao smiled politely after the innkeeper returned with a large pitcher of cider and four more mugs, "where does this story begin?"

"Great Living God," Elder Eman muttered at that same moment, handing the letter abruptly to his surprised companion and glaring at them both. "Where are the other three?"

"What?" Nebaya asked in surprise, caught off guard.

"The letter says there were five of you. Where are the other three?"

Ra'ah decided only the truth would do. "They were detained in Kathik."

"Detained?" the old man snorted gruffly. "Not surprising if the people there got the same letter."

"Peace, my friend," Elder Timao murmured to him as she quickly read the letter. "Oh dear. Yes, I see the problem."

"Problem?" Nebaya asked, confused by the interplay.

"Elder Sophia's letter speaks of five of you. Five witnesses to the 'event.'"

"Yes?" Nebaya nodded.

"Well, there are only two of you," she finished, expecting them to see the problem.

"Explain it like we aren't from here," Nebaya finally asked.

"Any matter of importance must have at least two to three witnesses," the woman explained patiently. "You apparently had five witnesses when you left Pethe. Why did you leave three behind in Kathik?"

"It wasn't exactly by choice," Ra'ah admitted in frustration.

"I can appreciate that it may not have been," she conceded with a nod of her head. "But based on what she is alleging your message is, two may simply not be enough."

"Will you at least hear our story?" Nebaya asked impatiently.

"Of course we will," Elder Timao smiled. "But we are just two elders of nine. And there is a reason Elder Sophia sent you to us. The others will be exceedingly more skeptical, depending on what you ask us to believe."

"That's for sure," Elder Eman chimed in. "So go ahead—tell us a good one."

Nebaya exchanged a worried look with Ra'ah and nodded for him to go ahead.

"I wish our friend Angelis was here, but the whole thing started seven nights ago," he began, hoping that he could tell the whole story clearly.

The common room was empty and the innkeeper was busy tidying around the far tables when the elders finally ran out of questions for them. They had listened patiently as Ra'ah had done his first telling, with Nebaya adding parts he either forgot, or, as in the case of Pethe, wasn't there for. Once he finished, they started asking questions, asking him to repeat certain parts of the story. Their questions had seemed endless.

"That's quite a story," Elder Eman admitted.

"It's all true," Ra'ah insisted.

"A bit of advice, son?" The old man looked at him shrewdly. "I've discovered that no one is ever convinced a story is true just because the person telling it insists it is. A story often stands or falls based on the teller's character as much as the truth of it."

"So you don't believe us?" The young man's countenance fell.

"Heavens above, the boy is daft," the old man grumbled to the table in general.

"What my friend is saying, Ra'ah," Elder Timao intervened, "is that establishing the truth in any report starts with knowing who the messenger is. Do you believe your own message?"

"Well, yes," Ra'ah stated in bewilderment.

"Then you shouldn't need to try to sell it to us." She held up the letter they had brought. "Elder Sophia sent this letter to vouch for the characters of you and your friends. Elder Shamar vouched for you to her. Even in the Valley, there are those who might deceive for their own ends, given the chance."

Elder Eman pointed his finger at Ra'ah. "You're asking yourself why the Living God would send a Maylak to five people on the fringe of society with such an important message. You listen to old fools like us and wonder how you can even spread that message when no one believes or trusts you."

"Yes, frankly," he admitted softly.

"I think it's in part His sense of humour," the old man said, sitting back and smiling. "But it's also because you five were available and open. Out there in the woods searching for answers in the Call."

"You know about the Call?" Ra'ah asked in confusion.

"You think because I'm an elder in a village like Meletsa that I don't know of or hear the Call?" He snorted. "I was young once, too. I wandered the forests of the valley once, looking for the source of my discontent, thinking I was looking for a community better than the one I left.

"What you don't understand is the Call isn't out there, in the forest outside the five communities. The Call has always been in here." He thumped on his chest. "The Call is the Spirit of the Living God pulling on your destiny, drawing you out of a complacent life. Eventually you realize that and find yourself returning to community. Eventually you come to realize that being in the forest looking for the Call is selfish, that you have to search for it in community. Contend with it in the community. And you find yourself contending with community for the sake of that same Call."

"I..." Ra'ah struggled with the words. "I haven't heard anyone describe it like that."

"The Valley has gotten quite complacent," the old man agreed. "We no longer teach truths that were once understood by all. I have long expected that something would come to shake us from our complacency."

"You think the Living God is behind what is coming to destroy us?" Nebaya asked incredulously.

"Behind it?" Elder Eman frowned. "No, He's not behind it. The world is a far wider place than our little Valley, full of the enemies of the Living God. Frankly, it was only a matter of time before those enemies might take the opportunity to finish what was started long ago.

"But He would definitely use it. Use it to stir the faithful out of complacency. And He's chosen five kids from the forest to be his harbingers. To shake the wise and disrupt the comfort of a lazy and forgetful people. To bring them all to a place they had forgotten during long years of comfort."

"The Mountain of the Living God," Ra'ah murmured, entranced by the old man's gruff passion.

"Partly"—the old man smacked the table—"but also back into the service and worship of the Living God, which the call to the Mountain truly represents."

"I think that is enough for one night," Elder Timao smiled gently. "Where will you be staying?"

"Here," Nebaya said. "We also have one more letter to deliver tomorrow."

"To whom is the letter addressed, if I may ask?"

"A Master Dunhamai," Ra'ah answered, stifling a yawn. "The innkeeper told us where to find him."

"Her," Elder Timao corrected. "Everyone in Meletsa knows her, if at least by reputation. Elder Eman, maybe you'd like to take them to see the Master in the morning?"

The old man nodded to them. "Dawn. We'll need to catch her early or we won't catch her at all. Although you may regret meeting her." His face broke into a cold grin. "She thinks my disposition is sunshine."

"Thank you, both of you." Nebaya bowed her head. "You give us hope."

"We all do our part," Elder Timao stated simply.

They retired to their room, exhausted. The last thing on Ra'ah's mind was uncomfortable: if Elder Eman was sunshine compared to Master Dunhamai, what were they in for in the morning?

17

Stand-Off

Anatellia awoke in her old bed to the sound of her young and inexperienced lady-in-waiting scurrying around the room trying to lay her clothes out for the day. *The poor girl is completely out of her depth*, Anatellia realized. But her mother's reason for choosing the girl was quite obvious. She wouldn't spare any of her own servants on her wayward daughter just so she could mistreat them like she had the previous evening. And she wouldn't waste resources on hiring an experienced girl. Scheming, conniving, manipulation, and threats, these were the bread and butter of their relationship.

Ever since her father had died when she was twelve and her mother took over the family business, the woman had bent all of her planning and will on Anatellia. She was determined to remake her daughter into her own image. Malik was right: she *had* been mother's favourite. The only daughter. Lady Raphael had been determined to leave the family legacy to her. It had forever broken the relationship between them all. *Well, everyone except David.*

She sat up in the expansive bed and stared around the dark room. The girl had clumsily laid out the dress she was to wear at the foot of the bed, and she was trying to bring in the ewer of water for the basin. Anatellia watched her quietly until she managed to set it on the table. It would do no good to make her jump.

"What is your name?" she asked when it was safe.

"Dana, my Lady." She jumped around and almost knocked the table over anyway.

"Relax, Dana," Anatellia sighed. "Would you get the curtains, please?"

The poor girl tripped over her own feet trying to get to the windows and pulled back the heavy curtains, allowing light to stream in through the sheer curtains behind. The light of the morning sun was just coming over the mountains across the valley, and it lit up the room with a warmth she doubted it had seen in the ten years since she'd left. She slipped out from underneath the covers and tentatively touched the cold floor.

"Wait, my Lady, I'll get you your robe and slippers." The girl was a gangly mess of arms and legs trying to go faster than her mind could direct.

"Relax, Dana," Anatellia smiled reassuringly. "I'm not my mother."

Dana wasn't comforted. "Forgive me, my Lady, but the head housekeeper said if I didn't do a good job, I'd be dismissed."

"Did she?" Anatellia felt her anger rising. "Well, let's make an agreement, you and I."

"Yes, my Lady?" The girl handed over her robe and set slippers on the floor at her feet. The slippers were obviously mismatched, which made Anatellia smile.

"Let's agree that while we are alone together, you will relax." She slipped her feet into the slippers and slid the robe on. "And together we'll make sure everyone knows you're doing a good job."

"Yes, my Lady." The girl looked confused, and then, looking down, realized the slippers were mismatched.

"Dana?" Anatellia put a finger under her chin and brought her head up.

"Yes, my Lady?" the girl whispered.

"Call me Lady Anna." She smiled at the girl's discomfort. "That is what my last lady-in-waiting called me, and I prefer it."

"Yes, my… Lady Anna," she stumbled.

"Good." Anatellia smiled and then regarded the room and the clothes laid out on the bed. "Let's get this day rolling, shall we?"

A knock at the door sent Dana scurrying, and Anatellia waited as she opened it a crack to see who was there. The sound of David's voice carried through, and the girl told him pointedly to wait while she announced him. With a soft click, she shut the door and returned.

"My Lady's, I mean…" she struggled, "…your brother David is here to see you, Lady Anna."

"Thank you, Dana," she laughed, tying the dressing gown around herself and heading for the door.

"My Lady," Dana called after her in shock, "your modesty, Lady Anna."

"Modesty?" Anatellia laughed. "This dressing gown could pass for a dress in some villages."

She left her tongue-tied lady-in-waiting in her bedchamber and entered the outer drawing room where David sat with his legs draped over a chair. He looked up when she came in and raised his eyebrows.

"Mother's going to love your choice of dresses this morning! But you're not twelve anymore, dear sister."

"What do you mean?" She looked at herself in the mirror. "Every inch of me is covered."

"You may be able to hide your beauty out there with your friends, Anna, but it's on full display back here," he warned her seriously. "Watch out for her machinations."

"I'm not sure what you mean," she said uncomfortably.

"Hmmm." He looked at her, and then, dismissing the subject, he smiled again. "What plotting can I help with today?"

"Did you meet with Nebaya and Ra'ah?" she asked eagerly.

"Yes. And I gave them the letters from your friend Daskow. He and Angelis are locked up in Mother's cellar and none too comfortable. Nebaya didn't come right out and say it, but she missed me. And Ra'ah's a nice guy." He watched her for reactions as he checked off his list.

"What? Yes, he is," she agreed distractedly. "So they are leaving for Meletsa?"

"Should have left this morning," he assured her with a smirk.

"What are you smirking at?" she asked in annoyance.

He shrugged. "Oh, nothing. Was I missed at dinner?

"There wasn't even a place set for you at dinner."

"Not surprised," he confessed. "I've made it a point not to show up whenever I can. She's got the door wardens reporting to her whenever I go out so she doesn't have to face the embarrassment of an empty seat at the table. How were our brothers and their wives for dinner conversation?"

"Silent," she admitted. "Mother has gotten very good at controlling the table in the ten years since I've been gone."

"Be careful, sister—she's gotten very good at a lot of things since you've left. Nothing is untouched by her control."

"Maybe you should get Daskow and Angelis out of the cellars," she murmured in concern.

"I'm already ahead of you."

"Oh?" She looked at him in surprise.

"Daskow mentioned he knew people at the university," David started in explanation. "And after talking to Nebaya and that Ra'ah fellow I decided it wouldn't be worthwhile to leave them here, so I came back last night with the intent of sneaking them out."

"They're gone?" she asked in surprise.

"Let me finish! It's my story," he scolded playfully. "When I came into the courtyard, who should I meet but Governor Taman coming out from dinner. Apparently you were exhausted and retired early?"

"I *was* retired," she corrected sarcastically.

"Ah, of course," he nodded in understanding. "She wouldn't want you being too free to talk until she ascertained how much of your training still remained. Anyway, the Governor was disappointed he hadn't had the chance to talk with you and took the opportunity to ask about your friends. I, being the helpful guy that I am, told him they were finding the accommodations cramped and less to their liking. So we agreed they'd be more comfortable at his estate, which as you may or may not know is quite close to the university."

"And?" She looked at him as he took a long pause to feel proud of himself. "Where are they now?"

"Gone." He showed empty hands like a magician. "Disappeared from their cell in the night. You're welcome."

"I hope Governor Taman can be trusted," she said, with a small measure of relief.

"I only gave you a brief description of the conversation that took place, Sis," he assured her. "The governor is as much an ally to you as any could be. Something is rotting in this city. You were good to get clear of it when you did."

"And now here I am, back in the spider's web." She shook her head.

"Better get dressed for the spider." He gave her a sympathetic smile. "Your day promises to be long and full of intrigue."

"Yay." She turned and walked back toward her inner chamber. "Can't wait."

She was in the middle of instructing Dana how to tie the corset straps of her dress when her mother burst into the room. The servant jumped and turned white as a ghost, but Anatellia just turned her head to regard her mother with icy eyes.

"Hello, Mother," she greeted coldly.

"Time has not healed you of tardiness," her mother noted in an icy tone as she crossed the room and pushed the fragile lady-in-waiting aside. Grabbing the corset straps, she pulled so sharply Anatellia gasped.

"Just strangle me with them and be done with this," Anatellia snarled.

"Silly girl." Raphael continued to work the straps. "I have no intention of wasting all the effort I've poured into you—all you've become in spite of yourself. You may have no love for me, but everything I do I do for you."

"Oh Mother, please!" she laughed through gasps. "Everything you've done, you've done for yourself."

"No!" The older woman grabbed her by the shoulders and spun her so they were looking eye to eye. "Everything that I've done for you has been so you could have opportunities I never did. You could have been the head of all the guilds after I was done with you. You still could be!"

"But you never asked me what I wanted, Mother!" Anatellia felt all of the frustration she'd held for fourteen years pour out. "Father died and you changed! Nothing I did was ever good enough after that! You stopped loving me and started moulding me. Moulding me to become just like you. And I hated you for it. I hated what you had become. I hated what you were turning me into!"

She didn't see the slap coming. Her face exploded in pain and she jerked her head back around to stare in shock at her mother. What she saw there was pain. Pain deeper than her own. It was there only briefly and then it was gone, her mother's eyes turning to ice as her jaw set like stone. Without a word she turned and left Anatellia's room.

She stood there in silence, her cheek stinging. Her anger drained out of her and left only a sense of shame at her angry words. *What am I doing? Why am I playing this game again?* She'd run away to avoid this game, this life. Nothing seemed to make sense. And through the confusion of all her thoughts, one fact stood out.

In three weeks, none of this would matter.

She sat back on the edge of the bed and let hot tears flow down her cheeks as Dana looked on helplessly.

18

A Fraternity of the Faithful

Daskow stood in the window of the room Governor Taman had provided for them after they had been sprung by David the night before. At first they had been unsure of the man's intentions, fearing they would be "disappeared," as Ange had put it. But the Governor showed them the letter that Elder Shamar had sent, and assured them that he meant no harm.

The Governor's estate was situated just off the grounds of the university—Daskow could see them out his window. A soft knock on the door announced Angelis, looking happy to be free of their cell accommodations. She was chewing on a piece of toast heaped with jam and giving him the "What are you doing?" look he'd come to know in the years since they had started travelling together.

"Breakfast is served, I take it?" He smiled at her as she nodded.

The outer room of the small apartment was beautifully furnished, and a tray of breakfast foods sat on the table in the middle of the room. He looked it over as he entered and grabbed a plate.

"The strawberry jam is incredible!"

"I'm wondering where these melons came from, myself." He took a bite of the juicy fruit before settling on a bowl of raspberries.

They feasted in silence, enjoying the sunny room for some minutes before Ange felt full enough to start chattering again.

"What were you and Governor Taman talking about last night?" She gave him an inquiring look. "Something about a fraternity of the fruitful?"

"Fraternity of the Faithful," he corrected softly.

"Yeah, them," she nodded as she jammed up another slice of toast. "They're a secret group or something?"

"The Fraternity of the Faithful," he repeated, "is a society of students and teachers who have devoted themselves to living their lives by the old ways. They are dedicated to seeking out the ancient paths."

"Paths? Like the one Anatellia took to find the Mountain of God?" She had a way of dragging explanations out of him.

He shook his head. "No, I mean like ancient beliefs and understandings that our forefathers had when they settled the Valley. We've lost much of the old knowledge."

"Like the Mountain of the Living God being an actual place and not just an idea," she said.

"Exactly!" His inner teacher was coming out. "The Fraternity was a group of men and women who would gather outside of class time to argue and discuss ideas like that."

"And you were a member."

"Yes," he nodded, choosing a strawberry from the tray. "And so is the Governor, it turns out."

"Really?" She was surprised that a politician would be part of a secret university society. Another thought occurred to her. "Why does it seem so secret?"

"Because many of the old beliefs and understandings have fallen out of popular favour," he admitted.

"Popular favour?" She scrunched her nose at the idea. "How are knowledge and truth dictated by popular favour?"

"How indeed?" Daskow nodded as he bit into another strawberry. "That is why the society exists, to protect truth and knowledge from the tyranny of popular thinking."

"Like what?" she pressed. "What kind of thinking is popular thinking?"

"Well, like the idea that the Living God is more of an idea than a person, for one thing." He searched for other examples. "And the idea that the holy texts are allegory and myth and very little actually happened the way it says it did. And of course the Mountain and Maylaks and all of that isn't real."

"That sounds sillier than anything I heard in Pethe. Do people really believe that?"

"Sadly, they do," he admitted. "Many people in the city think that way. They tend to look down on the villages."

She looked sad. "I hadn't realized. How haven't I seen that?"

"Because we avoid places where that kind of thinking is prevalent." Daskow handed her the last slice of toast. "And you and Ra'ah have grown up gloriously sheltered from those kinds of things.

There was a knock at the door and it opened to reveal the face of the Governor.

"Am I intruding?" he asked graciously.

"Not all." Ange jumped up to get the door. "And it's your house, anyway."

"Too kind." He smiled warmly at her. "I just wanted to let you both know that I've arranged a meeting of the Fraternity tonight, and I wondered if you wanted to work out your testimony by presenting it to me."

"You want to hear it first," Ange accused playfully.

"You are a delight." His smile increased. "And as refreshing as a summer breeze. If I was but half my age…!"

Angelis blushed and sat back down.

"Have a seat," Daskow offered. "We would do well to refine our story. This will not be a village meeting, after all."

"Indeed it will not." Governor Taman sat on a comfortable chair and waited for them to start.

"Ange?" She jerked her head up in surprise as Daskow called her name. "Do you want to tell it?"

"I'm out of my depth here," she admitted sheepishly. "I really am much better with village meetings."

"Don't sell yourself short." He smiled at her. "But this time I'll let you off the hook."

He set his plate on the table and settled himself back in the chair he'd chosen.

"We were camped on the slopes above Cardaya about a week ago," he began the now familiar story.

19

A Family Meeting

Anatellia strayed from her apartment a little after midmorning. Her fight with her mother had left her rattled, and she had sat for a long time with a cold cloth on her cheek, pondering what she had said and what she had seen in her mother's eyes. Ten years had not dulled her anger at all. It had just taken her mother's presence to bring it back.

What she had not expected, other than the slap, was the look of hurt in her mother's eyes. She couldn't recall a time when she'd ever seen her so vulnerable. So human. And despite what her anger might tell her, what she had seen was real. The fact that her mother had left her to her own devices after their fight was proof of that.

She wandered the hallways without any real destination in mind. Eventually she would make her way to areas she was pretty sure the staff had been instructed not to allow her into, but she was in no hurry. She was just preparing to go down to the main floor when the sound of a door opening brought her around. Two women were coming out of one of the apartments. With a sinking feeling, she realized she recognized both of them from the night before.

"Well, hello sister-in-law." The lead woman's voice had mastered contempt. "I'm surprised Lady Raphael has let you move about the house."

"Hello." She smiled crisply. "Forgive me, but I have forgotten your name. It's been ten years and you weren't nearly so forward when you were following Malik around like a puppy."

The woman's smile all but cracked. Anatellia wondered where her animosity toward this woman had come from. She was a little taken aback by her own cattiness. The other woman, Margaret, covered her mouth with her hand, hiding her own satisfied smile. Anatellia knew she had reason to feel sorry for that one.

She switched to a sincere smile. "Hello, Margaret. I was sad when we couldn't talk further at dinner last night. Perhaps you'd walk with me?"

"Absolutely." Margaret smiled and looked at her companion. "Do you need me for anything else, Lydia?"

"No." Lydia's voice was as brittle as her face as she turned on her heels and went the opposite direction.

"Edward was right about you," Margaret commented quietly after she left. "You are your mother's daughter."

"Edward said that?" Anatellia felt like she'd been stabbed through the heart. "How nice of him."

"Don't get me wrong," Margaret back-pedalled slightly as she offered Anatellia the lead down the hall, "you don't strike me as someone who'd use that strength to hurt the weak. Lydia hasn't been put in her place for years."

"I'm afraid Edward may be more correct than I want to admit," Anatellia confessed with a smile. "I left because I didn't want to become that person.

"We often end up becoming the very thing we run from," Margaret admitted sagely.

"My dear, how did you get stuck in this family?" Anatellia found herself liking this woman.

They took lunch together in Anatellia's drawing room. Margaret looked around in fascination as she ate. This apartment had been off-limits the entire time she'd lived in the estate. Edward always assumed that Mother had refused to accept Anatellia was actually gone, supposing that she would return one day and everything would continue. He'd thought otherwise, it turned out.

"And it appears he was wrong," Margaret mused, "because here you are."

"Not by choice," Anatellia confessed ruefully.

"I can't understand that." The other woman shook her head. "I mean, your mother is determined to groom you for an empire. She's already secured the leadership of the silk guild, and it's said she has designs on more."

"Mother has ambition and more to spare," Anatellia admitted. "But I want none of it."

"You'd rather be out there in the forest with your friends?" Margaret shook her head in wonder. "I can't imagine such a life."

"I don't *want* to imagine any other life," she countered wistfully.

"Well, when the Sacheth settlers arrive, it'll be much harder to find quiet places like that, I guess," Margaret concluded.

"Who?" Anatellia sat up straight.

"The Sacheth," Margaret repeated, confused that the other woman didn't seem to know what she was talking about. "The people from beyond the mountains that are coming to settle here with us? Edward said they should be here within the month."

"Margaret"—Anatellia kept her voice calm—"tell me everything you know about the Sacheth."

"I don't really know much more than that," she admitted, a little alarmed. "I heard Edward and Malik talking about them. Apparently Lady Raphael has brokered a land deal with them. They have a great country across the mountains, and she offered land for a trade deal or some such thing. Honestly, I know nothing of such matters."

"Oh Mother, what have you done?" Anatellia whispered softly to herself.

At that moment the door burst open and Malik stormed in. Behind him was the stocky captain from the day before, followed by David, who had an amused look on his face. They ignored the two women entirely as they searched the drawing room and adjoining bedchamber.

Anatellia sat quietly, watching David with amusement. Margaret looked absolutely scandalized.

"Malik!" Margaret stood and stared him down when he returned from the bedchamber. "This is not behaviour suited to a gentleman! Your sister's rooms should not be treated this way!"

"Shut up, Margaret," he dismissed her as he looked helplessly around the room. Finally, he fixed his gaze on his sister.

"Lose something, brother?" she asked sweetly.

"Where are they?"

"Your symbols of manhood?" She almost regretted taking the shot. This wasn't who she wanted to be. But this family brought out the worst parts of her and she didn't have time to play nice. "We saw Lydia earlier—you should go ask her."

Margaret continued to look shocked, and covered her mouth with her hand. The stocky captain simply left the room without looking back. Malik's face turned a horribly unhandsome shade of red and he came toward her, only to be restrained by David's hand. Anatellia smiled sweetly at them both to hide the horror of what she was becoming.

Dear Living God, she thought to herself, *deliver me from myself.*

"Where are your vagrant friends?" Malik clipped each word. She had to give him credit: he had more restraint in the moment than she did.

"They aren't here," she said flatly, stating the obvious.

"Tell me where they are."

She shook her head. "No. Even if I knew, I wouldn't tell you. Obviously."

"You're going to end up on the wrong side of this game you're playing, Sister," he threatened.

"I'm firmly on the side of the Living God," she said, standing up to face him. "If you see that as the wrong side, God help you."

"Mother's patience will not last much longer. Let's see if your Living God and all the Maylak will save you then."

"For the first time in our lives, I see you, Brother. When did you give up on believing?"

"When our father died and you stole my birthright!" he admitted bitterly in the moment. "I knew then that there were no loving or just gods."

"I feel sorry for you, Malik." She shook her head sadly. "Now get out of my rooms."

"I should go." Margaret slunk out the door as quickly as she could.

Malik stared at her for a long time and then turned and left. David made to follow, giving his sister an appraising look.

"David," she whispered softly, "stay. We need to talk."

"I'm almost afraid," he admitted. "Your tongue is far sharper and your manners much dulled since this morning. I trust your bloodlust is satisfied for now?"

She nodded sadly. "For now. Shut the door."

He did as he was asked and then came back and watched her in expectation.

"What do you know of the Sacheth?" she asked bluntly.

"Who or what is that?" he returned without hesitation.

"You honestly don't know?"

"Seriously, Anna, what is going on with you?" He sat down across from her in concern. "You disappear for ten years and then show up with your friends, get arrested, tell a story of Valley apocalypse, and emasculate our brother in front of our sister-in-law. That's a lot for one day, even for you."

"I had to make up for lost time," she joked sadly. "But joking aside, Margaret told me something I shouldn't have heard."

"Something about the Sacheth—whatever that is."

"Whoever," she corrected significantly. "It's whoever that is. And apparently, they are the people coming to the Valley at Mother's request. Margaret said they'd be here within the month. Malik and Edward know about it."

"I'm not worthy enough for family business," he admitted absently. "But if there are actually people coming, does that mean something else is coming with them?"

"What if it's *them*? What if the people Mother has made a bargain with are coming to destroy the Valley?"

"Wait, are we talking figuratively or literally?" he asked in confusion. "Mother wouldn't invite an army into the valley."

"Not knowingly."

"Caught between Mother and the Living God." He shook his head. "no wonder you're cranky."

"Have I mentioned you're my favourite brother, David?" She smiled sadly at him.

"What do we do?" he asked after a brief pause.

She plotted in her head. "We get a message to Daskow. He's got to spread the word in the city about these people. I just hope that Governor Taman isn't in on this secret."

"Why would Mother invite people into the Valley without telling the city elders and governors?" David asked the question that had been bothering her.

"She would have to tell some of them," she admitted. "But only those she knew would support her."

"But why invite them at all?" he pressed in bewilderment.

"Isn't it obvious?" She put herself in her mother's place. "She's setting herself up with more power. As the head of a lucrative trade deal with a foreign country. The first brokered deal of its kind between the Valley and an outside country. She could move all of the guilds under her authority."

"And you could be the heir to that empire," he pointed out.

"I'll let that suggestion pass, since you've never stood before a Maylak of the Living God." She shook her head. "But I will take her report over anything our mother might offer."

"Maybe you should think about slipping out with me when I go to see Daskow and Ange?" he suggested. "If what you say is true, Mother will be no farther behind you in reasoning this whole thing out. At what point do you go from heir apparent to threat in her eyes?

"I can't leave yet. I have to at least confront her. Give her a chance to explain what she's done."

"I don't think she's going to agree that she owes you an explanation," her brother shook his head emphatically. "But I'll be ready to get you out of the house once you realize that."

"You are…"

"Your favourite brother—yes, you told me!"

— 20 —

Practical Thinking

Nebaya and Ra'ah were roused by a soft tapping on their door. Fumbling in the dark, he reached for the lamp that the innkeeper had left them and turned the flame up, flooding the room with light. The tapping came again, more insistently, and Nebaya got up and put her ear to it.

"Who's there?" she whispered.

"It ain't maid service," a gruff voice responded.

Nebaya opened the door to see Elder Eman holding a hooded lamp. The old man gave them a glare and stepped into the room.

"I decided we should get to Master Dunhamai a little earlier than planned. Gather your stuff—you won't be back."

They exchanged alarmed looks, which the old man ignored

"If we hurry, we can catch breakfast at Elder Timao's," he added as he headed back out the door. "Be quick. I'll be waiting in the common room."

They gathered their things and blew out the lamp. The hall was dimly lit by a lamp hung by the stairs, and they hurried quietly down the hall after the stocky man. The common room was also dimly lit, and the man stopped to leave a note under the lamp on the bar. Turning, he motioned them out the door and into the early morning.

"What has happened that we're leaving earlier than planned?" Nebaya cut to the point when they were out on the street.

"Happened?" Eman regarded her from under his bushy brows as he lifted his hood. "Life happened. A merchant caravan arrived from the city last night and is leaving first thing this morning. Dunhamai always goes up the pass with the caravans these days, so we've got to catch her before they leave."

"That must be the same caravan we travelled here with," Ra'ah said.

"Well, if you'd mentioned that you'd arrived with a caravan last night we could have planned better," the old man muttered.

Ra'ah looked helplessly at Nebaya, who just shrugged. The elder set a pace that was surprisingly fast for a man of his age and size, and they put their heads down and followed him through the lamplit streets. The eastern sky was just beginning to lighten when they came to the Pass Gate, where the highway left the village and climbed into the rocky pass above the Valley River. Eman led them to one side where a tall grey-haired woman stood in a lit doorway.

"Dunhamai," Elder Eman greeted her.

"Eman." The woman's voice was low and disinterested. "Who are these with you?"

"Nebaya and Ra'ah. They have a letter for you."

"Strange. I don't get mail, as a rule." She regarded them coldly, her eyes staying longer on Nebaya. "The short kid is from Bato or I know nothing. But this one, she reminds me of her parents, I think.

"You knew my parents?" Nebaya asked a little tersely. Ra'ah thought back to Amon, the last person who had remembered her parents.

"I'm not sure," the tall woman admitted with a shrug. "But you and I have never met and yet you are familiar. The familiarity is old, so it's not a brother or sister you remind me of either. Hence, I probably knew one of your parents. You have a letter for me?"

"Oh, yes." Nebaya was caught off guard, and fumbled for the letter in her cloak before she finally handed it over. "Here it is."

Master Dunhamai snatched the letter from her and examined the seal in the light of the lamp. Ra'ah watched her mouth the words she was reading, and she looked back at Nebaya again. She finally broke the letter's seal and started to read it. Time seemed to slow down as she read. Ra'ah fancied he heard the wheels of carts coming up the road from the village behind them. The sky continued to brighten. Finally, she rolled the letter up with a deep sigh and fixed Elder Eman with a dark look.

"You got a letter of your own?"

"From Elder Sophia of Pethe."

"Did you bring it?" she asked pointedly, handing him the letter she had just read.

He nodded as he took her letter, and pulled the one they had given him and Elder Timao the night before out of his cloak. She took it and briskly unfolded it to read. Eman did the same with hers.

"Did they use these as pillows?" she asked as she read.

Eman glanced up at the two waiting young people before he continued to read.

They waited in the cold. Silence hung between the four as the sound of wagons become distinct from down the road. Finally she folded the letter she was reading back up and handed it to Eman. She regarded the two young people in silence for some time before speaking.

"There were five of you and now there are two. Did the wolves get the other three?" she asked harshly.

"What? No…" Ra'ah was caught off guard. "They were delayed in Kathik. We decided to come ahead of them."

"Delayed?" She regarded them. "More likely detained. In a way, the wolves likely did get them. Just not the black devils."

"What do you mean?" Nebaya demanded. "You speak like you know more than those letters could tell you."

"Ah, Little Sister." The tall woman regarded her in a different light. "It's not easy living black and white in a world of grey, is it?"

"I still don't know what you mean." Nebaya shrunk a bit in the face of the other woman's intense gaze.

She continued to stare. "Don't you? No matter. I know all about the black demons running riot across the valley. They came out of the pass over a week back. No one else saw them pass on the high slopes, but I did. Nothing escapes my notice around here. Dozens of them that night, none since."

"Why didn't you sound the alarm?" Nebaya accused.

"Who says I didn't, in my own way?" Dunhamai shot back. "But obviously my warnings didn't go anywhere, or you simply didn't know where the warnings came from. Either way, I did what I could."

"Enough." Eman stepped in, waving the letters. "What do you think of all this?"

"What do I think of this?" she repeated. "You already know what I think. I've already told you doddering fools what I think."

"Please," Ra'ah begged in frustration, "please tell us what you're talking about."

"I've been overhearing talk amongst the caravans," she explained. "Many of them are talking about the Sacheth. Some talk is friendly, other talk is fearful. Whatever the Sacheth are, their reputation goes before them."

"And Master Dunhamai feels that they are coming here," Elder Eman finished for her impatiently.

"I know they are." She glared at Eman. What's more, there are caravans overdue. Half a dozen at least." She looked back at the two young people. "Something large is moving up toward the Koreb Pass, and at the very least, nothing can get around it."

"That's your speculation," Eman insisted.

"True," she agreed. "The other explanation is that six caravans were destroyed by the black wolves and no one has returned to report it. And all six are her competitors."

"Whose competitors?" Nebaya caught the inference.

"Lady Raphael of the Silk Guild," the tall woman declared. "And to add to my suspicions, one of her caravans came out of the pass on time right in the middle of the overdue ones. So that eliminates the wolf theory, wouldn't you say?"

"I would say," Nebaya agreed quietly.

"What would you have the Council of Elders do?" Eman demanded. "We cannot take the word of one person, even if that person is you, Dunhamai."

"Some words ought to carry more weight than others," the Master declared pointedly. "Debate those letters and these kids' testimonies all you want, but in two days when I come back down from the pass, I'm going to take anyone who will listen to me and leave for the Mountain."

"You'll get your stubborn self banished!" he warned her.

"Upon my word, Eman"—she towered over him like a great bird of prey over a rabbit—"before the new moon rises again, you'll be wishing you were banished with me if you aren't with me already."

Eman tried to redirect the subject. "Your conspiracies need proof, that is all I'm saying."

"Proof?" The tall woman threw her hands up. "We used to be a people who heard the voice of the Living God and obeyed. Now we're a people of proof and reason. We are more refined in our thinking. So the Living God has to change how He communicates with us. He has to get more refined. He's only allowed to speak to us through logic and reason and dusty holy texts.

"Pay attention to the proof, old man. The drivers and merchants talk to me like I've taken the Oath. I've been hearing rumours of the Sacheth for months. The Sacheth are dominating our trade. The Sacheth are increasing their territories. The Sacheth are taxing trade routes. The Sacheth are making trade pacts for land deals. I've shared all of this quietly with you and that addled council!

"Now you've got five kids out of the forest claiming a message from the Living God. I haven't even heard their story, just what those letters say. Disaster is coming on the next new moon. Everyone must flee to the Mountain of the Living God. He is responding, calling His children to Him. And what are his children saying? Don't overreact? Show us proof? Send us more *convincing* proof?

"The proof that many people in this valley are going to get is slavery and death, if my guess is right." Her tirade carried her halfway into the street, following the retreating old man.

Ra'ah simply watched the whole exchange agape. The tall woman was like a force of nature—like a great grey wolf herself. His mind raced as he tried to process all of the new information. The Oath was the vow of secrecy that all guild members had to take, from merchants all the way down to drivers. Obviously they did not know that Dunhamai was not a guild member for whatever reason, because the punishment for breaking the Oath was the most severe punishment imaginable—exile. Some group named the the Sacheth was coming. Caravans had gone missing, and a Lady Raphael of the silk merchants seemed to be involved. He realized in all of his thinking that he had felt safer when it was a nameless unknown threat, like the black wolves. Now the threat to the valley was forming into an all-too-close physical threat. He felt somehow less safe, less sure of success.

"Master Dunhamai," Nebaya interrupted the tall woman's assault on the old elder, "Whose caravan was the last one to come out of the Pass?"

"Lady Raphael's, of the silk merchants," Master Dunhamai responded. "There are six other caravans that left here either before or at the same time as hers, and none of them have returned. And in the late spring and summer caravans are rarely ever that late."

"And whose caravans have been talking about these Sacheth?" she pressed.

"See?" Dunhamai gave a significant look at Elder Eman. "This girl understands the importance of asking questions."

"Would it also be Lady Raphael's caravans?" Nebaya pressed anxiously.

"Why?" The tall woman grew suspicious at her questioning. "The Oath restrains tongues even between the guilds, but all the caravans are bringing back rumours. I can't say hers more than others. But why are you so focused on her?"

"She's holding our friends," Nebaya admitted.

"She is? Wait…" Ra'ah looked at her in shock as he put everything together. "…This Lady Raphael is Anatellia's mother?"

"If your friends are detained by Lady Raphael, I would be very concerned for them," Dunhamai said. "She has a reputation for ruthlessness among the caravan teams."

"She is our friend's mother," Nebaya admitted. "We had a letter for her and when our three friends went to deliver it, they were detained."

"Detained? By whom? Lady Raphael herself or the city guard?"

"Well, by Lady Raphael I assume." Nebaya shook her head. "They were under house arrest at her estate."

The noise of wagons suddenly got louder as the caravan rounded a corner and came toward the Pass Gate. They all turned as the caravan approached. Master Dunhamai regarded the approaching wagons with a set jaw, and then turned and motioned them all back to her doorway.

"Listen very carefully, you three." Her tone was severe and her gaze was hard. "Every prophecy of the Living God has a component of expected interaction. He speaks and we respond. I fear our enemy may be responding to the message you have brought."

"What do you mean?" Nebaya challenged her. "What can we do to affect the message of the Living God?"

"That caravan coming up the road is a silk caravan," the tall woman stated flatly. "It isn't scheduled to pass through here for another week. Yet it left the city yesterday morning—I assume about the same time you two did. When were your friends detained? I'm betting the night before last."

"You're suggesting they're carrying a message to whoever or whatever is coming?" Elder Eman asked incredulously. "Why would anyone in the Valley, especially a respected merchant such as Lady Raphael, help an invading army conquer us?"

"What if she doesn't believe it's an army?" Dunhamai asked with exaggerated patience. "What if she thinks this is some kind of business arrangement? Some kind of trade alliance? She doesn't have to be in the know to be useful to whatever the Sacheth is."

"What are we going to do?" Nebaya had her eyes on the caravan that was now rolling past them through the gate. "What will *you* do?"

"I always go with the caravans to the top of the pass," Master Dunhamai explained. "No one knows that pass like I do. This caravan will be no different. I will go up with them and return in two days, as I said. When I come back down, it might be with proof. Either way, you two wait for me. Try to convince the village council of your message."

"But if they are in league with the enemy, shouldn't we stop them?" Ra'ah protested quietly.

"Stop them?" Master Dunhamai repeated incredulously. "How? When have we ever raised our hand to each other in violence? Will we start now? Even if I knew beyond doubt they carried the proof that would convince the entire Valley of what was coming, I would not raise my hand in violence to any other brother or sister in this Valley to get it. That is a dark road that would doom us all, and we should hope no one ever goes down it."

Ra'ah nodded to Elder Eman. "But surely he could stop them and have them searched."

"I doubt they would accept his authority to do so even if he could be convinced to try." She glanced at the old man while he shook his head. "And consider this, we would be revealing our suspicions to Lady Raphael and her friends out there beyond the pass. Do we know what they might do? No—you should focus on your mission. The Living God goes before us in this; we will do our best to follow Him and respond to what He says, and not try to do anything in our own strength or wisdom."

She grabbed her gear from inside the porch of her small house and slung it over her shoulder. The caravan had cleared the gate and was making its way up the slope. She watched the lead wagon ascend before turning to Nebaya.

"Be my voice with the council, Little Sister," she smiled. "They often need someone who sees things clearly through the grey to help set their course. It's time you embraced the Calling."

"Okay," Nebaya nodded, taken aback by her directness.

The tall woman turned and jogged out of the gate after the caravan. Her voice drifted back to them as she climbed the road.

"Be obedient to the Word of the Living God. Don't wait for proof to settle it."

They watched her catch up and pass the caravan. The drivers waved to her as she passed and the outrider guards nodded to her, happy that she had finally joined them. Tradition was a comfort they all took for granted, Ra'ah realized.

Elder Amon turned to the two and regarded them pensively from beneath his brows.

"Let's go get breakfast," he decided finally. "There is much to work out in this."

21

CONFRONTATION!

Anatellia made her way to her mother's study. Her thoughts were buoyed on a storm of emotion. That the great Lady Raphael could be the architect of the Valley's destruction shook her, but deep down it didn't surprise her. She went over how she wanted the conversation to go, rehearsing it over and over in her head. However, she knew the real conversation would likely look nothing like what she imagined.

Benjamin was just exiting the study as she approached. He raised his hand abruptly and shut the door firmly behind himself.

"Your mother is not seeing anyone," the man announced imperiously.

"Even her daughter?" she challenged.

"Especially"—he emphasized the word with force—"her daughter."

"Well, I must speak with her," she insisted, and then added, "it's an urgent matter."

"Frankly, Miss Anatellia, nothing you have to say would be urgent to your mother at this time." He dismissed her and remained planted in front of the door.

"Okay, let's try this." She put on what she assumed was the most calculating smile she could. "Tell Mother that if she doesn't want to talk to me about the Sacheth, I'll just go find Governor Taman and talk to him about them. I'll sneak out of this house and find everyone willing to listen to what I know about the Sacheth."

"I know nothing about what you're apparently threatening me with," he admitted coldly, "and you threaten like a child. Go stir up trouble with your brothers—or better yet, crawl back to the forest hole you've been hiding in all these years."

"Do not mistake honesty for childishness," she warned him, leaning in close to his ear. "You forget whose daughter I am. Am I making an idle threat? Can you risk that I might know about something that you don't?" She leaned back out and raised her eyes, waiting.

"You are the lesser woman," he snarled softly. "You will never amount to half what your mother has already become."

"I reject your assessment, old man. I will become who the Living God has called me to be, in spite of you all. Now go tell her that her daughter will see her."

He hesitated, his pride fighting with his doubt. Finally he knocked and opened the door, slipping inside and shutting it before she could think to follow. She waited outside the door for several minutes, wondering if the man had simply locked the door and found another way out of the study. Just as she reached for the handle to test it, the door opened. She didn't wait for the invite and stepped through.

Her mother's study was emptier than yesterday. Her mother sat at her desk, watching her enter the room like a cat watches the prey. With a dismissive wave she sent Benjamin back out of the room through the door her daughter had just entered. Anatellia stood still and returned her mother's glare, waiting.

"What do you know of the Sacheth?" Her mother's voice was emotionless and cold.

"Let's see..." Anatellia pretended to recall what she had already spent so much time thinking about. "I know that they are from a distant country. I know that you've made a trade deal with them in secret. I know that you've promised them land here. And I know that they are coming here now and will be here by the new moon. Quite a coincidence, that one."

Her mother looked at her in silence, her fingers tapping on the desk in the way that told Anatellia she'd hit the mark, or at least close enough to it. Her mother was deciding what she was going to do with her. She decided to push forward before that decision was made.

"How could you, Mother?" she accused. "How could you sell the Valley—our home—to these people? What are you going to do, knowing what the Living God has said?"

"I don't know where you've gotten this information from." The cold edge in her voice revealed emotion under the surface. "And I don't know who you're working with. But if you think I'm falling for this message you're purporting to be an actual Maylak-delivered missive from the Living God, you don't think much of your mother. What I can't understand is why you'd betray your family to work with one of the other houses."

"What?" Anatellia was taken aback. "You think I'm plotting with another merchant against you? Is that what you think? Mother, how deceived can you be?"

"I didn't raise my daughter to be a spiritual vagrant in the forest, subscribing to a bunch of Cardayan mysticism in the vague hope that the Living God will step out of holy texts and give her a hug," her mother shot back venomously. "And I certainly don't believe this donkey swill about Maylak visitations and message from God. And I'm not about to let my daughter and whoever is influencing her destroy the most lucrative trade agreement this city and this Valley have ever seen. The Sacheth union will bring us forward and reconnect us with the world outside. A world that has grown past us in the centuries that we've been hunkered down in the forest acting like barbarians."

Anatellia shook her head in disbelief. "Mother, what are you talking about? What have you done?"

"I've made a decision to move the Valley into the real world," Raphael declared triumphantly. "And there is nothing you or your friends or whatever group is behind you can do to stop it. And to be sure you can't interfere further with it, I've dispatched a message to them this morning. They will be sending others ahead of the settler caravans to help us restore order."

"Restore order?" Anatellia heart skipped a beat. "Do you even hear yourself?"

"This is for the Valley's good," her mother assured her. "There will be some transition pains, to be sure, but this is not the first trade pact of this kind that the Sacheth have successfully negotiated."

"How do you know? When have you ever travelled to these lands, met these people? Who made you the ambassador for the entire Valley?"

"You are still a child," her mother said dismissively. "You do not understand what drives trade with those outside the Valley. You never bothered to learn about where the silk comes from that gave you everything you ever wanted growing up. Where the spices come from. The fruit that cannot grow in the valley. For centuries we've stayed secluded and tentatively sent out caravans to trade for goods, scraping the bare surface of our potential. I was given the opportunity to bring us back into the world we left, and I took it."

"You've sold us to the enemies of the Living God for coin and power," Anatellia declared. "There was a reason our forefathers left that world and came to this Valley, Mother. There was a reason they set aside sword and shield, spear and armour, and chose a life of peace and seclusion. You may think it's all just myth and religion, but I don't. Thousands of others in the Valley don't. And the Living God certainly doesn't. You've betrayed us all, and the Living God has responded. You're on the wrong side of this."

"I never raised my daughter to be such a religious zealot." Her mother shook her head in disgust. "What happened to you?"

"I was adopted by a greater family." Anatellia's heart was suddenly filled with longing for her friends, "And a greater Father. One that will not die and leave my new family to the whims of a vain and fickle woman."

She turned on her heels and ripped open the door. She heard her mother rise behind her, but she didn't care and didn't look back. She was done.

22

A Different Kind of Meeting

Nebaya and Ra'ah quietly followed Elder Eman through the streets of Meletsa, each one lost in their fears and doubts. The meeting with Master Dunhamai had left them with both a certainty of the threat approaching the Valley and an uncertainty of the depth of conspiracy within the Valley itself. Nebaya seemed deeply troubled and agitated, and Ra'ah guessed it was centred around their friends trapped back in the city.

For Ra'ah's part, he felt a growing sense of despair as he considered what it all meant for the future. *What is coming for us? How are the black wolves involved?* He had a hard time believing they were natural. He thought about the dissolved tooth in the jar in his pack. *No, they are not natural animals,* he decided, *they are something else. And what of the Sacheth? If the creatures serve them, are they something just as unnatural?* The Maylak had suggested they were too strong to be resisted. The idea of something stronger and more evil than the black wolves made him shudder.

"We are taught nothing of the world outside this Valley," Nebaya noted out of the blue. "We trade with the peoples across the mountains, but we don't hear any stories about the lands beyond. Why do you suppose that is?"

"It's because of the Oath," Elder Eman responded immediately. "Those vows coupled with holy text doctrines."

"Elaborate."

"You have a big vocabulary for a hunter from the forests," Eman noted before continuing. "When we first started trading out of the Valley, the trading guilds were required to enforce a vow of silence about the lands beyond the Valley, and about the Valley when they interacted with people out there. The Guild Oath became an ingrained part of caravan society. To this day, you cannot get any member of the guilds to talk about anything they have seen beyond the pass.

"And all of it comes down to the warnings from the holy texts. Specifically warnings about keeping ourselves separate and apart from the lands we left and the peoples beyond the mountains."

"Hard to believe you can keep something like that secret when people are involved," Nebaya said.

"Well, it does come with severe penalties for Guild caravans if they get caught breaking their vows with outsiders."

"And all this time the Guilds could have been communicating with cities and people outside the Valley while everyone else has been blissfully unaware?" Ra'ah summarized.

"Undoubtedly," Eman nodded from ahead of them. "But we are unaware by choice. Ignorance is bliss, after all. With knowledge comes responsibility. Don't tell me you haven't thought about what would have happened if you just ignored that vision you all had on that mountainside and went peacefully about your business."

"The Valley would be destroyed," Ra'ah protested. "We couldn't let that happen. And we certainly couldn't dismiss what we saw and heard as merely a vision."

"And everyone would have been blissfully ignorant of it till destruction comes marching out of that pass back there." He jabbed a finger back the way they had come. "With knowledge comes the burden of responsibility. You had to act. And you bring knowledge to everyone else. And then they have the burden of responsibility and they have to act. But don't be surprised when people resist knowing in favour of ignorance."

"Because ignorance is bliss," Nebaya and Ra'ah finished for him.

He glared back at them, and then pointed to a house ahead on the riverfront.

"That's Elder Timao's house. Try to find your manners again before we get inside."

Elder Timao had been expecting them, as it turned out. They were brought by a servant through the house to a balcony overlooking the river. A table and chairs were set out and Timao was happily drinking tea and squinting out at the rising sun. She encouraged them to sit and eat and then fixed her stare at Eman.

"What did she have to say?" she asked him pointedly.

"Nothing really new," he admitted, handing her the two letters, "but the conversation revealed more details about these two and their friends."

"Oh?" She looked over at the two young people digging into the bacon and eggs. "How so?"

"Lady Raphael is holding the other three. Apparently one of them is her daughter."

"Ah," she nodded. "So Anatellia is a member of your group and returned to her mother's house. I wonder why she did that?"

"One of Sophia's letters," Eman concluded. "You three were close at one time, weren't you?"

"A long time ago," Elder Timao mused quietly. "When we were these kids' ages. But if Sophia sent Raphael one of these letters, the Lady would now know that there is a warning going throughout the Valley. So how does she react?"

"She seizes her daughter and her daughter's friends and locks them up in her estate," Eman declared, filling his plate with food.

"Which suggests that she doesn't want the message out," Timao continued, tapping her lips with her finger. "She doesn't try to get in front of the message, doesn't try to discredit the message, but tries to stop the message from spreading."

"Maybe she *is* trying to get out in front of it and discredit it," Eman suggested. "She just doesn't want to have to compete with her daughter the entire time she's doing it."

"I don't think so. Otherwise we'd have received letters from her or the governors and elders who are loyal to her. What did Dunhamai have to say to all of this?"

Eman grunted in disgust. "She's convinced Raphael has sold out the entire Valley. She's ready to come back down the mountain in two days and lead everyone who'll follow to the Mountain of the Living God, wherever she thinks it may be."

"She knows where the Mountain is?" Ra'ah asked in surprise.

"She says she does." Eman raised his hand to forestall further interruption. "She says she's been there, in circumstances much like what you shared about your friend."

"Anatellia," Ra'ah interjected. "It is Anatellia who has seen the Mountain."

"Whatever." He brushed it aside gruffly.

"Master Dunhamai is a woman of…" Timao paused to choose the right words, "…unique and diverse talents and knowledge. Everyone is wiser to not dismiss her out of hand."

"Anyway," Eman continued loudly, "She's coming down and taking anyone who will follow her up the Valley."

"So she believes the threat is real, and that it's likely this Sacheth group she's been hearing about," Timao concluded as she drank her tea. "And she's committed to following the instructions from the Living God that these young people have brought."

"Pretty much." Eman chewed a piece of bacon.

"Well, we've only got two days to debate this in council then," she concluded with a smile at the two friends sitting across from her.

"Pretty much," Eman repeated in disgust.

"Let's get you two prepared for what's coming." She smiled pleasantly as she waved the empty teapot at her servant.

Nothing could have prepared Ra'ah for what came after their quiet breakfast. The elders explained that each of them would be asked separately to tell their story, in great detail, before the council. They were encouraged to be completely honest and use their own words. They were warned not to use each other's phrases or conspire in any way to make their stories sound the same. The Council of Elders would ferret that out immediately. They reinforced the encouragement to tell everything and leave nothing out. When they were as satisfied as they could be that the two understood, they gathered them up and walked them to the centre of the village where the council hall stood.

The hall was a tall stone structure with wooden doors on one side of the main square. They led them through the doors and then to a small side room with a table and chairs and a door on the other side. This was the room where they would wait until called upon. The council would be gathering momentarily at Timao's request, and then they would get right to the matter at hand. And the two of them *were* the matter at hand, she assured them.

"Who wants to go first?" Elder Eman barked.

"Ra'ah," Nebaya volunteered, and then shrugged apologetically to him when he looked at her in horror. "Your version of the story will be what they judge mine by. Would you rather be second and wonder what I said and how I contradicted you the entire time you're talking?"

"She's right, young man," Eman laughed. "Take it and run."

"I guess I'll be first," he decided lamely.

"Good choice." The old man's voice sounded like gravel as the two elders left the room.

They sat in silence for a long time, expecting the door to open at any moment and for Ra'ah's name to be called. He didn't remember ever feeling this nervous. He wondered what was happening to the others in Kathik, and if they would have to face this kind of trial and interrogation. He missed them terribly.

"I miss Ange in moments like this," Nebaya admitted out loud. "She loves public speaking."

He nodded, smiling. Daskow was good at it as well, although he preferred teaching to singing and storytelling. He wondered again how they were doing—if they were alright.

The door opened and Elder Eman stuck his head in.

"You're up first, kid," he announced gruffly.

Ra'ah stood up and went through the door. There was a short hallway that led him to a large room with a great table and nine high-backed chairs around it. Eman led him to the foot of the table and sat down in a chair close to the end.

"Introduce yourself and give us your testimony," Elder Timao instructed him from the far end of the table. "Be as clear and thorough as you can be."

He nodded and took in the table. Five men and four women stared expectantly at him. In a corner of the room sat a man and woman with quills poised, ready to write. Two letters he recognized as the ones they had brought were spread open on the table in front of the elders. He took a deep breath and tried to relax himself.

"My name is Ra'ah. I am originally from Bato," he began. "My friends and I had set up camp above Cardaya a little over a week ago when we were attacked by a black creature of extraordinary size."

The two scribes were furiously writing, and everyone's attention was fixed on him. Finding courage in the telling, he proceeded to tell the entire story, stopping only to drink from the mug of water that had been set aside for him. He did what he was told and tried to be as honest and thorough as he could, picking his way through the events day by day right up to their arrival in Meletsa.

The elders regarded him in silence as he finished his story with the meeting of Timao and Eman in the Inn of the Loneliest Donkey. He looked to Eman and Timao to see if he should say any more, but they just nodded to him encouragingly.

Elder Timao stood up to address the council. "Shall we break for lunch or hear our second witness?"

"Myself, I would like to see if we could call on Kathik for the other three," one man said. "But since there are only two witnesses, let's hear her version of this tale and then we can question them over lunch."

Everyone nodded in agreement to this, and Eman stood and offered Ra'ah a chair off to one side. "You can stay here and listen, since you've already given your testimony."

"I expected questions," he admitted sheepishly.

"Oh, there will be questions," the elder who had spoken earlier assured him, "but why interrogate you twice? Once for the discrepancies you've created for yourself and once for the discrepancies created in your story by other testimonies? It's more efficient this way."

Ra'ah nodded and shut his mouth. Eman walked back down the hall and called Nebaya into the room. She looked much more relaxed than he had felt standing before the nine elders. She introduced herself and told the same story that he had, with much less detail and description. Every detail she shared was factual and to the point, as if she was speaking specifically for the ease of the scribes up in the corner. It felt like she was done in a fraction of the time he had taken. When she reached the part of the story that he had ended on, she looked to Eman.

"Did you already tell them about our conversation with Master Dunhamai?" she asked him pointedly.

"I have," Eman nodded uncomfortably.

"Do you need my account as well?"

"That will not be necessary," the man from earlier assured her. "Master Dunhamai is a well-known subject in this room."

She nodded hesitantly, considering whether to press the issue, and chose to remain silent.

They sent one of the scribes out to have lunch brought to them and seated Nebaya and Ra'ah side by side at the foot of the table, then started to ask questions. Through lunch and long into the afternoon they asked question after question about this part and that. They grilled Nebaya on things she had left out that Ra'ah had gone into detail about. They grilled each of them about the others who weren't there, the three friends held in the city by Lady Raphael.

Ra'ah felt like he was being slowly pecked apart by polite, patient birds. It wasn't that he felt they didn't believe him, it was just that they wanted something in the story he didn't think he had, or even things he thought he'd already given them. He was almost in a dazed state when they recessed for the evening.

Elder Timao came over and laid a hand on his shoulder. She smiled at them both and just nodded. Eman was blunter.

"Good job not lying," he snorted gruffly. "That made things a lot smoother than normal."

"That was smooth?" Ra'ah asked in surprise. "I feel picked apart."

"That's because you *were* picked apart," Eman assured him. "We're very good at getting all the meat off the bones of a story."

"So what will the council do?" Nebaya asked bluntly.

"Tomorrow we'll weigh your testimony and maybe call one or both of you back if something comes up that we missed," Eman explained almost gleefully. "Anything worth deciding takes time."

"Seems like you've only got two days," Nebaya pointed out.

"Dunhamai tends to act out her thoughts as she has them," the elder replied, "But she'll come to council before she takes the action she's threatened."

"I've prepared rooms for you at my house," Elder Timao told them. "Spend the day tomorrow and rest. Your job is done for now."

They both nodded wearily, seeing no reason to argue. And after the last couple of days, they were both exhausted.

23

A Small Family Rebellion

If Angelis had tried to imagine a perfect village for Daskow, she could not have done better than this. The Fraternity of the Faithful met in a windowless hall deep inside the very guts of the university. She'd never been in a room so full of quiet people in her life, everyone's attention glued to Daskow as he related their story with all the minute detail that he could muster—and none of the exciting tidbits she would have added to keep the audience interested and engaged. And even without the tidbits, these people were stuck on his every word.

She shifted in the seat and glanced at the Governor sitting beside her. He was a romantic intellectual, she'd come to realize, far more than he was a politician. And he was apparently quite high up in the Fraternity. Everyone seemed to defer to him when he entered the hall with her. They even had some of the best seats reserved for them.

Daskow finished up with his story, revealing their unfortunate detainment in the cellars of Lady Raphael. The moderator stood and thanked him, preparing to open up the floor to questions. Governor Taman explained the process in soft whispers as she watched in fascination. She had never taken part in a secret society meeting before.

Her attention was grabbed by a rather dishevelled young man running up from the back. He said something urgent but unheard to the moderator and the moderator looked up to the Governor in concern before responding back to the young man, who ran back out the door at the back.

"Something is afoot," the Governor whispered. "Be ready in case we need to leave, Miss Angelis."

A disturbance rippled through the hall as three people entered. Ange almost jumped up in delight as she recognized the two tall figures with the young man. Anatellia and David were dressed in riding clothes, and Anatellia looked positively fierce.

"Miss Anatellia has escaped her mother's clutches," Governor Taman murmured. "And judging by the look on her face, she's about to blow open her mother's secret schemes."

"What makes you say that?" Ange asked in deep curiosity. She had to admit she'd never seen that look on Anatellia's face before.

"Because I am familiar with her mother, and that is her daughter in all her mother's glory," he whispered back. "And I have been suspecting things about Lady Raphael's scheming for some time, and I believe your friend is about to confirm much of it."

"Intriguing." Ange tried out the unfamiliar word from her vocabulary.

"Indeed," the Governor chuckled softly.

Anatellia and her brother approached the moderator on the dais and she asked the man something. He shook his head. She said something else and he looked perplexed, looking first at Daskow and then up at the Governor.

"Let her speak," the Governor called down, to the murmurs of the crowded room.

Anatellia approached the podium and said something to Daskow, who pointed up to where Angelis sat. Anatellia looked relieved and then focused her attention on the hall.

"Men and Women of the Faithful, my name is Anatellia Beth Raphael."

The crowd stirred. Ange could feel the tension in the room rise. Some people were looking to the exits.

"I have asked to speak to you tonight on the gravest of matters," She gestured to Daskow. "My friend Daskow has already told you of our encounter with the Maylak over a week ago in the forest above Cardaya. He has told you about the dire warning the Maylak gave us, and he has no doubt told you of our attempts ever since to warn the Valley of its impending doom."

She paused as her words drifted away into the hall. She looked over at her brother and up toward Ange and the Governor. She seemed to be deciding something, but the decision was made quickly.

"I'm here to share shocking news with you all, to the shame of my own family." The room was dead silent now. "My mother, Lady Raphael, has been in negotiation with a group calling themselves the Sacheth. She has made a business agreement with them. A trade agreement. And they are coming to collect on that agreement. They are to arrive with the new moon. The same new moon when the Maylak has promised our destruction will come."

Chaos erupted in the hall. People stood up shouting, demanding proof, asking her what could be done to stop them. The moderator stood in front of Anatellia and slammed a gavel on the podium until everyone settled down.

"What are we going to do about this?" someone shouted from the back. The room erupted again and the moderator took several long minutes to bring about a semblance of calm, but it was apparent he'd lost the room.

"Governor," the moderator looked up at him, "As our highest-ranking member in attendance, I need to yield the floor to you."

"This was inevitable," Taman sighed. "Come on, my dear, let's go join your friends."

Ange followed him down the stairs of the hall to the platform that held the podium. She found shelter beside Daskow as the Governor took the stand, calling for order. Everyone became silent.

"As many of you know, the Fraternity of the Faithful has always held the possibility that we may be faced with opposing the very city leaders and other people in high positions of power within our Valley." His voice carried over the room. "Although many believed this opposition was simply an intellectual exercise, the events being discussed here tonight reveal another terrible reality. We have been betrayed."

Voices rose in anger as the room erupted in chaos. The Governor raised both hands, silencing everyone.

"I do not suggest violence and open rebellion, but rather we take up the Call of the Living God, as it is brought to us by these young people and so clearly explained by our brother in the Fraternity, Daskow. We must take this warning to every person who will hear it—as far as we can extend our network, even to the very edges of the Valley. We must make sure every person within our circles of influence has a chance to hear and obey. To do otherwise would make us as guilty of their blood as those who would bring this calamity down on us. Will you all do this with me?"

There was much nodding in the hall. Anatellia leaned close to his ear and whispered something, He nodded and offered her the podium again.

"One other thing I need to share with you. My mother heard the warning my friends and I brought with us. She has sent that warning ahead to her contacts with the Sacheth. We may not have as much time as we once did."

The room became dead silent. One university student at the front raised her hand. The Governor nodded to her and she stood.

"Let us spend this time working out exactly what was said by the Maylak of the Living God and discerning the wisest plan of action," the young woman declared. "Often prophecy is misinterpreted and action misplaced. Tomorrow is soon enough to act."

There was murmur of approval at this suggestion, and Daskow stepped forward to the podium and motioned the other two to join him. Ange wasn't sure what to expect, but stepped forward with Anatellia.

"We submit to your questions," Daskow told the crowd. "Let the truth be a lamp to our feet."

Hands were raised and Daskow pointed to them one at a time. The night became full of questions, questions, and more questions. Seats were brought out for those at the podium and still the questions came. Ange had at first thought the questions would all be for Daskow and Anatellia, but once the Fraternity members discovered she was a wealth of perspective and insight they peppered her with more questions than the other two. She felt like she was on trial. The questions died down slowly and Ange had started to nod off in her chair when the Governor stood and addressed the room.

"I believe we've run out of new questions. Let us now act on what we've learned."

Everyone stood up and started to file out of the hall. The friends were led by gentle hands out of the building and across the university lawns. The sky was oddly bright in the east.

"They interrogated us all night," she protested loudly.

"And they barely scratched the surface of what you had to say." Anatellia laughed softly as she put her arm around her friend.

"I missed you," Ange confessed as she leaned into her. "You smell like horse."

Laughter carried into the dawn as they made their way to the Governor's house.

24

WAITING…

They spent all that day in the apartment provided by the Governor. He came in just as they had devoured a late breakfast and informed them that they were the talk of the city leaders. Apparently Lady Raphael had taken the extreme measure of accusing her vagabond daughter of stealing a horse from the family stables and running off with various family treasures. David laughed hysterically but Anatellia was not amused.

"You possess something she wants back," the Governor pointed out gently. "You have the power to uncover her and leave her exposed to her enemies in the city."

"What will she do when she finds out I've already left her naked for all to see?" Anatellia wondered.

"You should stay out of sight for awhile," Taman concluded sagely. "The rumours will already have reached her ears. And she will already be recloaking herself in more lies."

David left with the Governor to check on the horses in question in the Governor's stables. It had seemed like a good idea the afternoon before to take them, since two rich merchants riding through the city was as common as farmers in a village. But now she regretted bringing her old horse into the whole affair. Geran had taken good care of Storm all these years, but now if they were caught her mother might just decide to make an example of him.

She sighed and closed her eyes, listening to the sounds of the university grounds through the open window. Ange watched her for a long minute and then couldn't keep silent any longer.

"Do you think Nebaya and Ra'ah are okay?" she asked softly.

"David passed on our message and gave them the letters," Anatellia assured her. "They would have gotten to Meletsa last night."

"I hope they weren't arrested there."

"Why would they be?" Anatellia asked in exasperation.

Ange shrugged. "I don't know. I don't know how far your mother's arm extends."

"I somehow don't think it extends that strongly into Meletsa," Anatellia said sleepily. "They don't take too kindly to that kind of politicking."

"Anatellia?" Ange asked softly.

"Hmmm? What?"

"Are you trying to sleep?" she whispered, ducking the pillow thrown from across the room.

Daskow appeared later that afternoon in the uniform of a university student. Ange looked at him appraisingly and complimented him. She hadn't ever seen him dressed in such finery.

He smiled and tossed her a bundle. "Try those on. Our help is needed."

"What are we doing?" She unwrapped the bundle to reveal a student's outfit for herself.

"We're helping get the word out." He raised an eyebrow at her as she looked at the clothes in disdain. "Is there a problem with those?"

"I don't like skirts."

"Consider it a disguise! Come on, people want to meet you."

"Meet me?" She jumped up and took the clothes into the next room. "How exciting!"

"Did you bring me a change of clothes?" Anatellia murmured from the chair where she'd been sleeping.

"*You*"—he emphasized the word with a finger point—"are public enemy number one. You're the second subject on everyone's lips."

"Who dares be first?" she grumbled.

"Turns out it's the Living God," he answered happily. "Our message is spreading, catching the rumours and igniting them. People are already getting ready to leave. Demanding answers. The whole city is abuzz."

"That'll make Mother happy." She turned over and found a more comfortable position.

Ange came out of the bedroom dressed in her university student clothes. She twirled; the skirt flared off her ankles and spun around her legs. She considered herself in the mirror.

"Can I keep it?" she asked happily.

"They are yours," Daskow answered with a laugh.

"Have fun, you two." Anatellia waved at them dismissively.

Anatellia ate dinner with Governor Taman in the apartment. He came with the meal and an offering of a book he thought she might like to read.

She ran her hand over the rich gilding of the cover as she ate listlessly. "I haven't held a book in ten years," she murmured. "What does this title mean? *A Journey through Smoke*?"

"It's a fanciful tale," he said between small bites. "An apocryphal account of the Journey to the Amatta Valley as remembered by Simon the Apostate."

"Really?" She looked at him with wide eyes. "Why, this is absolutely priceless! And absolutely heretical. I love it."

He smiled. "I thought you might. There are often snippets of truth even in works such as that. I'd be interested to hear your thoughts."

"Thank you." She sighed and returned his smile. "I hate being stuck here."

"Well"—he shrugged—"You kicked the hornet's nest."

"I guess I did."

Daskow and Ange arrive late in the evening to find her still curled up in the chair they had left her in. She acknowledged them with a small wave, but refused to move her nose from the book. Ange gave Daskow a "she's your problem" look and announced her mission to find late night food. Daskow came over and bent down to see what she was reading.

"Where on earth did you get that?" he breathed out as he read the title.

She looked at him over the top edge. "Governor Taman, of course. Have you read it?"

"Only pieces," he admitted in awe. "I didn't know there was still a complete copy left in the Valley."

"Really?" She suddenly felt awkward holding it. "I thought it was just really rare."

"It suffers the infamy of taking a different perspective on the Valley than some of the more popular texts available," he said sarcastically.

"You mean it contradicts holy texts."

"Not outright," he said, studying the cover. "Just the interpretations."

"Like what?" She set the book on her lap.

"Like in Journey, it suggests the forefathers were actually going to the Mountain of the Living God…" He made a motion with his hands, signifying hitting an obstacle. "And they stopped short when they came to the Valley."

"So?" She didn't see the difference.

"So the Valley wasn't where they were supposed to stop, according to Simon's story," he explained.

"Oh!" She looked at the book in surprise. "That's uncomfortable."

"Can I read it after you?" he begged.

"Ask the Governor," she teased him.

25

Dreams

The next day Nebaya and Ra'ah woke up in the house of Elder Timao and ate a leisurely breakfast alone on the balcony above the river. The elder assured them as she left for the council hall that if they were needed, they would be sent for. As the morning dragged on and no one came for them, they started to get bored. By the time lunch came around, they were getting desperate for something to do. Ra'ah eventually found himself in Timao's kitchen talking spices with her cook; he was still there when Nebaya wandered through looking for a cork.

"Going fishing?" Ra'ah asked with a laugh.

"Well, we're not supposed to wander out of the house," Nebaya confessed in frustration.

"So how are you going to fish?"

"You'll see!" She smiled as she brandished two wine corks in victory.

When Elders Timao and Eman arrived home that evening, they were surprised to find freshly caught fish and fresh baked bread for dinner.

"Where did you go to catch those, Nebaya?" There was a slight rebuke in Timao's tone.

"Off your balcony," the huntress said. "I had to use all of my line."

"I have a library if you need something to do tomorrow," Timao offered with a smile.

"Tomorrow?" Nebaya looked at her in frustration, "I was hoping you would come back with a decision tonight."

"We need to discuss a little longer," Timao explained as Eman eagerly set into supper. "And we need Dunhamai's report when she gets back. This is not a decision for anyone to take lightly."

"I think I might go out to the Pass Gate tomorrow morning after breakfast," Nebaya said. "If that would be acceptable."

"By all means," Eman replied between mouthfuls of fish and bread. "Your testimonies aren't in dispute."

"I'll join you," Ra'ah offered.

"You could always bake me some more bread like this," Eman said. "No good bakers in Meletsa."

The next day in Kathik passed much like the one before. Daskow and Ange went out right after breakfast to continue spreading the word. David had disappeared the day before on an errand for Governor Taman. And the Governor himself was out of the house on his own business.

That left Anatellia alone with the book. She devoured it like nothing she'd ever read. Daskow had said it had a different perspective on the Valley's founding, but she began to feel uncomfortable how accurate it was in describing the Valley and the Forefathers' journey from slavery and certain destruction into a land all of their own. It read more like a history book than an apocryphal story. All of it, except that throughout the pages, the search for the Mountain of the Living God was the centrepoint. And that was a direct contradiction to the teaching that the Valley had been their destination all along.

She paused only to find herself food and a pot of tea. She found herself at the end of the book as the sun was setting over the mountains across from the university grounds. She sighed as she closed the book on itself, thoughts buzzing in her head like moths to flame. The mission that the Maylak had brought to them little more than a week before seemed to dovetail into the book in her hands. Somehow it was all connected.

She got up and set the book on the table just as Ange and Daskow walked through the door.

"Food?" Angelis looked at the almost empty table with sadness.

"I was about to go scrounge something up," Anatellia said as the door opened again to allow the Governor and his servant in with dinner. She threw up her hands. "Never mind."

They all sat and ate in the silence of good company. When they had eaten their fill, they sat back and Ange told them about their day. So many people with questions! People were starting to prepare for the trip up-Valley. The city guards were everywhere.

"Apparently news has spread through the market like wildfire," she announced excitedly. "And everyone is demanding answers from your mother. I heard she's had to place a guard on the gates of the estate!"

"That will do nothing to improve her mood," Anatellia mused. "What news from the city council, Governor?"

"The council is, quite frankly, a divided mess." He shook his head. "One thing this chaos has done is reveal those who are in league with, or at least on the same side as, your mother. They will be deadlocked till winter."

"They don't have until winter."

"Then you understand the problem. On a positive note, there is so much chaos in the city that they have all but stopped looking for you."

"That's good news, I guess…" She picked up the book and handed it to him. "Thank you for the loan of the book."

He shook his head, refusing it. "Not a loan, my dear—a gift."

"I couldn't…!" she stammered, glancing at Daskow, who eyed the book almost greedily. "Daskow says it's exceedingly rare—maybe priceless."

"So are you." He smiled and wrapped both her hands around the book. "A rare book for a rare woman. A rare leader as well, if I'm not mistaken."

"Thank you." She sat back and wiped a tear.

"I am thinking it might be time for you three to think about moving on," he said after a silence. "There is still Bato to tell, and I cannot help but feel it is getting dangerous for you to stay here."

"But we want to continue helping," Ange protested.

"He may be right," Anatellia admitted. "My mother will not stop trying to turn this to her advantage. And she will not stop looking for us, even if the guard has."

"And the harder she is backed into a corner, the more dangerous she becomes," the Governor added. "Do not underestimate Lady Raphael."

Anatellia nodded. She hadn't wanted to think about how her mother might react to all of this—but she simply had to ask herself how *she* would. And when she looked into the darker places of her soul, she found no good answers.

"I think we should sleep on it," she said, looking at her friends. "But I tend to agree with Governor Taman."

They all nodded, finding no reason to say more. The morning would be better for arguing, when everyone was fresh.

Nebaya sat bolt upright, drenched with sweat and stifling a cry of alarm. In the bed across from her, Ra'ah rose sharply. He looked as white as the sheets in the waxing moonlight that was coming in through the open window. He looked over at her and shook his head.

"I had a dream," he whispered.

"Me too."

"Master Dunhamai was in trouble…" he started to tell her, but she raised her hand.

"The sun was rising above the mountains. The river was below her and she could see the valley through the peaks."

"But she was being chased by black-cloaked men and wolves," Ra'ah finished. "How did we have the same dream?"

"Get dressed. We have to help her."

He immediately got out of bed and dressed himself. Just a short while earlier he would have asked more questions, but the last few days had driven that need out of him. He wrapped his travel cloak around him and then stopped as she handed him his bow and quiver. Her look was hard and steady as he hesitantly accepted them.

"No time to wonder if you can or if you're ready," she assured him. "Now is the time to act."

They came out of the room they shared and hurried down the stairs. No one in the house stirred as they left through the front door. They made their way at a jog through the deserted early morning streets and came to the Pass Gate just as the eastern sky started to lighten.

"How far up do you think she is?" he asked Nebaya in worry.

"Trust," she breathed out as she shook her head. "We just have to trust. Come on."

She set up the road at a jog. They left the lights of the village far behind, and the moon had long disappeared into the west. By the light of the stars and the brightening eastern sky, they kept to the road as it rose up into the Koreb Pass. They reached the entrance of the pass just as the light of the rising sun broke over the peaks of the mountains across the Valley. The road continued to climb up along the river gorge below, and they saw a point far away where they assumed the summit lay.

They continued to run up the slope—there was no way they could miss anyone on the narrow road bordered by mountain on one side and gorge on the other. The sun was fully above the mountains, like in their dream, when they reached what they thought was the summit and stared down the length of a long road that climbed gently for miles across a desolate mountain plateau no wider than the one they had just come up.

Running toward them was the distant form of Master Dunhamai, and behind her bounded black shapes. With a shout Nebaya rushed forward, seeing the need to close the gap between them. Ra'ah clumsily grabbed back for an arrow and started running after her. *Too slow. Too late,* he thought.

Whether it was a trick of the morning light or the tall grey-haired woman was much swifter than he thought, the distance between them melted. Nebaya stopped and drew from the white quiver a bright white arrow. With a fluid motion and barely a pause she released one and then another. The two black forms nearest Dunhamai tumbled to the ground to move no more, but others were gaining.

Suddenly the tall woman stumbled and fell just short of Nebaya. The younger woman fired three more arrows, bringing down three more black foes. Ra'ah jumped up and closed the distance between them, running behind his companion to the obviously wounded Dunhamai. The woman was struggling to rise while holding a jagged wound on her side. He slipped under her arm and lifted her to her feet.

"Where did you kids come from?" she gasped.

"Just out for a stroll," he responded flippantly, moving back toward Nebaya without looking back.

Two more arrows left Nebaya's bow in rapid succession, the last arrow striking flesh uncomfortably close behind him. She shook the next arrow out of the white quiver and nocked it, holding it ready, but she didn't fire. Ra'ah risked a look back. Black bodies lay sprawled across the road, some obviously wolf-like, but two were frighteningly human. Nothing moved behind them on the gentle slope.

"Are there any more?" Nebaya asked the other woman.

"I don't know," she admitted through clenched teeth. "Not close, I think. But there *will* be more."

"We have to get her back to the village." Ra'ah kept walking.

"Maybe we should look after that wound?" Nebaya looked at Ra'ah and Dunhamai questioningly.

Dunhamai answered for him. "No—get me out of this pass and then worry about my wound."

"You heard the woman," he agreed.

"You two go; I'll catch up," Nebaya commanded. "I'm not leaving behind those arrows."

Ra'ah nodded. "Hurry. She could use your height to move faster."

Anatellia, Daskow, and Angelis woke up simultaneously with gasps. The dream had been so vivid. They stared at each other in the dim lamplight as they caught their collective breath.

"How strange is that?" Ange looked between the two others. "To each have a dream wake us at the same time."

"You had a dream, too?" Daskow asked through heavy breaths.

"Well, yeah." Ange looked at Anatellia. "And so did she, by the look of her."

"It can't be coincidence," Anatellia breathed out. "Ange, what was your dream?"

"Your mother was chasing us all around your house," she recounted, the dream still fresh in her memory, "and you were trying to get us out, but every turn we took, she was there ahead of us. And David was there and he kept shouting 'back, back, back' and motioning us to go the way she didn't expect, but you ignored him. And then we rounded a corner and could see the forest ahead of us for some reason, but your mother was already there and she had men with bows and they fired at us and then I woke up."

Daskow shook his head. "That was a very accurate description of my dream as well."

"Mine, too," Anatellia nodded.

"What does it mean?" Ange asked, flopping back on her pillow.

"It means we should probably listen to my brother, wherever he is," she replied.

"We need to leave." Daskow sounded anxious. "And we need to go to Meletsa."

Anatellia shook her head. "Not Meletsa—we want to go up-Valley toward Bato."

"Does Ange need to repeat herself?" Daskow stared across the room at her. "Would it help if I told you Governor Taman sent your brother to Meletsa last night?"

"What?" Anatellia leaned over and turned the lamp up, and then glared across the room at him. "He did what?"

"Governor Taman sent David to Meletsa with letters for the Council of Elders," Daskow explained. "He left under the pretence of visiting the market pubs so the guard at the gate wouldn't be suspicious and report it to your mother. He'll be there by morning. And we shouldn't go to Bato and leave this city between us and the others. Not to mention that our dream seems like a pretty clear warning not to move in a direction your mother would suspect. And don't forget the letters for Bato are with Nebaya and Ra'ah in Meletsa."

"This all seems pretty clear to me," Ange nodded in agreement.

Anatellia threw her pillow at her. "Fine. One thing is sure—I've had my fill of home."

They got up quietly and packed their things. Anatellia smiled at Daskow when they caught Ange trying to stuff her new clothes into her pack, already full with all of her other garments.

"You might have to get rid of something one day," Anatellia confronted her.

"I don't get rid of anything until I've got all my use out of it," Ange insisted as she adjusted the straps to her pack.

They quietly made their way out into the hallway and passed the Governor's study. They stopped when they saw a light under the door and knocked. Seconds later the door opened and Taman peered out at them.

"Took my suggestion to heart, eh?" He smiled at them. "Can you at least wait till breakfast?"

"We all had a dream," Ange said by way of explanation.

"You all had a dream?" He seemed confused, looking at each of them.

"The same dream," Ange explained further. "It was not very nice."

"I understand." His face said he didn't entirely. "Where are you going?"

"Meletsa," Anatellia replied. "We're going to meet up with my brother and the others."

He nodded. "Wise. How do you plan to get out of the city without being seen by the city guard at the gates?"

"We haven't exactly figured that out yet," Anatellia admitted.

"I have a novel idea." He smiled knowingly. "Stay for breakfast and I'll get you through the gate with no one the wiser."

"Fine," Anatellia agreed. "Your idea is probably better than anything I could come up with."

"Oh, it is! Run to the kitchen and ask my cook to get breakfast ready while I borrow Daskow for a bit."

An hour later they were seated around Taman's table, enjoying an ample breakfast in peaceful silence. Daskow had returned from whatever errand the Governor had sent him on just before they sat down to eat. When the girls asked him what he'd been up to, he just smiled and said "You'll see!"

Breakfast complete, they regathered their things and Taman led them through the predawn streets toward the city gate. Just as they came to the last bend, a crowd of young people suddenly surrounded them and started walking down the final stretch toward the surprised city guards. Anatellia and Ange found themselves bordered on every side by particularly tall university students, shielding them completely from the guards who were protesting the mob's sudden exit from the city. Several of the students stopped to explain the impromptu field trip as the bulk of the mob carried the three safely away into the market streets, where they dispersed suddenly with laughter and waves. As quick as that, they were standing alone with the Governor again next to a market stall.

"I cannot believe that worked," Anatellia laughed quietly.

"Like I said," Taman smiled, "novel. A peculiar event, but nothing that they care to explain or report."

Ange hugged him. "We'll see you again soon."

"Take care of yourselves. You are important to what is happening in this Valley."

"We will," they assured him.

They turned and hurried through the slowly stirring market, wanting to put as much distance between themselves and the city as they could.

—— 26 ——

Reunion

The journey back down out of the pass seemed to take forever, although in reality it took very little time at all. Nebaya had quickly recovered her arrows and rejoined them, her face pale and her eyes haunted. Without a word she slipped the other woman's free arm around her shoulders, and together the two of them all but carried the wounded guide down out of the pass. Dunhamai was as motivated to get back down as they were, and despite the pain she was obviously in, she kept the pace that they set without a problem. They did not speak at all until they came down the hill in sight of the gate.

"Take me straight to the council chamber," she demanded. "They can tend to this while I talk."

"What happened up there?" Nebaya demanded harshly. "Who were those men with the wolves?

"Forgive me, Little Sister, if I only want to tell the tale once," the older woman answered. "I do owe you both my life, and likely many others will owe you theirs as well before this all plays out. Thank you."

Mollified, Nebaya led them through the gate and down through the village. People going about their morning business stopped in shock as they passed, everyone recognizing the Master. A crowd quickly gathered behind them, although no one offered to help, realizing that they could do no better than the two young people blazing a trail through the village to the council hall at its centre.

They burst through the outer doors and proceeded right into the council chamber, where the elders had already gathered for the day's debating. Everyone stood in surprise at the sight of the old woman supported between Nebaya and Ra'ah. A few went to call for the village healers, and others had chairs and a cot brought from somewhere in the building.

Elder Timao looked at them with admiration. "I wondered where you two were off to so early this morning. But how did you know where go and find her?"

"That story is for later, if at all," Dunhamai cut her off, propping herself up on the newly arrived cot as a healer tried to get at her wound. "There is an army approaching from the other side of the pass. I saw it at a great distance from the top of the Koreb. We have to flee up the Valley, and we also have to send rangers into the pass and slow them down."

The elders stared at her in shock and horror. They knew better than to openly question her report. Nebaya and Ra'ah stared at each other over her cot. Ra'ah thought he saw his question written on her face—they'd all thought they would have until the new moon.

"How long do we have, Dunhamai?" Eman asked bluntly.

"The main army is still far, far away. I only saw the smoke of its fires on the horizon. But I saw those faithless caravan drivers meet up with a group much closer after we parted ways. Then a patrol of dark demons waylaid me as I hurried back here. I would have been dead in the pass if these two hadn't appeared out of the dawn to save me."

"How big is the closer group?" another elder pressed.

"I do not know," she admitted. "But the amount does not matter if we do not prepare. Any number of soldiers coming out of the pass would be devastating. We are hopelessly unprepared for a war of any kind."

"What do you suggest we do?" Elder Timao asked.

"What I told Eman you should do when I went up the bloody pass two days ago," she snarled as the healer struggled to work. "Gather everyone who can't fire a bow and send them up Valley to the Mountain. These young ones know where it is—at least roughly; they will be able to get close enough. And they've got to go, too. They are summoned."

"Wait"—Nebaya looked down at her—"what?"

"You're summoned to the Mountain, Daughter of the Living God." She gave the younger woman a penetrating look. "You and your brother here. You've got to get there as soon as possible."

"How do you know that?" Nebaya sputtered in confusion. "We've got to finish our mission."

"No." The woman shook her head, pain flickering across her expression. "I hear it so clearly in the Call. The charge has changed. You must leave with the tall blond messenger."

"What messenger?" Nebaya demanded. "What are you talking about?"

"That messenger." The grey-haired woman jerked her thumb back over her shoulder as a shadow crossed the doorway and a familiar face looked into the council chamber.

"Excuse me," David cautiously stepped into the room, "but I've been sent with an important message from Governor Taman of Kathik. I'm sorry if I'm interrupting."

"No, young man, come in." Eman shook his head in wonder. "It appears we were expecting you."

"Hello, Nebaya." David winked at her as she simply stared at him. "It looks like you've seen some excitement here as well."

"We've got to go back," Ra'ah explained to David as they ate on the steps of the council house. "We're called to the Mountain."

"Says who?" David asked simply.

"The woman on the cot in there. She said you'd come, and that we need to leave with you back to the city."

"Okay." David took that in stride. "I assume you can ride?"

"Well, no," Ra'ah admitted.

"Looks like you're going to be learning," David replied, "because I'm here with two horses and I'm going back to the city with two horses. Nebaya can ride with me."

"I'd rather run the entire way," Nebaya assured him from the doorway. "We'll walk."

"Suit yourself," he shrugged. "But I've got to get back, and I'm leaving after we're done eating here."

"We'll go get our gear," she told him, motioning for Ra'ah to join her.

Ra'ah got up, stretched, and joined her to walk back to Elder Timao's.

"So you agree with her?" Ra'ah asked when they were out of earshot.

"Yes," she nodded. "When she spoke, I felt the truth of it, if that makes any sense. I feel an urgency to go."

Ra'ah nodded. He felt it as well. Like they were being urgently called from a long distance by a great voice.

"We need to go get the others," he realized.

"I don't understand how or why, but they are on their way here." She simply shrugged when he looked at her.

They quickly packed their gear and were out the door and back to the council chamber before the sun indicated midmorning. The sense of urgency was increasing for both of them. They found David watering two horses from the well in the centre of the village square.

"You two ready to go?" he asked impatiently.

"We should say goodbye," Ra'ah suggested.

"No need," Master Dunhamai called from the door to the council house. She stood with Timao and Eman and waved them over. "You must leave and not look back. I do not understand the meaning, but you have an appointment to keep. May the Living God go before you and behind you, and keep you until we meet again. Goodbye, Little Sister. Goodbye, Little Brother."

"Goodbye," they echoed awkwardly, looking at all three.

They returned to David. He had adjusted the saddle and stirrups on the black horse, which he kept calling "Storm." He secured their packs and helped Ra'ah mount the animal, and readjusted the stirrups accordingly,

"Riding a horse isn't as simple as just sitting on it," he explained. "You've got to stand in the stirrups and take weight off your butt. You guide the horse by squeezing with your knees. The reigns are for stopping, mostly."

"Mostly?" Ra'ah asked nervously as he sat atop the animal.

"Look, it's going to be a crash course," David admitted. "Hopefully more figuratively than literally."

He swung up on his own horse and extended a hand to Nebaya, who just glared at him.

"I would have given you Storm to ride, but we both know how the last horse ride ended for you. Unless you've learned since then?"

She glared harder at him but took his hand, and he swung her up behind him.

"Ok, Ra'ah, here we go." He gave his horse a kick and it sprung off down the street.

Ra'ah gave his horse a similar kick, and with a snort Storm shot off after the other horse, with Ra'ah already trying desperately to stay on.

"It's going to be a long ride for that boy," Eman muttered to the two women as they watched them disappear around a corner.

27

An Unexpected Appointment

Ange, Anatellia, and Daskow made good time down the Meletsa highway. They all agreed that it felt good to be out of the city. The highway was a familiar one to them, and they laughed and sang as they set a brisk pace that would get them to Meletsa before sunset.

They stopped and ate lunch by a mountain stream that flowed down and under the road and then continued on their way. An hour or so later they stopped under the shadow of an avalanche shelter and stared out at the Koreb pass and the village of Meletsa in the distance. The day was hot and they were loath to step out of the cave-like shade of the cool shelter.

Something caught Ange's eye as she stared down the road. She shaded her eyes and squinted to try to see better.

"Hey Daskow, what do you see there?" She pointed down the slope of the road.

"Two horses with riders," he said as he tracked her gesture. "Coming pretty quick."

Anatellia came over to see what they were looking at.

"What is that behind them?" she asked as she tried to make out the images through the shifting of the summer heat off the road. "The mirages made it difficult to see."

"More horses?"

"Those are black wolves," Ange squeaked.

The galloping horses were much closer now. They could make out three riders bent over the saddles. One of the riders looked to be desperately trying to stay on the animal.

"That's Storm," Anatellia realized. "Living God, that's David and the others."

They started wildly calling and hollering as the horses approached the avalanche shelter in earnest. Behind them by about a mile were the leaping black forms of a dozen wolves. David's horse sprang suddenly forward at his urging, bearing down on them with frightful speed. Storm seemed to lag behind, threatening to veer away from the dark overhang and off the road.

Anatellia stepped out, and putting her fingers to her lips, issued a piercing whistle. The black horse turned back onto the road with a snort and toss of its head. David's horse passed under the shelter and he reined up next to them with a clatter of hooves

Storm flew up behind and stopped dead in front of Anatellia. The snow-white face of Ra'ah appeared over the horse's neck as he desperately tried to stay on. The horse simply put his head down and bumped Anatellia in affection. She patted the horse's nose and looked up at the petrified Ra'ah clinging to the horse's neck.

"See what I mean about horses?" she teased as she helped him unceremoniously to the ground.

"What are we going to do about the wolves?" Daskow asked in panic, pointing to the quickly approaching pack.

"Don't worry." Nebaya had already slipped off of David's horse. "This is not the first pack Ra'ah and I have faced. David, take Storm and move behind us. I'd rather not get kicked by a panicking horse."

"What are you three doing out here on horses?" Anatellia couldn't help but ask, despite the approaching wolves.

"We've been called to the Mountain," Ra'ah blurted. "Change of plans."

"What?" Anatellia turned on him in confusion. "What are you talking about?"

"No time; they're here." Nebaya nodded down the road. The wolves rushed up, but they stopped short of entering the shelter. They spread out around the perimeter and watched the six with hate-filled red eyes.

"Glad to see we haven't been abandoned." Ra'ah exhaled a held breath.

"What are you talking about?" Anatellia repeated as she looked nervously at the pack slowly surrounding them. "Why aren't they coming under the shelter?"

"The wolves are afraid of the Maylak," Nebaya said.

"Do you see any Maylak?" Anatellia's voice lifted in panic as she watched the black wolves circle.

"Don't worry—just trust," Ra'ah assured her.

The wolves circled farther around and one of them stepped into the shadow of the shelter. Nothing happened; emboldened, the wolves started closing the circle with ever-increasing speed.

"Nebaya!" Anatellia screamed as she pulled her knife. The bows they had been given had been left in Kathik, an oversight she now regretted. How were they going to fight off so many wolves?

A great wolf gave up on simply circling and leapt the distance between them in a single coiled bound.

Time seemed to stop entirely.

The five friends stood in wonder. David and the horses seemed frozen in comical fear, and the wolves hung suspended in various poses. The wolf that had leapt at Anatellia hung in the air close enough for her to touch it. Nothing moved around them; there was no sound but their ragged breathing.

They stood that way until they felt the presence behind them. Turning as one, they beheld a Maylak greater than any they had yet seen. He carried a great sword that rested on the ground.

They stood before him in silence; his very presence washed over them, driving away all fear and pain and concern. They didn't know how long they stood like that before he spoke, but when he did his voice swept over them like waves of power and peace.

"You are Summoned," he told them. "You are summoned to the Mountain of the Living God. He has risen a standard. You are Called."

They look at each other in wonder. Did he need an answer? Ra'ah was the first to step forward.

"I will go."

Ange and Daskow both stepped forward.

"We will go."

Nebaya stepped forward.

"It is my life to serve—I will go."

Anatellia stared in wonder at the Maylak and her friends. She felt so unworthy of them or this task. She felt small. She locked eyes with the giant Maylak and made her decision.

"I will go," she whispered. "Though the way is long and the road is hard, I will go."

The Maylak nodded and gripped the sword before him. A great burst of light lashed out, sweeping around them like the waters of a great flood, lifting and encompassing them and sweeping them away.

A sudden blast of light and wind knocked David off of his feet, and he lay for long seconds stunned on the ground. Just moments before the air had been full of the sound of the wolves and the panicked horses and his sister arguing with her friends; suddenly, all he could hear was the wind whistling through the rocks. Coming to his senses, he jumped up and stopped, stunned. Everything—every*one*—was gone. The wolves, the five friends, everything they had carried: gone in a flash.

He turned a full circle in shock. Not only were his friends and the wolves gone, but so was the road. The roof of the shelter was gone too, revealing the ever-rising slope of an avalanche path that rose up the steep mountain slope. All around him was nothing but natural rock, green grass, and trees. Trees everywhere.

"Wait a minute," he muttered to himself in shock as he spun around toward the river.

The green avalanche path fell away at his feet to terminate at a tree line at the base of the slope. Before him spread a valley he didn't know, although it looked oddly familiar. Trees covered the broad valley floor in all directions, revealing a pristine and untouched wilderness. With rising fear, he turned his head and looked back down the valley in the direction he was sure he had just ridden. There, at the end of the valley, rose a rocky and bare slope up into the cleft of the rocky pass that he knew was the Koreb. But there was no road, no Meletsa, and absolutely no cultivated fields anywhere within his sight.

"Living God," he whispered as he turned to look up the valley where field upon field should have been. There was nothing but forest.

A sudden movement caught his eye from the edge of the avalanche path. A man in a forest green cloak that did little to hide the fact that he was also wearing armour stood up from a campfire that David had failed to take in until that moment. The man looked at him in wonder, and he stared back in shock. A sword swung at the man's side as he motioned broadly for the tall youth to join him.

"Friend," the man called, "surely you are a Friend of God to appear so. Come over and share a meal with me."

David continued to stare. His mind simply stopped trying to make sense of what his eyes were trying to tell him. He looked out again at the Valley, which was no longer the Valley. It was like everything had been erased in a flash. His sister, her friends, literally everything else in the Valley, all gone. Everything except he himself and the two horses. And this guy, wearing armour and carrying a sword, something that hadn't been done in the Valley since the time of the forefathers.

The man stepped onto the green grass of the avalanche path with a look of concern. "Friend, are you alright?"

"Alright?" David's voice sounded too high in his own ears. He realized he sounded a little hysterical. He decided that was okay. "No, no I'm not alright. I'm far from alright."

"Come." The man gestured to his campfire. "Come and sit. I am a friend and you are safe, whatever your trouble. What is your name?"

"My name?" David walked forward with the horses like he was in a trance. "My name is David."

"Hello David," the man smiled reassuringly. "My name is Simon."

The story continues in

Book 2 of

The Amatta Valley Chronicles: A Banner Extends

Gone! Everyone and everything simply disappeared in a great flash of blinding light, leaving David standing alone with the two horses.

Not only his sister and four friends, but the road, the farmland, and the village in the distance have disappeared as well. With the help of a stranger named Simon, David comes to realize the horrifying truth about where—or rather when—he is.

Bewildered, David finds himself being dragged deeper into the plans and purposes of a Living God that, up until this day, he has barely believed in.